"Why, shaggy-hair Joe...I never expected a beauty compliment from you."

"Stop talking like that, Brit." He placed his fingers beneath her chin, tilting her face up to his. "Stop talking and kiss me."

She froze. A deer in his headlights.

And then she laughed, shaking her head, loosening his hold. "You almost had me."

He did have her. He had his arms around her and she relaxed. He kissed her.

A simple act. Four lips. Two hearts. One beat.

It didn't feel simple. It felt complex and intense and terrifying.

He had no right to kiss her. Kissing implied intent. He was broke, with a daughter to provide for. His world was imperfect when she deserved perfection.

He had no right to kiss her. Kissing opened the door to heartbreak. He couldn't stand to be left or betrayed by another person he loved.

He had no right to kiss her. And yet he did.

And for a moment, everything felt perfect.

Dear Reader,

Welcome to Harmony Valley!

Just a few short years ago, Harmony Valley was on the brink of extinction with only those over the age of sixty in residence. Now the influx of a younger generation is making life in Harmony Valley more fun for its gray-haired residents than afternoon television.

Brittany Lambridge dreams of being an upcycle artist. Although she pays the bills by working in her grandfather's barber shop, she's been commissioned to make a driveway gate with a luxury car grill. Now all she needs is a luxury car grill. She thinks she's found one in an abandoned car cemetery next to a closed auto-repair shop. Too bad Joe Messina bought the defunct garage the day before Brit tries picking the place. This single dad refuses to let Brit take anything away until he identifies the owners of the abandoned cars. In the meantime, if Joe wants to make a living fixing cars, he's got to prove to Harmony Valley that he's no longer the bad boy they remember.

I hope you enjoy Joe and Brit's journey to a happily-ever-after, as well as the other romances in the Harmony Valley series. I love to hear from readers. Check my website to learn more about upcoming books, sign up for email book announcements (and I'll send you a free sweet romance read) or chat with me on Facebook (MelindaCurtisAuthor) to hear about my latest giveaways.

Melinda Curtis

www.MelindaCurtis.com

HEARTWARMING

Marrying the Single Dad

———

USA TODAY Bestselling Author

Melinda Curtis

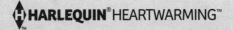

Recycling programs
for this product may
not exist in your area.

ISBN-13: 978-0-373-36813-6

Marrying the Single Dad

Copyright © 2016 by Melinda Wooten

This edition published by arrangement with Harlequin Books S.A.

For questions and comments about the quality of this book, please contact us at CustomerService@Harlequin.com.

Printed in U.S.A.

www.Harlequin.com

Award-winning *USA TODAY* bestselling author **Melinda Curtis** is an empty nester. Now instead of carpools and sports leagues, her days go something like this: visit the gym with her husband at 5:30 a.m., walk the dogs, enjoy a little social media, write-write-write, consider cooking dinner (possibly reject cooking dinner in favour of takeout), watch sports or DIY shows with her husband, read and collapse in bed. Sometimes the collapse part happens before any TV or reading takes place.

Melinda enjoys putting humor into her stories because that's how she approaches life. She writes sweet contemporary romances as Melinda Curtis (Brenda Novak says of *Season of Change*, "found a place on my keeper shelf"), and fun, steamy reads as Mel Curtis (Jayne Ann Krentz says of *Cora Rules*, "wonderfully entertaining").

Books by Melinda Curtis

Harlequin Heartwarming

This book is dedicated to those who—like my heroine—dare to dream. Sometimes it just takes one person to have faith to make you believe in yourself.

CHAPTER ONE

"WHAT DO YOU think you're doing?" a deep masculine voice bellowed across the overgrown, wreck-strewn field in Harmony Valley.

Brittany Lambridge jumped and thunked the back of her head on the hood of the ancient BMW sedan. Add headache to her list of injuries this morning.

"I told you we'd get caught," Regina whispered. Brit's sister was the queen of *I told you sos*.

Brit stepped back from the decaying car, rubbing her head beneath her baseball cap. The nip of early morning bit into her scraped knuckles while dewy knee-high grass hid her feet. She peered to the left, then the right, but the rusting, abandoned cars were still rusty and abandoned. No one else was in the flat patch of land with them. No one driving past on the two-lane highway bordering the field. No one stood near the thick blackberry bushes along the river. And she'd been told the car repair shop and nearby house had been empty for at least a decade. Had she imagined the voice? Or… Brit stopped rubbing her head and faced her sister.

"Don't look at me." Regina rolled her artfully made-up brown eyes and said with disdain, "I'm not a ventriloquist."

"No, but you hate helping me with my art."

"I love helping you and your *hobby*," Reggie corrected. "I just worry about getting bitten by angry, territorial spiders or snakes, or—" she glanced around nervously "—angry, territorial property owners."

"Didn't you hear me?" An angry, territorial-looking man appeared from behind a dented gray minivan. "I said, what are you doing here?"

Guilt, disappointment and a feeling she couldn't name froze Brit more completely than a complicated updo with too much hair spray.

The man strode forward. Broad shoulders, muscular arms, rumpled black hair and… Brit stopped cataloging his parts because that hair glinted almost blue in the sunlight and made Brit's fingers twitch for her hair-cutting scissors.

"Oh, my," her twin murmured wistfully,

having already forgotten her fear of getting bitten.

A thin boy appeared next, wearing light blue, grease-splotched coveralls like Brit's and a preteen's poor attempt at a sneer. He slouched against the minivan's rear fender, thrusting his hands in his pockets. His dark brown hair stuck out from beneath a faded green baseball cap.

Brit's fingers twitched again even as Shaggy Man drew closer. As a licensed beautician, bad hair drove Brit crazy. As did the feeling she could now name: artistic appreciation. Shaggy Man was like a Pollock painting—a riot of energy that was perfect chaos. She couldn't look away.

The man stopped ten feet from her, propping hands on hips. His black T-shirt and blue jeans had seen better days, while those bladed cheekbones and ice-blue eyes had probably appealed to a fair share of women. Everything about him said he was the kind of man her mother had warned her and Reggie about while they were growing up—tempting, dangerous, a man more concerned with who warmed his sheets at night than who made his coffee in the morning.

"That car is mine." Those cool blue eyes of

his skated across the landscape with chilly calculation. "Leave."

Reggie glanced at Brit.

Who reminded herself about big-girl panties. She unwound guilt, brushed out disappointment and gripped her defenses as firmly as the socket wrench she'd been using to remove the BMW's grille. "I was told this was Harmony Valley's vehicle graveyard." That the deserted cars and trucks were fair game for picking.

"The garage over there, this land and everything on it used to belong to my father." His stance remained as rigid as his words, at odds with that distracting, rule-breaking hair.

"But…" Used to belong to? *Shoot and darn.* "It's yours? The garage and the land?"

His glacial gaze found hers, so cold it crackled between them like icicles on eaves before they plunged to the pavement. "Papers went through yesterday."

A day late. That should have been the title of her life story.

"Let me handle this," Reggie said, half under her breath. She waded through the tall grass toward trouble. In her tight jeans and off-the-shoulder sweatshirt, she looked like she was walking across a catwalk, not the junkyard.

"I'm Regina. I manage the B and B in town."
An overstatement. Their grandmother owned
the modest B and B that Reggie hoped to buy.
"And this is my twin, Brittany. She uses junk
for her arts and crafts projects."

Arts and crafts?

Brit bristled. How was she ever going to
be taken seriously in the art world if her own
family dismissed her efforts? "Upcycle artist,"
she muttered, although based on the iceman's
smirk, the damage was already done.

"I'm Joe Messina. That's Sam." Joe didn't
come forward to meet Reggie. He didn't even
remove his hands from his hips. He held his
frown and his ground, not being the type to
shake hands with trespassers or fawn over
beautiful women.

Couldn't Reggie see that?

Apparently not. Reggie cast a confused look
over her shoulder. Being the twin who'd gotten all the good bone structure, Reggie wasn't
used to being overlooked, trespassing or not.

A breeze blew the wild grass and Joe's unruly hair. The wind swirled and tugged and
then, when neither Joe nor the grass bent, it
died out.

Brit's hopes of free materials for the gate

ornament she'd been commissioned to create nearly died along with the breeze. Nearly. "This grille is doing nothing for you. It's just sitting here."

"I'm not parting the car out." Joe stepped around Reggie to better glare at Brit.

"Here it comes," the boy said quietly, rubbing at the unruly hair at his neck.

"I'm going to get that car running and sell it." The determination in Joe's words would have had Brit believing him if it hadn't been for the age of Joe's clothing and the dismissive tone of the boy's comment.

She turned to the forty-year-old BMW. The faded paint and oxidized patina were nearly a work of art in themselves. But the tires had sunk into the soft dirt so deeply the sedan sat on its axles; the wheel wells were rusted nearly clear through; and the interior looked as if something furry had taken up residence. "Have you gotten a good look at this car? You'll need several years and several miracles to restore it." Brit swallowed her pride and lifted her voice. "I'll give you fifty bucks for the front grille."

His jaw worked. He half glanced at the boy

and then back to her. "Do you have the cash on you?"

Knowing the answer, Reggie headed toward Brit's small beat-up gray truck.

Brit barely had fifty dollars in her bank account, which was one reason she'd moved to Harmony Valley in the first place. Creating upcycle art wasn't cheap. Nor was living in San Francisco. "Well…"

"Then it's not for sale." Joe closed the distance between them and slammed the hood. His gaze drifted to the BMW's interior and the frost in his icy eyes thawed a smidge. He may have high hopes for the cars in this field, but he'd learn soon enough that building castles in the clouds would be easier than fixing anything here for resale.

Brit loaded her tools into her toolbox and followed Reggie.

She'd wait a week, let reality set in and make Joe a second offer.

Maybe then he'd take twenty-five.

"GRANDPA PHIL IS a simple man. Cold cuts and white bread. Bills paid by check and sent via the post office." Reggie was in glass-half-empty mode now. "He's going to fire you for this."

Her sister didn't have to sound so gleeful.

"Technically, he can't fire me if I'm renting a station from him. But if he does—" Brit unlocked the door to her grandfather's barbershop and propped it open "—you can say *I told you so.*"

"Hurry up, then. I'd rather be in and out before he gets here." Reggie picked up the back of the rust-speckled antique bicycle and the metal mermaid rider Brit had welded to its frame. "What did you think of Joe?"

Brit hefted the heavy end of her sculpture and backed into the shop. "I think he'll give me that grille for five dollars by Memorial Day." In her dreams, maybe. But she always dreamed big. At least she had until Dad died.

"I meant…" Reggie waddled in with her end. The rear wheel spun between Reggie's legs and the green aluminum mermaid tail swam over her shoulder. "What did you think of tall, dark and frowning?"

"He could use a haircut." Just a trim. A crisp cut would imply he'd been tamed. Who tamed a raging storm? "Set it down here." When the bike rims rested on the ground, Brit soaked in the familiar ambience of the place. It may only be a two-person barbershop, but it had the stations and the shampoo sink of a salon, much like the places Mom had once worked in.

Brit eyed the large framed mirror hanging over the chairs in the waiting area. A beer brand was stenciled in block letters in the middle of the glass, rendering it useless in a beauty shop. Looking at it made her feel uninspired to do hair or art. "I can't work with that hanging behind me all day."

"Don't change the subject. You thought Joe was cute, too." Reggie smoothed her hair using her limited reflection in the mirror. "Admit it."

"That man is not cute." Snowflakes were cute. Kittens were cute. Snow tigers were lethal. "Focus, Reggie. Mirror down. Mermaid bicycle up." Brit tried not to look in the mirror. She really did, but it was impossible not to. Not to look, not to compare.

Two women. Sisters. Anyone could see they were cut from the same cloth. Long, dark brown hair. Mahogany eyes. Wide smiles beneath pert noses—granted, Brit's wasn't as pert and she could mention more differences than similarities. For years, Brit hadn't realized she was any different from Reggie. Not when they were five and enrolled in Miss Deborah's School of Dance, where Reggie was placed front row, center stage, and Brit was relegated to the back row with the other gigglers. Not when they were eight and they'd sung in the school's holiday choir, where Reggie sang front and center, while Brit was assigned to the end of the middle riser next to Olivia Paige, who blew the biggest gum bubbles Brit had ever seen.

No. It wasn't until they were twelve that Brit's averageness relative to Reggie's beauty sank in. That year, they'd been allowed to wear make-up when they'd gone to the sixth-grade Promotion Dance. Reggie had put on war paint like a professional model, while Brit had declined. Reggie had danced to every song, each one with a different boy. And Brit? She'd sat on a bench against the wall with Margaret Hilden, whose leg was in a cast. Brit had held back her tears until they'd returned home. And then she'd cried on Mom's shoulder, on Dad's shoulder, even on Reggie's shoulder.

Later, she'd fought the hiccups while Mom tucked her in bed. She'd kissed Brit's forehead and whispered, "You have an inner beauty, honey. You'll always look better and be more popular if you wear makeup and cute clothes."

Even at twelve Brit had understood what her

mother was telling her: *you're the ugly duckling who'll never be a swan.*

Mom loved her, but Mom was in the beauty business, which was all about appearances.

Brit and Reggie had shared the same womb. The same bedroom. The same beat-up pickup their father used to drive. But they weren't identical. Reggie had won more points in the gene pool. Reggie looked like she hadn't ingested a carb in years, while Brit looked like she and carbs were on a first-name basis. And from the day of the Promotion Dance, they'd begun to go their separate ways. Reggie ascended to the throne of mama's girl, while Brit became Dad's sidekick. He was a metalworker and liked to tinker on cars.

The summer after the Promotion Dance, the neighbors had met to discuss turning their street into Christmas Tree Lane with lots of lights and decorations. Mom proclaimed they had to do it, but since she was always busy working or being a dance mom, and Dad hated yard duty—he'd taken out their front garden years ago and replaced it with rock and cacti—he had decided to create a metal forest for Santa.

He brought home his welding equipment,

along with scraps from the metal fabrication company where he worked. Brit watched him lay out sheets of metal on the garage floor like mismatched puzzle pieces. But when he welded them together, they created the most amazing seven-foot-tall trees. At her suggestion, they took old car parts and a muffler he hadn't yet hauled to the salvage yard and welded them into woodland animals—birds, bunnies, reindeer. Having learned nail art from Mom, Brit painted each creation, adding to the impression of whimsy and movement. They'd highlighted everything with lights. The lawn was unique and beautiful. Brit was hooked.

She quit Miss Deborah's dance studio, much to Reggie and their mother's dismay. She quit spending so much time on what she wore, although she still didn't go anywhere without makeup. She quit worrying so much about things that she couldn't control, like whether or not a boy liked her.

Despite this split, the twins remained close. But they went to different colleges—Reggie to study business, Brit to study art. In a reversal of Mom's expectations, Reggie had supported herself by working in a hotel, while Brit had supported herself by working in a beauty salon. Did Brit miss sparkly costumes, fancy hair and dance recitals? Sometimes. Did she miss propping up the wall at all those school dances she refused to go to? Not at all.

What she did miss was her dad. He'd died last year of heart disease after a series of heart attacks and surgeries that robbed him of his strength and spirit. It was a painful and scary end to a man she'd once thought would live forever. And his absence left a chasm between Brit's artistic dreams and her ability to create art. In a word, she was blocked. She hoped this move was a new beginning.

"She's beautiful, Brit." Reggie touched a spun, floating aluminum tress of red mermaid hair and then met Brit's gaze in the beer mirror, a gentle smile on her face. "And so are you."

Brit's throat crowded with love for her sister.

"And don't give me any of that ugly-duckling crap. Joe thought you were beautiful, too." Reggie's smile turned wicked. "He couldn't keep his eyes off you."

Heat rushed to Brit's cheeks. "From his perspective, I was trespassing and looting. He wanted to put the fear of God in me." That wasn't lust in those cold eyes of his.

Brit gestured that they pick up the bike and lean it against the shampoo sink in the corner.

"It ticked Joe off that he didn't succeed in shaking you." Reggie was still grinning. "Guys like a challenge."

"Correction." Brit peeked behind the beer mirror to see how it was hung, glad to find a thick wire and two big hooks. "You like a guy who's a challenge. I like nice guys." Ones who didn't suck the emotional energy—the lifeblood of Brit's creativity—out of her. "Grab the other side of the mirror and lift."

"Hanging your sculpture here worries me." Despite her reservations, Reggie did as asked and helped Brit store the mirror in the back room. She returned to stare at the mermaid. "Don't put this up. It's a barbershop, Brit. There's no future for you here."

"Agreed. But that doesn't mean I want to work in a plain box, or give up hair and go halfsies on the B and B with you." Brit pulled two utility hooks from her coverall pockets and considered where to put them in the wall. "This is just to fill the gap until my art career takes off."

"Do you know how many artists are self-sufficient?" Reggie, being Miss Glass-Half-

Empty, said. "You wouldn't be on your feet all day if you owned half the B and B. You'd have plenty of energy and time to make more pieces like this." Was that a hint of desperation in her voice?

Impossible. Reggie had emotional shock absorbers to take life's bumps in the road effortlessly. She planned her future like an airline pilot planned the route to his next destination. She'd never be desperate. Besides, she'd been talking about running the B and B for years. It had been her favorite topic with Dad.

Brit studied Keira's flowing lines. The effortless wave to her hair had taken days to achieve, with Dad on the sidelines cheering her on. She'd never sell Keira because she'd never create anything as perfect as the mermaid again. If she created anything ever again. *Geez. Now, that's maudlin.* And Reggie was waiting for an answer. She tossed her a question instead. "Do you know how many B and Bs make a profit?"

"Touché," Reggie murmured. That didn't stop her from presenting her case. "But owning the only rooms for rent in this town will be profitable when the winery becomes more popular." Wine-thirsty tourists were already making the trek to this far-flung corner of Sonoma County. "Can't you see that?"

"The only thing I can see is a blank wall. You know white space bugs me." Brit walked to the truck for a drill and a hammer.

A few minutes later, Keira hung on the wall. Her aluminum hands held the handlebars and the rest of her swam whimsically above the bike as if she was riding underwater.

Reggie stepped back to view the piece. "People will want their hair cut just to get a look at her."

"My wallet hopes you're right." Regardless, there was something about the mermaid's balanced, carefree movement that made her breathe easier. "This sculpture… It's the first one I've created that made me feel like a real artist." One that other artists could respect. One that Dad could be proud of.

Before Keira, people had looked at her creations and said, "How nice." Which was their polite way of covering their real opinion: *What is that supposed to be?* Brit could always sense the truth by their carefully modulated tone of voice. Which made her resentful of their need to try to be kind. Which made her hate anything other than the truth in all aspects of her life.

Reggie hugged her. "Leona wants you to come to dinner tonight. And I want you to be my partner in the bed-and-breakfast, but if you become the next art world sensation, I won't complain."

"Much." Brit smiled at her twin. "Lighten up. You'll buy out Grandmother Leona and be a success without me."

Reggie didn't look so sure.

CHAPTER TWO

"You should've sold the lady the grille." Sam spoke with the gravitas of an eleven-year-old who knew everything as she washed her hands in the chipped kitchen sink in the apartment over their repair shop.

Joe couldn't smile like a good dad should've at his daughter's wisdom. His smile had gone the way of cement shoes off the end of a deep-water pier. "She wasn't serious about paying." If Brittany had been, she would've gotten out her cash then and there.

"We don't work on wrecks," Sam said. "We work on performance machines."

Oh, for the luxury of ego.

Gone were the days of big-screen TVs in every room, recliners with heating massage and vehicles with air-conditioned leather seats. Joe took in the neglected bachelor pad. The brown couch with wooden arms must be from the 1950s. The small Formica table in the cramped dining area didn't seem any newer. And he'd bet no amount of scrubbing would remove the scuff marks in the gray linoleum.

Joe had traded in the good life. In return, he hadn't been arrested and had kept custody of Sam. He'd get used to the lack of finer things. He might never get used to being forced to choose between the uncle who'd saved him half a lifetime ago and Sam.

Sam, who needed to understand this was their new reality. Uncle Turo and his larger-than-life lifestyle was no longer an option.

"Those cars in the field?" Joe pointed out the window. "Those are the kinds of cars I used to work on when I lived here as a kid." The kinds of cars that were going to provide for him and Sam for the next five to ten years. Less for good behavior.

"Ew." She'd said that the first time they'd entered the apartment this morning. And again when she'd seen the hard-water stains in the toilet. And once more when she'd spotted a garden snake slither into a hole in the wall of the garage office.

That had made Joe want to say *ew*, too.

Once they were rid of the trespassers, they'd finished unloading the truck and trailer that had their beds and few belongings—the possessions the FBI let them keep. Only then had he spared a glance to the house he'd grown up in. The one he refused to live in.

Besides bad memories, there'd be too much square footage to heat or cool for it to make sense for him and Sam to move in there. He'd barely looked at the barn in back where the family had once kept their personal vehicles. It was practically drowning in blackberry bushes and would probably have more spiders and snakes than either he or Sam was comfortable with.

Instead, he'd chosen the apartment his grandfather, and later his Uncle Turo, had lived in. He focused on being thankful that he hadn't done anything illegal, and concentrated on rebuilding his life and his daughter's.

"We'll inventory the cars in the field later and find out which ones we own." He wouldn't sell a car he didn't have the legal title to. He led Sam downstairs, noting midway he needed to repair a soft tread. "We'll start work on whichever one's in the best shape once we get some paying customers."

"Dad," Sam said with lawyerly seriousness. "There is no *best shape* in that field."

There was no best shape in his memories of this place either. Everywhere he looked he saw Uncle Turo. Around the field there were still remnants of the dirt track Uncle Turo had made for him and his brothers to race their motorcycles. In the kitchen cupboard he'd found an old container of Uncle Turo's favorite spice, and his business cards were stacked behind the service counter. Everywhere he looked there was a memory of how Uncle Turo had shown up and held the family together after Mom left and Dad fell apart. It made Joe's decision all the more painful.

He'd made the right choice, the only choice, a father's choice. That didn't mean he didn't feel the consequences of his decision in the guilt rooted in his throat, the anger planted on his shoulders or the regret twined around his heart.

For Sam's sake, he'd bound his guilt, his anger and his regret deep inside him. Only occasionally did the bindings unravel, crowding the air out of his lungs.

He pushed through the office door to the parking lot and unhitched the trailer he'd towed from LA. What would the trailer be worth? Enough for car parts to restore a wreck in the field? Doubtful. But doubtful was better than nothing. "Let's go into town and pass out some flyers." He'd typed them up and had them printed at one of those office-supply stores in Santa Rosa. "Who knows? We might get lucky and find someone with car trouble."

"Sell the grille," Sam repeated, opening the passenger door of their pickup. The hinges sounded like a wire brush being dragged over rusty sheet metal. "This truck is pathetic."

"It's a classic." Joe tried to believe it, tried to infuse his words with optimism. "Even a pathetic truck can be the best of a bygone era."

He'd bought the cheap red pickup last week. After a bit of work, the big block engine ran with race-car precision. The rest of it wouldn't have been out of place in the field behind their garage.

The women picking their field for treasures had been driving a similar "vintage" truck, which was surprising. They'd looked like sensible sedan drivers. Although...

Maybe not Brittany. Stained coveralls and scuffed work boots said one thing. Short, black, polka-dot-painted fingernails and carefully applied makeup said another. Something about her didn't add up. She didn't look like she knew how an engine worked, much less how to pop the hood. But she'd held the socket wrench with confidence and had tucked it into a full toolbox, one lacking pink-handled tools.

Athena would've liked her. Athena would've taken Brittany's money for the grille. Or the promise of it.

His wife had always been too trusting in others.

Joe's head throbbed. Memories flashed. The wet road. The unexpected turn. The smell of a hot engine and cold blood.

It was better to focus on the here and now.

Joe took in the peeling paint on the garage's outer walls, the small cracked-asphalt parking lot, the roof shingles that looked as if a gusting wind would blow them free. He needed something new to focus on. The here and now was demoralizing. He wasn't in Beverly Hills anymore. There were no luxury cars waiting to be fixed. No roar of precision machines in service bays. No rumble of commands left in Uncle Turo's wake.

Uncle Turo would've liked Brittany, too. But he would've sold her the entire BMW plus an expensive service plan.

Joe's phone rang, playing the opening notes

of "Jailhouse Rock." He'd programmed the main number from the Los Angeles County jail.

Joe's head hammered harder, the pain moving behind his eyes as he let the call roll to voicemail.

He tossed a short stack of flyers advertising the opening of their business on the bench seat and climbed behind the large white plastic steering wheel.

"I miss Uncle Turo." Sam turned a too-innocent gaze toward him. "Do you think he's okay?"

"Yes," Joe lied, because eleven-year-olds shouldn't worry. "Forget Uncle Turo. Now it's you and me." That's what his brothers, Gabe and Vince, had told him when the law finally caught up to Turo. *Get out. Get away. Protect Sam.*

"So…this is our home?" Sam sighed with all the melodrama of a silent film heroine.

Joe didn't know what angle Sam was working, but he needed to keep her on the straight and narrow. "This is the end of the road. Home sweet home." He started the engine, listening for any inconsistencies, which was challenging given his pounding head. Hearing none, he put the truck in gear.

"We should send Uncle Turo our address."

A muscle in Joe's eye twitched. He drove past neat rows of vineyards, which were serene and picturesque, but he missed the frenetic pace of LA and the kaleidoscope of vehicles of every make, cost and color.

Sam sighed again, perhaps upset that her request to communicate with Uncle Turo had fallen on deaf ears. "Do I have to start school on Monday? I can wait until fall to go back. You can't run the garage on your own."

Or perhaps they were revisiting the argument about how this move had made her realize she didn't need school.

Their arrival coincided with spring break. The school in Harmony Valley was minuscule, nothing like her old school with hundreds of kids. Or what Joe had experienced growing up here.

More than a decade ago, the mill—the biggest employer in town back then—had exploded and shut down, causing a mass exodus of young families in need of regular paychecks. Joe's family had been among them. Eventually, the schools had closed as more people left. Now, after nearly becoming a ghost town, Harmony Valley was poised to thrive. Joe intended to take advantage of being the first repair shop to resume business. And Sam could take advantage of the low teacher-student ratio. The Harmony Valley School District had just reopened and had one teacher for a handful of elementary school children.

"Dad." Sam's voice shrunk to the level of wistfully made wishes. "Remember when Mom used to buy me new clothes before school started?"

With his head pounding and his eye twitching, Joe felt as worn-out as a tire on its third retread. "It's April, Sam." And they didn't have money for new clothes. Uncle Turo had seen to that.

"Yes, but…" Sam turned to look at him, a petite version of Athena's classic features with puppy-dog brown eyes. He might have been won over if not for the hint of dogged determination in the set of Sam's mouth. That came from his side of the family. "Dad, it's a new school."

"Sam, you'll be in class with a handful of elementary girls. They won't care if your clothes aren't new." People in Harmony Valley were different. Or so Uncle Turo used to say. Joe didn't remember if that was true. When last he'd lived here, he'd been a hell-raising, angry teenager, more concerned with rebelling against authority than being accepted.

At sixteen, he'd viewed everyone over the age of thirty as the enemy. They'd either driven too slow or complained he drove too fast. They'd lived happily within the boundaries of society, while he'd felt rules weren't for him. He hadn't appreciated that the very things he resented about Harmony Valley had protected him as a child. Not until he'd needed a safe harbor for Sam.

Now he hoped what Uncle Turo said was true, because he wanted to provide his kid with an environment that didn't judge her for her great uncle being a crook.

Joe drew a steadying breath, willing his eye to stop twitching and his head to stop pounding. Starting over wasn't supposed to be so hard. "Why don't we put up flyers at the bakery first?" Sugar. It was just the distraction Sam needed. They could afford a little sugar, couldn't they?

Sam slumped, staring out the window as Joe turned onto Main Street and down memory lane.

At first it seemed nothing had changed. The cobbled sidewalks, window awnings and old-fashioned gaslights remained. There was the pawn shop and the pizzeria. There was the barbershop where he'd gotten his hair cut. There was the bakery, and farther down, the Mexican restaurant.

A second glance showed him that time hadn't stood still. The corner grocery was dark. The ice-cream parlor where kids used to go after school was vacant. The stationery store had been taken over by something called Mae's Pretty Things.

Main Street had been the heartbeat of town. Bustling. Never an empty storefront or an empty parking space. Now it felt deserted, despite a few scattered cars.

They parked, grabbed the flyers and went inside Martin's Bakery. Again, there was a sense of time standing still. The same mismatched wooden tables and chairs, framed yellowed photos from the bakery's past on the wall, fresh sweets in the glass case. The smell of rich coffee was new. And the place was surprisingly crowded with retirees—which was great. They'd drive dated cars that didn't require expensive diagnostic equipment that rivaled the cost of sending a man to the moon.

Conversation died almost the same time as the door swung closed behind them.

The familiar feeling of his youth, of not belonging, prickled Joe's skin and tensed his shoulders. He longed to hide behind a motorcycle jacket and a sneer.

"Dad." Sam edged closer to him. "Why are they all…"

He thought Sam was going to say *staring.*

"…so *old?*"

Someone chuckled. The crowd released a collective sigh. The young woman behind the counter waved them over with a sunny, welcoming smile. Joe's sense of déjà vu receded.

Now was the perfect time to announce the garage was back in business, before conversations resumed.

Words stuck in the back of Joe's throat.

He'd never been much good at public speaking or composing smooth sentences. Joe and his brothers had grown up on the wrong side of the river. Their parents weren't perfect or even well liked. Dad had mental-health issues that made him unpredictable and volatile. Mom liked to argue with anyone about anything. Their parents and status in life made the boys self-conscious, but had also given them a tough core that held up the chip Uncle Turo later placed on their shoulders.

When Turo came to town, he'd given them an outlet for their resentment—motorcycles— and, not being a fan of mama's boys, he'd encouraged their rebellious attitude. Not exactly the best way to help them fit into small, sleepy Harmony Valley, but a blessing to three teens longing for a guiding hand. Any guiding hand.

But that was in the past. Joe was done with motorcycles and mischief. He was a single dad. A business owner. A responsible taxpaying citizen of Harmony Valley.

Joe cleared his throat and stepped forward. "I'm Joe Messina and this is Sam. We're reopening the garage over by the highway."

"Messina?" A thin old man squinted at them. He wore a red tie-dyed T-shirt and had a gray ponytail hanging down his back. "One of Tony Messina's boys?"

Joe nodded.

"I'm Mayor Larry." The aging hippy eyed Joe as if unsure how to tally his vote. Perhaps assuming Joe's opinion was favorable, he added with all the enthusiasm of a politician, "Welcome home."

"Are you the Joe Messina whose mother used to be in the quilt club?" A wrinkled woman with short purplish-gray hair sat in the window seat. She wore a hot-pink tracksuit and had a quilt square in her lap. She stared at them with kind curiosity. "Her pinwheel quilt blocks were exquisite."

Joe nodded, breathing easier.

"The Joe Messina who was a lineman on the high school team?" asked an elderly Asian man with a walker next to his seat. The table in front of him held a checkerboard, pieces midgame. "The one who lost his temper and punched the other team's quarterback?"

The mayor wrinkled his brow.

"Uh…" Joe barely dipped his head, very much aware of Sam at his side. This was like entering a room of talking elephants. They hadn't forgotten anything. He hoped they didn't mention his dad. But he prayed they didn't mention Uncle Turo.

"The Joe Messina who set fire to the gymnasium?" This from a beefy senior with what looked like orange cat hair on his red polo shirt. He sat across from the checker player and might have been the fire chief back in the day.

"That fire was an accident." Grabbing Sam's arm, Joe moved toward the main counter. A large tablet above the cookies flashed a message: Read Today's Blog (Zucchini and Jalapeño Cookies with Sweet Lime Glaze). "I think that's enough reminiscing for one day."

A well-dressed brunette paying for her coffee turned to give him a teasing smile. "Man, it sucks to be you." It was Regina, the B and B manager and would-be car-part thief. She was too pretty and high-maintenance-looking to pick auto parts regularly. No. It was Brittany who was the brains of that outfit. "Makes me glad I didn't grow up here. My past remains in the past, if you know what I mean."

Regina didn't seem the type to have a dark past. Her sister, on the other hand… He'd bet she and that wrench of hers were trouble.

"Do you have fifty dollars now?" Sam said in a voice that was far too businesslike for a kid. She widened her eyes and her smile, having been taught how to work a crowd by one of the best crooks in the family tree. "I can sell the grille to you."

"Samantha Ellen," Joe said sharply. Sometimes his daughter was too big for her coveralls.

Regina stared at Sam as if working through a complicated math problem.

"It's my property, too." Sam jutted her delicate chin. "It's the Messina *Family* Garage."

"Samantha?" Regina's gaze flicked up to Joe's hesitantly.

What was there to be hesitant about?

"Samantha," Regina said again, firmly this time as she looked Sam in the eye. "You can ask Brit about the grille. She buys junk like I buy new clothes. All the time." With a tug at her gray sweatshirt—which hadn't been made for sweating—Regina took her coffee and left.

"I remember you now," the mayor said to Joe. "I was confused because all the Messina boys had long hair, drove fast and had a penchant for getting into scrapes."

"All in the past," Joe assured him. Vince had a decent job on an oil rig in the Gulf Coast, Gabe was overseas with the military and Turo was behind bars.

"You still have long hair." The woman with purplish-gray curls didn't sound reproachful. She sounded flirty. "I bet women *love* that rebellious scowl of yours."

"Eunice," the blonde behind the counter scolded. She was in her twenties with a friendly face that was naggingly familiar.

"Nine times out of ten," the former fire chief said in a loud voice, suggesting either a need for hearing aids or a grudge against accidental arsonists, "long hair and getting into scrapes go hand in hand."

"Hey," said the tie-dyed-T-shirt-wearing mayor as he flicked his long gray ponytail. "I resemble that remark."

While the fire chief apologized, Joe spied his reflection and overgrown hair in the glass bakery case. He knew he needed a haircut, but it'd been at the low end of his budget priorities.

"Ignore them." The woman behind the counter grinned. "They're…a conservative bunch. But harmless." Her bright smile, short blond hair and lack of a history with the Messinas should have soothed him. "I'm Tracy. I think… you went to school…with my older brother. Will Jackson?"

So much for a lack of shared history.

"I remember Will," Joe said tightly. Mr. Golden Boy. Mr. All-American. Mr. Could-Do-No-Wrong.

"Now, Will," the former fire chief boomed. "There was a boy who turned out right."

Joe's shoulders locked as tight as the old BMW's carburetor was sure to be. He'd been hoping for a new start. For anonymity. Maybe some leftover goodwill from the past. The Messinas hadn't been all bad...had they?

Samantha took his hand. "My dad turned out all right." So young to be his fiercest supporter.

What did it say that she also defended Uncle Turo?

Joe had to do right by her. He *was* doing right by her. He'd make the citizens in Harmony Valley see he was reformed.

Look on the bright side, Athena would have said. *A new start.*

Don't apologize for who you are, Uncle Turo would have said. *Stand tall.*

So he had long hair? At least it wasn't winter and Joe wasn't wearing his black leather jacket. And he hadn't ridden into town on a Harley. Wouldn't that have played to type?

On the other hand...

He brushed his fingers through his hair. A haircut to show the conventional crowd he was respectable wouldn't hurt. The barbershop was down the street, and Phil Lambridge used to cut his hair. At least he had until Joe took Leona Lambridge's new Cadillac for a midnight joyride on a dare from Vince and got caught.

CHAPTER THREE

"Don't change another thing."

Brit pulled her head out of the supply cabinet filled with sixty years of barbershop supplies. She stared at Grandpa Phil, at his sweet lined face and his short-sleeve, wrinkled white button-down. He looked as outdated as the decades-old box of men's hair color in her hand.

That will not *be me fifty years from now.*

"I'm not changing anything." Brit added the box of hair color to the already full trash can. "I'm cleaning."

"Something's changed." Grandpa Phil's hands shook as he held the open newspaper, but they didn't shake with anger. His hands always trembled nowadays. "You hung an old bicycle on my wall. What will you dig out of the trash next? A pair of worn sneakers?"

"It's called upcycling. Repurposing things that have been thrown away. People like it. *I* like it." She may be a beautician by trade, but in her heart she was an artist. An artist who'd been commissioned for her work.

"People don't like change," Grandpa Phil said, raising his newspaper higher so she couldn't see his face.

"Meaning you? Or your customers?" Few as they might be. "Or perhaps those retired friends of yours who like to gossip and play checkers all day at Martin's Bakery?"

"I'll have you know that playing checkers keeps me mentally sharp." Phil turned a page and rattled the newspaper. "I'm sharper than the reporter who wrote this article on local crime in Cloverdale. He said they arrested a catfish."

Brit didn't bother explaining the social-media term that referred to taking on a false persona to scam someone. The fact that the reporter was accurate would only make Grandpa more upset. And given that Brit wasn't exactly in a Zen mood, she didn't need him wound up, too.

"Now, don't change anything else or you can go live with your grandmother like Regina did."

Brit contained a shudder. Grandmother Leona was the Captain Bligh of Harmony Valley. She ran a tight ship and just being around her made Brit want to mutiny.

When Reggie announced she needed a break from corporate America and was moving to Harmony Valley to run a B and B—Leona's B and B—Brit had been happy for her. And truth be told, she'd also been a tad envious. Had Brit taken a running leap toward her dreams of being an artist? Nope. There'd been too many excuses—Dad's death, bills, the price of scrap and metal—and too much doubt—she'd talked through the logistics of almost every project with Dad. Could she create her art without him?

If she wasn't careful, she was going to be eighty and her only legacy worth noting would be Keira.

So she'd followed Reggie to Harmony Valley. She'd convinced Grandpa Phil to rent her a station in the barbershop and a bedroom in his home for figures significantly below those she paid in San Francisco. She told Reggie she was moving to the small, remote town in the easternmost corner of Sonoma County to lend her support. And she'd told herself that she'd work half days at the shop and the rest of the time on her art.

The barbershop door opened and the town

council began to enter. The three elderly women had stopped by earlier to introduce themselves, and this time they'd brought gifts—cleaning supplies.

Brit sighed with relief.

"Here we go," Phil muttered.

"We thought you could use some help cleaning." Agnes planted a bucket and a mop near Phil. Her stature—small and unassuming—was at odds with her nature—big and confident. Her pixie-cut hair was as dull gray as Phil's, but her eyes were sharper than Brit's thinning shears.

Rose danced in, holding the broom like a waltz partner. She was as slender as a ballerina and her ivory chignon was just as tight as it would be if she was performing in a ballet. "Will you be coloring hair, Brittany?" Rose dipped her broom partner. "I'm thinking of becoming a redhead."

"The world isn't ready for Redheaded Rose." Mildred trundled in, a spray bottle of disinfectant hooked on her walker. Her snow-white curls stood stiffly. They'd been unrolled hastily and hadn't been combed out. In a way, Mildred reminded Brit of Mrs. Claus...if Mrs. Claus wielded a walker and squinted from behind thick glasses, ready to review the unruly elf brigade. "Where are you putting the hair dryers? I don't see any hair dryers."

"Ironic, Mildred." Rose spun with the broom. "Since you don't see."

Brit revised her assessment of Mildred's hair from unrolled hastily to unrolled by feel.

"My hearing is just fine, Rose," Mildred said sternly, banging her walker around so she could use the built-in seat. "The hair dryers will be perfect underneath that thing on the wall."

Brit tried not to be upset by Mildred's calling Keira a *thing*. She'd save her emotion for critics with better eyesight.

"We aren't getting hair dryers." Phil rattled the paper more than usual. "This is a barbershop."

"Grandpa, I'm paying you rent so I have a spot to do women's hair. I deserve half the space." Especially since he wasn't using any. He hadn't cut one head of hair yesterday and based on the dust on his station, he hadn't cut any hair in weeks.

"The electrician I know said he'd be here Monday." Agnes had wasted no time assessing Brit's needs and wasn't shy about pitching in. She poked around the supply cabinet and held up an inky black toupee with her thumb and forefinger. "Whose was this?"

"Crandall's." Grandpa Phil lowered his paper and his gray eyebrows. "His wife didn't want him buried in it and thought someone else might use it someday. Why do we need an electrician?" He'd been at Martin's Bakery when they'd stopped by the first time and wasn't privy to their conversation.

"I don't want to blow a fuse and cut the electricity to the entire block when I plug in the hair dryers," Brit said briskly. "Do you know how much electricity a chair with a hair dryer attached uses?"

Before Grandpa could answer, a figure appeared in the barbershop's window.

Joe stood outside the glass, looking just as dangerously handsome as he had a few hours before. Dark hair, dark glare, dark outlook toward others. He reached for the door just as his ice-blue gaze connected with Brit's. His hand paused in midair.

"A customer's gonna get away." Grandpa Phil lurched out of his chair and shoved the door open. "Never mind the chitchat. The barber is in." He stepped out on the sidewalk, letting the door shut behind him.

"It's one of those Messina boys." There was awe in Agnes's voice. "I recognize the long black hair. They were a handful—too much for Tony with his other challenges."

"They should have gone to prison." Rose held the broom like a staff. "Painting the water tower green for St. Patrick's Day. Racing those motorcycles up and down Parish Hill." She pounded the broom bristles into the floor. "Why, one of them nearly burned the gymnasium down. It's a miracle they didn't kill themselves, much less anyone else."

"I always admired how they drove those motorcycles," Mildred said, reminding Brit that someone had once told her Mildred raced cars back in the day. "Not everyone knows how to take a corner at speed." She adjusted her thick glasses and blinked toward the doorway. "They used to be the most handsome young men in town. How does he look?"

"Like he could charm you out of your car keys and you wouldn't report him for stealing," Rose begrudgingly admitted. "Long hair. Blue jeans. Boots. All he's missing is a leather jacket and a motorcycle."

"There were more like him?" Brit was glad Reggie wasn't around to hear the wonder in her voice.

As one, the town council ladies nodded.

Brit needed to regain her perspective, focus on the man's flaws. "Did any of the Messina boys have a good haircut?"

"Nope. Unkempt troublemakers. Every one," Agnes said with a dreamy sigh.

"I have to admit." Rose began sweeping, but it was more like a ballroom dance. "Messina men improve with age."

"Sam!" the object of the women's infatuation called out loud enough they heard him through the glass. "I'm getting a haircut. Wait for me here." Joe pointed to the curb.

"Okay, Dad," came a high-pitched prepubescent reply. A familiar figure—slight, in blue coveralls—appeared on the sidewalk. Sam plopped onto the curb, booted feet in the gutter, slouching and drinking from a Martin's Bakery to-go cup.

Phil ushered Joe inside and into his chair. "What are you looking for today? Trim? Buzz cut? Mohawk?"

"Trim." Joe spared Brit a look that was stay-away contemptuous.

Lighten up, dude. It wasn't as if I made away with anything this morning.

Phil opened a drawer at his station. It took him several tries to clench a folded drape with his age-spotted fingers.

The first inklings of apprehension worked their way through Brit. She'd noticed Phil's tremulous hands for years, but hadn't made the leap to what that meant in terms of him cutting hair. She couldn't let him cut anyone's hair. At least, not with scissors. "How about a buzz cut, Mr. Messina?"

Phil's head came up. "Messina?"

"No, thanks." Joe stared at Brit as if she'd teleported from another planet and offered him a ride on a unicorn.

Phil was stuck on Joe's last name. "You're one of those Messina boys who used to live here?"

Joe sighed, as if being recognized was the worst news of the day. "Yes."

"Is that…" Rose glided gracefully to the window with the broom, which took skill, considering she looked to be nearing eighty. "Is that a girl?"

Brit's attention turned to the child on the sidewalk. The child she'd assumed was a boy because of the shapeless, grimy coveralls and an equally grimy baseball cap. Brit had gone through a tomboy phase after the devastation of the Promotion Dance. She, of all people, should have recognized a girl beneath the trappings.

"Hell, yeah, Sam's a girl," Joe said defensively. "Anyone can see that. Brittany's sister just called her by her full name in the bakery." But this last was said without Joe's typical iceman tone.

Agnes and Rose exchanged doubtful looks.

"Wow." Brit should have felt better that other people assumed his daughter was a boy, too, but she didn't. The little girl had probably been called a boy more than once and she was getting to an age where those remarks would register and sting. "Poor Sam."

"Poor Sam." Joe snorted like a bull about to charge. "You don't know what you're talking about."

"Sam…" Agnes said evenly. "As in *Samantha*?"

"Yes," Joe ground out.

"What's going on?" Mildred asked, squinting toward the window through her thick glasses.

"I see someone, but can't tell if it's a boy or a girl."

"Exactly," Rose said.

"SHE'S A GIRL." Joe kept his voice down, but that didn't stop his eye from twitching. "What's wrong with you people? Brittany was wearing coveralls this morning and I didn't mistake *her* for a man." Granted, Brittany filled out her clothes differently than his daughter did.

The barbershop had fallen silent. Uncomfortably, painfully silent. And he guessed it wasn't because Phil was trying to remember if Joe was the Messina who'd taken his ex-wife's car for a joyride.

Joe refused to turn and look at Sam, unwilling to validate their perception. Lung-deflating doubt—that he wasn't a good father for a girl—tried to suffocate him.

"Hard to tell gender nowadays," Phil said, interrupting Joe's panic attack. He flung a plastic drape over Joe's lap. It smelled musty and unused, kind of like the garage apartment's shower curtain. "If she's a girl, you might want to buy a pair of pink coveralls." He fumbled with the drape snap at Joe's neck. "Which Messina are you?"

"The only Messina in your chair," Brittany said, moving behind Joe so she was visible to him in the mirror. She widened her eyes and waggled her eyebrows at Joe in some kind of undecipherable car-part-thief code. "Anyone can wear pink or coveralls nowadays, Grandpa."

Grandpa? The Lambridges were among the most upright, uptight citizens in town. Was Brittany a beautician with an innocent hobby? A woman willing to pay for car parts like a law-abiding Lambridge? Or was she cut from the same cloth as Uncle Turo? The kind of person who cut corners. The kind of person Joe couldn't afford to have in his life anymore.

"It's common to mistake gender at that age. There's no bumps or curves or whiskers to go on." Phil's hands fumbled in a drawer for something. "Plus there hasn't been a Messina girl in town. Ever."

"That's not exactly hard science, Grandpa." Brittany gave Joe an *I can't believe you don't understand me* look.

"You still haven't told me." Phil picked up a pair of scissors with hands that shook. A lot. "Which Messina are you?"

"I'm Joe." Finally, possibly too late, he'd

cracked Brittany's code. Her brown gaze reflected his worry about scissors and unsteady hands. Joe shifted in the chair and moved his gaze in the mirror to the antique bicycle on the wall behind him, the one ridden by a playfully curved, brightly painted, aluminum mermaid. It was nothing he'd expect to find in a barbershop. But then again, he'd expected a barber with a reassuring hand. "Hey, Phil…um…are you okay?"

"He's quick, that boy." The woman sitting in the walker chuckled. "Took me another five minutes in that chair before I panicked."

"I'm fine," Phil said cheerfully, as if he hadn't heard Mildred. "Never better."

"Your hands…" Joe met Brittany's gaze again. He'd never admit it, but his gaze might have been pleading.

Brittany laid a hand on Phil's forearm. "How about I give Shaggy Joe a trim?"

"You?" Joe choked out. What did this wrench-wielding woman know about cutting hair? Maybe Joe should take his chances with Phil.

"Yes, me. I'm licensed to trim." Brittany gestured to a framed certificate on the wall.

If Brit was a beautician, her appearance shouted thirty-five-dollar haircut. She may have worn coveralls earlier, like Sam's, and her dark brown hair was mostly hidden under a cap, like Sam's. But that's where the similarities ended. Phil's granddaughter had rhinestones on her baseball cap, sparkling threads in her thin pink sweater and in her black leggings.

Truthfully, he didn't mind the leggings. Brittany had a nice pair of legs. But he did mind the salon-like sparkle if it meant he'd pay more for a simple haircut.

"The man sat in my chair." Phil raised his scissors like they were the torch held by the Statue of Liberty. Unlike Lady Liberty, Phil's hand wavered, bringing Joe back to his original dilemma.

"Phil, I…uh… I'm Joe, the bad Messina you remember." In truth, Joe's two older brothers had probably raised more hell than Joe, but a man had to bail when sharp objects were near arteries. "I'm the one who took Leona's car for a joyride."

"Joe, Joe, Joe." Phil tsked, lowering his unsteady hand. "Leona said she'd given you permission."

Only after Uncle Turo had talked to her.

"Don't be nervous," Phil said. "I used to cut

your hair all the time when you were a kid. And I don't hold grudges."

"True," the old woman in the walker said, leaning forward and peering at Joe through bottle-thick lenses.

Joe caught Brittany's gaze in the mirror once more.

"Don't look at me." Brittany held up her hands. "I tried to save you."

"My hands have been like this for years," Phil said, a twinge of annoyance in his voice.

"True," the rail-thin senior by the window said, pounding the bristles of her broom on the floor.

Phil stared at his scissors. His wrinkled features maintained a tentative hold on defiance. "And I haven't cut a client yet."

"Also true," said the short old woman with the boyish haircut.

As if to prove a point, snip-snip went Phil's scissors in the air. Except Phil nearly poked Joe's eye out with the sharp blades.

"The operative word being *yet*," said the lady with the broom. "Don't young people film disasters nowadays? Who has a camera?"

Joe eased forward in his chair, the words *I've changed my mind* forming on his lips.

"Let me do this one, Grandpa." Unexpectedly, Brittany ran her fingers through Joe's hair.

Joe stopped thinking about leaving.

Brittany's fingernails skimmed across Joe's scalp, lifting his hair and letting it fall back down. Her touch was mesmerizing.

The last person to mesmerize Joe was Uncle Turo, suspected felon.

"After all," Brittany said, "starting Tuesday, I'll be doing pin curls and petal teases."

"I wanted a dye job," the broom lady said in the tone of the misunderstood.

"You can cut my hair for ten bucks," Joe said gruffly. He could barely afford that.

"Joe makes it sound as if you should pay him for the privilege, Brittany." The woman sitting in the walker chuckled. Behind her glasses her eyes were starting to look like something you'd see in a fun-house mirror.

Or maybe that was because Joe's eye was twitching again.

Phil tossed his scissors back in a drawer. "Outmaneuvered by my own kin."

Joe might have breathed easier if not for the realization that Brittany was as wily as Uncle Turo.

"I'm going to Martin's to play checkers."

The man walked with an uneven gait as shaky as his hands. Somehow he managed to hold the door open for Sam to come inside.

Brit's fingers were still working their thirty-five-dollar haircut magic on Joe's mane, making him wish he had thirty-five dollars to spare on a regular basis.

"I'm Agnes." The diminutive older woman came closer to get a better look at what Brittany was doing to Joe's hair. "Are you the only Messina opening up the garage?"

"Yes, ma'am." He and his brothers had inherited the garage and house when his father overdosed, but they'd done nothing with it beyond paying taxes. He'd bought out his brothers with every penny in the bank the FBI hadn't seized.

The thin, regal woman with the broom swept closer. She looked like a grandmother of one of his classmates. The woman who volunteered every year to help with the class play as long as it was a musical. And her name was...Rose.

"No Mrs. Messina?" Rose asked. She never seemed to stop moving.

"She's dead, ma'am."

Sam sank into a chair beneath the mermaid, glancing at a stack of magazines on a low table.

She didn't react to the statement that her mother was dead. She'd spent half her life without a mother. Almost all her life without a caring grandparent. And now, no Uncle Turo.

If Sam didn't react, Brittany certainly did. Her fingers stopped exploring the texture of his hair, making Joe remember how everyone in Harmony Valley was in everyone else's business.

"You know…" Joe slid forward in the chair, away from Brittany's magical touch. "The haircut can wait."

Brittany's fingers brushed over his shoulder. "The town bad boy could use a haircut to look respectable."

He agreed. Why did she have to be right? It was going to take another decade for the older residents to forget what he'd done. "For ten dollars." Not a question. Not negotiable.

Unfazed, Brittany drew her ponytail over her shoulders, revealing a purple streak amid the rich brown. Coveralls and colored nails? Shop tools and beauty techniques? She was a tangle of contradictions he had no intention of unraveling. "I'd trim your hair for the grille."

The verdict was in. Brittany was more like Uncle Turo than a Lambridge. "I don't barter."

Especially when he wasn't sure who owned the car.

The woman in the walker scooted forward. "Are you talking about a barbecue grill?" He recognized her now. Mildred Parsons. He used to cut her lawn every summer. That is, until Uncle Turo came to town. "Every man needs a barbecue."

"Dad doesn't grill. He uses the microwave and a Crock-Pot." Sam giggled *like a girl!* "Brittany wants a car bumper from the field near our repair shop."

"Whatever for?" For once, Rose stopped moving.

"I incorporate old bike and car parts into art." Brit gestured to the mermaid riding the bicycle on the wall. "Things people no longer want can be made into something everyone can enjoy."

Joe looked at the sculpture more carefully, finally recognizing the bike for what it once had been—an early motorbike, probably from around 1920. It had rims, but it was missing tires and an engine.

"That motorcycle was worth a lot of money." Before it'd had all that curling aluminum welded to it, it'd been worth more than a new roof for the garage. What Brittany had done to that antique was blasphemous to a motor-cyclist. To him. In fact, to anyone who revered the past, and wanted to restore and protect it. Uncle Turo may not have a good moral com-pass when it came to the law, but he revered the art of a good machine.

"It's still worth a lot of money," Brittany said crisply, spritzing Joe's hair with water.

Two of the old ladies went to stand beneath Brittany's creation, admiring it. After a mo-ment, Sam joined them.

"I'd like to upcycle the BMW grille." Brit began snipping Joe's hair in back. "A contrac-tor in Malibu hired me to create a driveway gate with a vintage automobile look. The grille would be perfect cut in half. When the gate is closed, it'll look like a car is coming out at you."

"Cool," Sam, the traitor, said. She was young and susceptible to bad influences.

The anger he'd wadded into his chest for the past few weeks tried to break free. He couldn't save Athena. He couldn't save Uncle Turo. But he could definitely save his daughter and that car. "I won't let you ruin it. I won't let you put a grille on a gate with your arts and crafts glue gun."

"I'd weld it." Brittany fixed him with a hot stare that could have welded Joe to his seat. "I'd use a blowtorch. Same as I did with my mermaid, Keira."

She'd given her creation a name. Sam would find that fascinating. Next thing you know, Sam might find picking junk on someone else's property without permission fascinating, permissible even. Joe's need to keep his daughter grounded had him lashing out. "Girls who cut hair and paint their nails don't use blowtorches."

Caught in the cross fire, the three old ladies fell silent, watching their exchange with interest.

"That's a little sexist." Brittany sounded unruffled. She continued to fluff his hair. But the heat remained in her gaze.

Despite a healthy dose of self-loathing—*what kind of dad said things like that in front of his daughter?*—Joe leaned into Brittany's touch. It was a dare. A stupid dare. But he'd spent weeks keeping his emotions in check. It wasn't fair that this woman—this trespassing thief—undid the links anchoring his equilibrium.

Brittany didn't back down. She held his gaze in the mirror. And then she firmly tried to tilt his head into his chest. "Look down."

"No," he rasped, holding his head up.

"It's okay to be scared, Dad." Sam misread Joe. She came to stand next to him and found his hand beneath the drape. "He doesn't get his hair cut often."

A riot of feelings burned their way through his chest and churned through his stomach. He was a bad dad. He should be protecting his daughter, not the other way around. He should have realized sooner what was going on at Turo's garage. He should have known the money he'd been earning the past few years from Turo was too good to be legal.

"Don't cut off much," Sam said to Brittany, still holding his hand, still too trusting. "My dad's never had short hair."

"I'm not shearing him like a sheep." Brittany snipped away, her touch less than gentle. "I'm just giving it shape."

"No," Joe protested, sounding less like a man resentful of the corner he'd been trapped in. "I want it short and respectable."

"I'm not sure you'll ever pull off respectable." Brittany's chin nearly touched his crown as she pulled the hair above his ears along his cheekbones. "With a face like that..." Her cheeks turned as ripe as a Red Delicious apple. "Well, anyone can see you're not a banker."

The older audience's chuckles locked Joe's frown in place tighter than a wing nut on a long screw.

"She's right." Sam grinned.

"Cut it short," Joe said through gritted teeth. "I need to be respectable."

"Why?" Mildred said from her walker. "I've always thought respectable was boring."

"And people don't come to Harmony Valley to be boring." Rose moved about with the broom as if she were waltzing.

"That's right." Agnes placed her age-weathered hands on his daughter's shoulders, although she was barely taller than Sam. "People come here to be true to themselves."

Joe knew being true to himself wouldn't get him any customers. But when Brittany finished his haircut, Joe had to admit he felt more like himself—a man who didn't second guess himself, a man who dealt with life head-on.

"About that grille..." Brittany began.

"I might have sold it to you if you planned to put it on another BMW." Joe stood, digging in his back pocket for his wallet. "Clearly, you don't understand its value."

"Clearly—" Brittany glared at him "—you don't understand the value of art."

CHAPTER FOUR

"JOE THINKS YOU'RE a stripper." Mildred nodded to Brit after Joe and Sam left the barbershop.

One moment, Brit had been fine. Satisfied Joe left looking better than when he'd walked in. Relieved that he and his closed-minded attitude were gone. And the next...

Brit did a quick check of her cleavage and backside in the mirror above her station. Nothing was exposed, but she felt as if she'd shown something. Her hands shook as much as Grandpa Phil's. "I am not a stripper."

"Of course you are," Mildred said matter-of-factly, tugging at a stiff curl. "A stripper divests cars of their parts. Joe's a purist. He'd rather preserve the entire car."

"He'd rather spin his wheels and go nowhere." Brit bit her lip to keep from saying more. She knelt and rummaged in an unpacked box of her salon equipment, unable to stop herself from adding, "The cars on his property will never run again."

"Never say never." Rose swept Joe's cut black locks into a pile. "I heard the Messinas were running a repair shop for famous folks and their fancy cars."

"Those Messinas have motor oil running through their veins." Mildred sounded wistful. "If they had the right parts, they could fix anything. Trouble was, we couldn't always get the right parts out here."

"Oh, come on." Where had Brit put her teasing combs? "There must be twenty cars in that field. If they were mechanical savants, I find it hard to believe they couldn't find parts for that many vehicles."

"Well…the Messinas aren't responsible for all those abandoned wrecks." Agnes returned to poke around the supply cabinet. "I hate to admit our constituents are irresponsible, but—"

"Our constituents are irresponsible." Mildred ran her fingers through curls on the other side of her head, making her hair look as if she'd been electrocuted. "Ten years or so ago, when the garage closed, there may have been one or two cars in that field. But ever since then—"

Agnes raised her voice like a teacher trying

to regain control of her class. "I won't name names—"

"Crandall Barnes. Haywood Dillinger." Rose was more than willing to call her neighbors out.

"But—" Agnes ignored Rose "—when you're old—"

"Don't make excuses for them," Mildred said.

"—it's easier to just give something up!" Agnes was practically shouting now.

Brit found the plastic box of combs, chose a pick and stood, her shoulders stiff with almost-too-good-to-be-true hope. "So they aren't all Joe's cars? What about that BMW?"

Rose and Agnes looked to Mildred.

"A BMW? That would be… It was driven by…" Mildred closed her eyes and clamped her mouth in a squiggly line. "Why can't I remember who owned that car?"

"Because you're old," Rose said baldly. "I can't remember what I had for breakfast yesterday."

Would a registration card have survived in the BMW's glove box? Could Brit sneak out there again and check?

An image of lowered brows over glaring

blue eyes loomed before her, more off-putting than a beware-of-dog sign. But she wasn't much good at heeding warnings.

Take cutting Joe's hair, for instance. Those thick midnight-black locks were perfect for styling. A beautician's dream. She'd ignored his bluster and steered through the storm even when his frigid eyes warned her away.

Thank heavens Reggie hadn't seen her while she was working or she'd have called her out—there'd been too much unnecessary touching going on. The man had an energy that spoke to her. She just didn't want to learn his language.

Yeah, cutting Joe's hair had been sweet torture. She hoped she never had to do it again.

Right now, she had a different cause for itching fingers—Mildred's unfinished curls. "Can I tease out your hair, Mildred? On the house."

"Oh, dear." Mildred hunched in on herself. "Are my curls that bad? Why didn't someone tell me before Hiro saw me at the bakery?"

"They looked fine this morning for your beau," Agnes soothed. "You've just been worrying them."

"Into a mess," Rose stated.

"I wish I could see better," Mildred bemoaned.

Brit took that as permission, and once she got in the rhythm, the tension in her shoulders eased.

Agnes resumed her attack on the supply cabinet, while Rose swept Joe's hair into a dustpan.

"I used to see every detail," Mildred said, half to herself. "Road signs. Social Security checks. My reflection..."

Rose interrupted Mildred's pity party. "Brittany, my dear, can I book you for a hair appointment?"

Brit surveyed her work. Mrs. Claus looked much less frazzled. "If you're serious about going red..."

"I am. Book me. Now, please."

"Rose, what's the rush?" Agnes picked up a can of shaving cream that was so old it'd rusted on the bottom.

Rose nodded toward the window. Brit glanced over her shoulder, and then turned completely around.

Several cars were parking outside. White-haired ladies tumbled out like sea foam on a slow-cresting wave.

"Are they all coming here?" Brit asked. There must have been a dozen of them.

Another car pulled up, just as full as the others. The barbershop tide had turned.

"Word must have gotten out." Agnes dumped the shaving cream in the trash. "We haven't had a beautician in town since Minna's closed."

"She ran a salon out of her garage. Drafty as all get-out." Mildred patted her hair gingerly. "She died about eight years ago."

"Tuesday morning," Rose whispered urgently to Brit. "Nine thirty."

"Okay." Brit hurried to her station, flipped open her appointment book and penciled Rose in.

And then the wave hit.

"Do you offer perms?"

"Will you be doing nails?"

"I'd like a wet set and tease."

In no time, she'd taken a full week's worth of appointments. Had she thought she'd only work half days? She'd barely have time for a BMW reconnaissance, much less setting up a workshop at Grandpa Phil's.

It's only the first week. The excitement will wear off, she told herself.

Trying not to listen when a small, fearful voice inside hoped it might be.

"WE DON'T LOOK like we're open for business." Sam crossed her skinny arms over her skinny chest and gave her best impression of teen-age contempt. "With all the dust and grime and cobwebs, we could film a horror movie in here."

Joe kept his mouth shut and his opinions to himself.

The horror had begun a month ago when the FBI confronted him outside a diner on his lunch hour. They were building a case against Uncle Turo for a number of things, including accepting stolen property, money laundering and racketeering. Did Joe know anything?

Joe hadn't. Not until the two feds started talking. Then his brain had shifted into over-drive, putting together pieces that seemed in-nocent and random before. People bringing in cars that no longer ran and receiving cash. Guys trading motorcycles for engine work on street racers. Cars sold "on consignment" for unknown clients. He hadn't paid much atten-tion. He was too busy working and raising Sam to realize his uncle was a crook.

Which was why when they'd asked Joe if he knew where Turo kept numerous stolen cars, he'd been unable to answer. He didn't know.

"You can cooperate," Federal Agent Haas had said, not believing Joe was that naive. "Or we can bring you up on charges of obstruction of justice and send you to prison for five to ten years." He'd handed Joe his business card. "Oh, and by the way, I love your daughter's softball swing."

The FBI had been watching his daughter?

Joe hadn't been able to speak. He'd sat in his pickup for several minutes before he trusted himself to drive. He wanted to call Vince and Gabe and ask for their advice, but he already knew what he'd have to do. There was only one way to ensure Sam wouldn't lose another parent. Sell out Uncle Turo to the feds in a sting operation.

The horror continued. The garage doors were open, but not even the breeze could clear out the dank smell. Grime. Dust. Long-neglected tools hanging from hooks attached to pegboard on the walls. The wooden shelves were strewn with odds and ends. The workbench was brown, warped Formica. An ancient tow truck sat on deflated tires in one of the two service bays.

It was a far cry from the clean chrome fixtures of Messina's Garage in Beverly Hills.

Soon Joe would be working on junkers, not Jaguars; beaters, not Bentleys. But what choice did he have? After Turo was arrested and his assets frozen—including the bungalow Joe and Sam had lived in—Joe had to put food on the table somehow.

"Give it until Monday," Joe said. "Word will get out and cars in the bays will change things."

Sam sighed with her entire body. "Can't we hire someone to make the garage presentable? At the old garage—"

"I was an employee." Joe spoke evenly, trying to keep weeks of fear and anger from his tone—none of which was directed at his daughter. "I was hired to fix cars, but had no say in how the garage was run." Or in which laws Uncle Turo decided to break.

"Uncle Turo..." Sam hesitated. She knew Uncle Turo had been arrested, but didn't know why. She came to stand in the midst of the empty service bay. Almost in the exact spot Joe had been the day Uncle Turo had come to town after Joe's mother left. Sam worked her lips mulishly. "Uncle Turo—"

"Uncle Turo..." Joe glanced out the open doors, half expecting to hear a motorcycle rumble or explosive laughter heralding Turo's approach.

The only sound was a bird. It chirped and tweeted and sang like this was the best day on the planet.

That bird was so wrong.

Maybe he should listen to that voicemail he'd gotten earlier, the one left by the caller with the "Jailhouse Rock" ringtone.

Or maybe not.

"Uncle Turo isn't here to give you a free pass." Joe yanked a broom from its cobwebbed cupboard in the corner and began knocking down the thick tendrils that hung from the ceiling.

Thunder rolled in the distance. No. Not thunder. It was a motorcycle engine.

The hair on the back of Joe's neck rose.

"Uncle Turo! I knew he'd come to bring us home." Sam ran into the parking lot.

It couldn't be. Turo was locked up in the LA County jail, awaiting trial. Bail had been denied.

The sound of the engine came closer, silencing the bird. Joe could relate. He couldn't speak either. His throat was thick with *damn you*s and *thank God*s.

It took him a moment to register the cadence

of the bike. It wasn't the untamed, throaty grumble of a Harley. It wasn't the deep, refined rumble of an Indian. It was the high-pitched whine of a small bike. Economical. Down-market.

Joe lowered the broom and turned, not to see who it was, but to register Sam's disappointment.

He saw it in the slow slide of her innocent shoulders. The leaden creep of her arms around her broken heart. The waver to her chin as she fought tears.

The motorcycle put-putted past under the legal limit.

Sam's feet broke a speed record as she raced upstairs, slamming every door. To the office. To their apartment. To her room.

The rafters above Joe shook when she flopped on her bed, showering him in dust.

This was his life now. He had to be grateful. He and Sam. They were together.

It could have been worse.

Though it was hard to think of worse when you'd hit rock bottom.

"DIDN'T YOU CLEAN enough for one day?" Grandpa Phil stomped into the kitchen, a grumpy expression on his face.

Brit stopped scrubbing the refrigerator shelf she had in the sink and glared at him. "I should have taken one look at your kitchen and left." When she'd moved into his little house days ago, she'd been too tired to register the degree of kitchen filth and had been too busy settling in to do anything about it.

Phil shrugged. "I'm not as fastidious as your grandmother." Who'd divorced him twenty years or so ago.

"I was considering sleeping in my car and renting a port-a-potty." Or bedding down in the back room at the barbershop. Her arms ached from scrubbing. Now she understood why her family had stayed with Grandmother Leona the few times they came to visit. "You can't let things go like this. Here, it's not healthy. And at the shop… You can bet we'll get a surprise inspection by the state board. We have to keep things clean."

"The state board isn't coming here." He mini-stumbled on a loose square of linoleum, catching himself with a hand to the door frame before she could reach him.

"Are you okay? Maybe you should sit down."

He shuddered to his full height, nearly six feet. "I'm fine. I could stand here all night."

He listed to one side a few inches and gripped the door frame tighter. "When I agreed to let you stay, I didn't think you'd want to clean and decorate and change everything *here*. I'm single for a reason."

"Because you like to live in squalor?" Brit deadpanned.

He made a rumbling noise like an old hound dog when roused from its nap by an intruder.

"No offense, Grandpa—" Brit patted his shoulder "—but I'm too busy to catch every germ you've deposited in this house in the past two decades."

"I can see I'll have no peace in my home from now on." He lifted his face to the ceiling, practically howling with displeasure. "Or in the shop. I've operated my business since the country's bicentennial. Forty years and no complaints or citations." He stomped into the living room in that unsteady, endearing way of his. "It says *Phil's* on the window, you know."

"I'm sorry you're upset." She left the shelf dripping in the sink and followed him.

The living room was torturous to her artistic sensibilities—plain white walls, a stained and lumpy tan couch, a scratched oak coffee table. No knickknacks on the mantel. No pictures on the walls. No personality. Nothing he'd regret leaving behind if Leona wanted him back tomorrow.

"I'm not upset."

He was. And she thought she knew why. "You know, I didn't come here to take over for you."

Just as Phil reached the couch, he spun and dropped in a heap of scarecrow-like limbs that sent coils squeaking. "That's not what the ladies in town think."

Holy wet set. "They're wrong."

"Not usually." He jabbed the remote in the direction of his boxy old television. It came on loud enough to end the conversation.

Demoralized, Brit returned to the kitchen. She hadn't moved here intent on building a thriving business or forcing Grandpa into retirement. She returned the shelf to the near-empty refrigerator, put away the cleaning supplies and thought about how she'd feel if someone came into her business—*into her home*—and began changing things.

She walked back to the living room, took the remote from Grandpa and muted the television. "I'm sorry I took down the beer mirror." Not sorry enough to put it back up; just sorry that

Grandpa Phil was bent out of shape. "I'm sorry I went through your cabinets and cleaned the place up." Despite it being long overdue. "And I'm especially sorry that women in town are excited to have a female hairstylist." Because that meant less time to devote to her art.

Her hobby. Arts and crafts.

The terms slid beneath her skin like barbed fishhooks, snagging her pride, dragging down her confidence. What if Keira was a fluke? Everyone loved her, but plenty of artists were one-hit wonders.

Grandpa Phil gave a full-body huff. "You know how women are—wanting a shampoo and comb out once a week. Word will get out. This is just the beginning. You're going to be busy."

"Phil's is an institution in town," she soothed, sitting next to him, flattening the sofa's worn, noisy springs. "I'm not trying to replace you. Heck, I'd be happier poking through these women's garages than through their hair."

Phil perked up at that. "I know people in town who'd love to get rid of their junk."

"Great. Hopefully, they want to give it away." Her operating budget was nil. She was going to have to put her beauty supplies on credit tomorrow when she drove down to Santa Rosa. "Donations accepted."

"Duly noted. Now…" Smiling, he patted her knee. "What's for dinner? I've been living on frozen burritos and cereal."

"Dinner is whatever Grandmother Leona is making." Brit watched his wrinkled smile fade. "I'm sorry. I've been summoned."

"It's okay." Phil took back the remote. "I like frozen burritos and cereal."

THE MOTORCYCLE WAS RETURNING.

Joe had completed a first pass at cleaning the garage, the first of many it'd need. He'd just plugged in the battery charger and hooked it up to the tow truck when the put-put cycle came to a stop in the lot outside the garage.

"Hey, there." The rider was too big for the motorcycle, too old and too misguided. He'd stuffed himself into bright red riding leathers that looked two sizes too small. It might have explained his stiff gait. "I heard the garage was reopening. I'm Irwin Orowitz. Barbara here could use a tune-up." Irwin gestured to his very small, very sedate motorcycle.

It wasn't a "hog." It wasn't even the kind of

bike you named. Brittany's mermaid sculpture was more deserving of that honor. It was the kind of motorcycle "real" bikers made fun of with terms like *scooter* or *two-wheeled hearse*, because the rider seldom knew what they were doing. But Joe couldn't afford to joke with what might be a paying customer.

As Joe was in the process of swallowing his opinions and putting on his best customer-service expression—*if not to smile, then at least not to scowl*—Irwin hitched up his too-tight, too-short pants.

This was proof. There was a hell. And Joe had fallen into it.

"Um…" Joe sought to cover his horror by rubbing an old towel over his face, as if wiping away sweat. "Bertha…er…Barbara didn't sound so rough."

"My *Barbara*…" Irwin stopped a few feet away from Joe, propped his hands on his hips and performed a hip swivel Elvis would've been proud of. "She's got no get-up-and-go anymore."

Joe doubted she'd ever gotten up and gone anywhere really fast. Irwin, on the other hand, needed to go get some pants that offered more room at the waist.

Sam peered through the window in the door to the office. Her eyes were red-rimmed and her hair was limp beneath her cap. She pushed open the door, which squeaked—like everything else in Joe's life lately—and drew Irwin's attention.

"Another generation of Messina boys in town." Irwin beamed, his smile rounding his already round face.

Another person who thought Sam was a boy?

Joe's eye twitched. "Well. There's me." He patted his chest. "I'm generation two. And my *daughter* is generation three."

"G3," Sam murmured with a meek smile, coming to stand next to Joe. "Cool."

"Messinas are back. This is wonderful news." Irwin's beam brightened. "You Messinas used to buzz around town on your motorcycles."

He'd never buzzed in his life. Joe's eye spasmed hard enough to pop out of his head.

"It's what inspired me to buy a motorbike when I retired." Irwin rearranged his belly this time.

"Dad," Sam whispered, tugging on his sleeve. "Are you okay?"

Be nice, Athena would've said.

Treat your customer like your mistress, Turo would've said.

"So." Joe tried to put a smile on his face, but it felt more like a grimace. "Bet... Berth... *Barbara* needs a tune-up."

CHAPTER FIVE

"GRANDMOTHER LEONA, BRITTANY is here," Reggie called, gently shutting the door behind Brit before dragging her across the Victorian's foyer toward the dining room. "You didn't dress for dinner." While Reggie had changed into a teal floral-print dress and white flats. She added in a whisper, "And you're late."

"I had to cook something for Grandpa before I left." She'd microwaved his frozen burrito while he'd poured himself a bowl of cereal. She'd worry tomorrow about stocking the house with healthier options.

Their footsteps echoed on hundred-year-old oak floors. The Victorian had been built to impress, but despite being filled with beautiful antiques, it felt as cavernous as the chest of the Tin Man before he'd earned his heart. They'd stayed here as children the summer their parents contemplated divorce. They'd cleaned the house, they'd run errands, and they'd done so silently at Leona's insistence. They'd half joked that Grandmother Leona thought they were the Cinderella twins.

This was the house their father had grown up in. If Brit had never been here before, she'd have thought there'd be pictures of Dad scattered around. He was Phil and Leona's only child. But there weren't any pictures. Not of Dad, not of Phil, not of the twins. On the bright side, there wasn't a program from Dad's funeral last summer either.

Brit wrinkled her nose over the hated smell of lemon polish and... "It smells like—"

"Liver and onions," Reggie whispered.

Brit tried to turn around, but Reggie had the grip of a professional bouncer and continued to propel them forward.

"Eat it and look grateful." Reggie gave her a final push into the dining room. "It's the only thing she's good at cooking."

"Don't kid yourself," Brit whispered back. "Cooking is her favorite method of torturing guests."

Grandmother Leona liked making people uncomfortable the way a clown liked to make people laugh. Not that you'd see Leona's lips curl in a smile at the reaction of those served her liver specialty. But her satisfaction would be there in the sly upturn of her voice.

The smell of liver was stronger in the formal dining room and couldn't be masked by onions. Brit's stomach executed the U-turn her feet wanted to do. For sanity reasons, she resorted to being a mouth breather.

"Brittany." Grandmother Leona backed through the swinging kitchen door, carrying a serving platter full of steaming liver and onions. She wore a plain blue cotton dress with long sleeves, one of which held a handkerchief tucked at her slender wrist. Her peppery-gray hair was in a smooth beehive and she wore Great-Grandmother Rambling's pearl choker on her thin regal neck. "Sit down," Leona said, her tone a command. No *please*. No warm greeting. No hugs for a granddaughter she hadn't seen in close to a year, the last time being Dad's funeral.

Brit had felt more welcome in Joe's field this morning.

Leona set the platter down and took the seat at the head of the table, indicating the twins should sit flanking her. "Regina tells me you've rented space at the barbershop." Her grandmother dished liver onto a plate and tsked. "Four years in college. You shouldn't be engaged in a trade."

"I'm an artisan working to make ends meet." Self-doubt lumped in Brit's throat, giving her words the gravelly feel of uncertainty.

"Is that what they call beauticians now?" Leona had a knack for slipping a barb between people's defenses. "Artisans?"

Brit declined the bait. She accepted her plate of liver and claimed two sourdough rolls from the full bread basket.

"One roll is enough, Brittany." Leona arched one silver brow. "Carbs live on hips."

Brit wasn't a child anymore. She wouldn't let Leona make her feel like a wing-clipped duck on a pond during hunting season. She didn't return the extra roll. Instead, she turned the conversation to Leona's one weakness: Phil. "I should take the leftover rolls to Grandpa Phil. He's having cereal for dinner." Which sounded more appealing now than it had thirty minutes ago.

Leona stiffened. "He needs to eat more fiber and protein. A healthy diet will make him live longer. We should all learn from what happened to your father." She couldn't even call Dad by his first name.

Her grandmother's apathy prodded Brit's rebellious streak. "Phil's freezer is full of frozen burritos."

Reggie had taken her first bite of liver. She looked like a bug had flown into her mouth.

"There might be enough liver leftover to send Phil a serving." Unlike most people her age, Leona had a way of frowning that minimized her wrinkles.

"He'd like that." Not the liver, but that Leona had done something thoughtful for him. Poor dear was still stuck on his ex. The why was a mystery.

The liver was thin. Brit cut hers into baby-sized bites and began hiding them under the mashed potatoes. This wasn't her first liver rodeo.

"I booked two guests for next weekend," Reggie said proudly. "They bought the wine-tasting package. That's fifty dollars more a night."

"Don't mention dollars at the dinner table." Leona didn't seem impressed with Reggie's accomplishment. "I'm assuming you invited Brittany over because you've finally agreed to my terms. I can't sell the Victorian to just one of you."

"Yes." Reggie set down her knife and fork on the far side of her plate, the way you did at restaurants to indicate you were done. She didn't look at Brit. "We agree."

We?

Brit choked on a bite of mashed potatoes. Maybe because a small piece of liver had made its way onto her fork. Maybe not. Maybe because she was choking on Reggie's lie.

Leona stared at Reggie with calculating eyes. And then she laughed. "I smell desperation."

"It's the liver," Brit said, half under her breath.

Reggie mentioned a crazy sum of money. She did not mention that Brit had refused to be her business partner.

A smart woman would have backed away from the table. A smart woman would have abandoned her twin to face Leona alone.

Brit sat very still.

"The money might be acceptable," Leona said, as a queen might say a jewel-encrusted crown could use a few more Hope Diamonds. "But I have other conditions to the sale."

"More than me being on the contract?" Brit asked in a strained voice.

Reggie had yet to meet Brit's gaze, busy as she was selling her lies to Leona.

"Yes. I want to live here until the day I die." Leona looked like she was playing her trump card. She was almost smiling. "Rent-free."

Deal-breaker.

Brit met Reggie's gaze across the liver platter and shook her head. Once upon a time, she and Reggie had been masters of twin-speak. Back before the Promotion Dance, Brit had been able to tell what Reggie was thinking before she started a sentence. And now? Her twin-speak was tuned to a different frequency. Was Reggie actually considering Grandmother Leona's proposition?

"I may only be in a trade," Brit ventured into the silence. "But I know a bad business deal when I see one. The answer is no."

Reggie looked more stricken than when she'd been chewing the liver. What was wrong with her? She'd been a shark in hotel management. And now? In the course of twelve hours, she'd been pushed around by Shaggy Joe and Grandmother Leona. Maybe Reggie did need a business partner. Just not Brit.

"There's a travel writer in town who happens to think I'm a draw to the B and B."

Leona cut her liver into neat, even squares. "I'd throw in breakfast."

"As in, you'd make it?" At Leona's nod, Brit pushed her plate away. "I'm out." She made a dignified run for the door.

"Wait." Reggie scurried after her, following Brit to the front porch and closing the door behind her.

"You lied to her." Brit struggled to keep her voice low. Lying was something she couldn't do. "I'm not buying this place. It gives me the creeps."

There was no mistaking the desperation in her twin's eyes. "I can't make this work without you."

"Good, because it's not meant to work." Brit sped toward the stairs, willing to forgive the lie if only to erase the trapped look in Reggie's eyes. "Run away with me, Reggie."

"No." Reggie lunged for Brit's hand. "Not yet. She's going to get used to the idea of selling. And her terms will change."

Brit slipped her hand free. "But mine won't."

"Can't you just—" Reggie's gaze swept the porch "—go along with it?"

"No. This house is her greatest love." Bigger than her love for Phil. "I won't lie to her about something so important."

Now there was more than desperation in Reggie's brown eyes. There was anger. "You have to."

"Why? What's going on?"

Reggie backed to the door, turned the knob. "This is a good deal for you. More money than cutting hair. A better gamble than your so-called *art*. You have to see that you were meant for more than digging through the trash or rummaging through a junkyard like some crazed homeless scavenger." She disappeared inside, shutting the door behind her with a soft yet piercing click.

Brit clutched the stair railing. She expected harsh criticism from Leona and perhaps even Mom. But Reggie had always been positive about Brit's creative passion, accepting of her modern expressionism. Reggie loved Keira. She was proud of Brit's accomplishments. Why, just this morning...

She's beautiful, Brit. And so are you.

But then there'd been...

Arts and crafts.

A better gamble than your so-called art.

Rummaging through a junkyard like some crazed homeless scavenger.

Brit straightened, still in pain but refusing to break. She couldn't keep standing here where Reggie would see or come back out.

Reggie had lied to Leona about Brit's involvement in the purchase. Reggie had apparently been lying to Brit about things for years. Reggie was just like everyone else who paid Brit's art lip service, who thought her time was better spent outside the workroom, away from the blowtorch, away from her passion.

Brit was lucky to be passionate about two things—hair and metal. She wasn't passionate about the B and B. She had to focus on what was right for her, not on Reggie. She had to set aside the sharpness of her sister's words and ignore the betrayal. She had to believe in herself.

Easier said than done.

She turned away from the Victorian. She'd prove to Reggie that her art was more than bits and pieces of trash and junk. And the best way to do that was to make something she was excited about and invested in, and something that sold on the merits of the idea alone: the BMW gate.

The sun was setting. She pointed her feet

toward Grandpa Phil's place. All she needed was a flashlight and some nerve. And stealth. No headlights to give away her presence. She could walk to the bridge that was near Joe's place. She'd make a night run to the BMW, looking for its registration papers. She'd be brave. And hopefully that bravery would restore her ability to create art.

"I'M DONE CLEANING. I want a car to work on." Sam tossed her sponge into the bucket at her feet and gestured weakly toward the dark field across the road, the one illuminated by the light from the service bays and little else. "Those wrecks out there don't count."

"Everything counts." Joe kept scrubbing the wrench to the beat of a song by one of those boy bands Sam loved so much. The music crackled from the single-speaker AM radio he'd found under the counter. Turo had insisted they leave most of Dad's tools when they'd left Harmony Valley, which was turning out to be a blessing. Joe hadn't been allowed to take any tools when they left Southern California. His father's tools had rusted in the humidity, but it wasn't anything a good scrubbing with a sponge and some WD-40 couldn't fix. "We've cleaned enough for one day. Why don't you try to start the tow truck? It's been charging all afternoon." And the tires were holding air.

She moved off with heavy-heeled reluctance.

Crickets chirped their last good-night before the evening turned chill and silenced them. In the distance, bullfrogs sang bass to the boy band's falsetto. The river would provide some dinners if Harmony Valley didn't provide enough customers.

A few minutes later, the tow truck gave a mighty cough, belching a big breath of burnt air into the service bay, and then died.

Sam stuck her head out the driver's window. Her chin barely cleared the sill. "Does the phrase *lost cause* mean anything to you?"

Not when it applied to everything in the garage. Joe set the wrench down. "Tell me your diagnosis."

She resettled her baseball cap on her head and frowned at the dashboard. "I suppose the distributor cap could be wet."

"Ah, my little prodigy." He almost felt like smiling. "You've forgotten rule number one of engine operation."

"Argh!" She slapped the steering wheel with one palm. "Lubrication?"

"That's right. Let's take the engine apart, check that the gaskets are still good, and then put it back together and lube everything up." Luckily, he'd brought several canisters of different-grade motor oil. What he didn't have were gaskets.

An hour later, they had the engine mani-fold, carburetor, hoses and air filter laid out on the floor. The dinner hour was long gone. Joe supposed the stew in the Crock-Pot would be close to overdone by now. "We can't put it back together without gaskets. Why don't you head upstairs and serve dinner? I'll close up down here."

She scampered off, more like his little girl than she'd been since Uncle Turo had been ar-rested.

Joe turned off the radio and then the shop lights. The lone light from the office lit a path to the service bay.

His cell phone chimed with its regular ring-tone. Sad to say, Joe recognized the number. Sadder still that recognizing the caller ID prac-tically cut him off at the knees. "Agent Haas, what can I do for you?"

"Mr. Messina…" The federal agent who'd arrested Uncle Turo paused as if he hadn't been prepared for Joe to answer. "After much searching, we've been unable to locate the high-end cars and car parts your uncle stole."

"Allegedly stole," Joe said, locking his knees in place.

"We know he received several stolen vehicles and parts. We've arrested several accomplices." The agent's tone wasn't registering good cop or bad cop. It didn't threaten or comfort. It was rational and factual and determined, which was scary. "We think you know where Turo hid everything."

"Um…no," Joe said with all the finesse of the petty criminal Agent Haas and the rest of Harmony Valley seemed to think he was.

"Where did he hide them, Joe?"

"I don't know." Joe was relieved it was the truth.

"Turo called you today. What did he say?"

He knew that? How had he known that? And if he did, then he'd be able to access Joe's voicemail. He would have heard the silence on the other end of the line. "I didn't pick up and he didn't leave a message."

"I need you to get him to talk."

Joe swallowed. "Why would he talk to me?

By now he knows I'm the one who ratted him out."

"He kept a stable of rats, Joe. And yet, you're the only rat he called." Agent Haas didn't believe Joe. If their situations had been reversed, Joe wouldn't believe him either. "I'll give you ten days to locate the stolen goods. And then I'm coming for a visit to Harmony Valley." He hung up.

Sam moved around upstairs. Crickets chirped. Bullfrogs sang.

Normal. All normal. And yet, Joe gripped the countertop so he wouldn't fall. The guilt was overwhelming. He couldn't protect Turo. He couldn't protect Sam.

He should be angry. At Turo for putting him in this position. At Agent Haas for treating him like Turo's accomplice. At Athena for not being here when he needed her. Anger held him together. But he wasn't angry. He was a dad who might have his daughter taken away for something he didn't know anything about. And that made him afraid. He preferred the anger.

Joe struggled to fill his lungs with air.

A light flashed across the road. The kind of slim beam from a small flashlight. Near where the BMW was.

"It can't be," he muttered, charging out of the garage and across the road with speed fueled by welcome anger.

Brittany had the car door open and was bent over, rummaging in the glove box. She hadn't bothered with coveralls this time. The sparkly threads of her clothing glimmered like winking stars in the inky sky.

"What do you think you're doing?" he growled, as territorial as a junkyard dog who'd been kept on a short leash for too long.

Brittany bumped her head on the door frame. "Why are you always sneaking up on me and yelling?" She straightened, rubbing the back of her head.

"Because you're always trespassing." He refused to feel sorry for her.

"Someone told me these cars were abandoned." She set her hand on her hip. She'd been caught. Most people would be running or apologizing.

"Was this the same someone who told you there were free pickings here?"

"No." There. There was some remorse. "I was checking for registration. If this car isn't registered to a Messina—"

"Possession is nine-tenths of the law." His

frustration level was redlining. His head should be pounding. His eye twitching. Instead, he felt alive and sure of himself for only the second time in weeks. The first being this morning when she'd had the BMW's hood up.

She groaned. "I need this, okay? I need it more than you do. Not that you'd understand. Me being a stripper and all." She marched toward the river, which meant she had to go past him. "I should have given you a buzz cut."

"And I should call the cops." That was the last thing he wanted to do.

"Cop. Singular. Sheriff Nate." Her tone implied she had no qualms about getting out of any legal trouble he made for her. "He made an appointment for a haircut."

Whatever cachet he'd achieved as a mechanic to the stars meant nothing on this side of the river. "Just because I'm a Messina doesn't mean you can steal from me."

"I wasn't going to steal anything." She stumbled as she passed, smelling of lemons and lies.

Joe grabbed hold of her arm, not sure if he was being a gentleman or if he planned on conducting a body search. "But you knew I wouldn't approve or you would have asked me."

"Dad? Dad. Dinner's ready."

They were so close, he heard Brittany's stomach rumble. Although it was so loud, he could have heard its thunder from the shop.

"Who's that?" Sam wandered into the parking lot. "Is it—"

"It's Brittany," Joe said before Sam could ask if Uncle Turo was here.

Her stomach rumbled again. Louder this time.

"Did you hear that?" Sam stopped at the edge of the field and glanced about. "Is there a cat out there?"

"That was me." Another chink in Brittany's blustery armor. "I didn't have dinner."

"You didn't eat?" Sam shifted into nurturing mode, a soft scold in her young voice. "Come eat with us. Dad makes plenty because he likes leftovers."

Joe hated leftovers, but they cut down on the number of dinners he had to cook and made good economical sense.

"I don't want to impose." Brittany's stomach practically roared in disagreement, making Sam laugh.

Joe held on to the sound as firmly as he held on to Brittany.

"Besides," the trespasser said. "I don't think your dad wants to invite me to dinner."

"Your stomach has the growlies. I won't take no for an answer." Now Sam sounded like Uncle Turo, competent and in charge. "It's the neighborly thing to do."

"She's not our neighbor," Joe muttered, even as a small voice in his head whispered, *She makes Sam laugh.*

"Dad." Sam heaved a long-suffering sigh. "This is a small town. Everyone is our neighbor." And then she laughed again.

"Don't you dare refuse her," Joe said to Brittany.

"IT SMELLS DELICIOUS." Nothing like liver and onions. And certainly better than frozen burritos or cereal. Brit was almost happy she'd been caught.

She wove through the mazelike stacks of moving boxes to stand out of the way, taking in the dingy white walls, dingy beige curtains and dingy gray linoleum. Not that she was a snob, but Grandpa Phil's place was looking better and better.

The living room, galley kitchen and small dining area were one combined area. The furniture wasn't purposefully retro. It was just plain old. Really, all the place needed was a good cleaning—the theme of the day—a coat of paint and some throw rugs and pillows to make it look less forlorn.

And then her gaze caught on the framed pictures sitting where a television should have. Joe standing with his arm around a curvaceous woman in black leather boots and jacket. She was staring at Joe adoringly and Joe…he was smiling at the tiny baby in her arms—warmly, tenderly, no hint of ice in his gaze. An older man stood behind them, his hands on Joe's broad shoulders. He had the same dark, unruly hair as Joe. But his smile was different— playful, perhaps a bit slick.

There was another picture, one of a young Joe standing a little apart from two older boys, so alike in appearance they had to be brothers. Their jeans were too long, their multicolored striped T-shirts too short, but that didn't handicap the promise of gorgeous men in the making. A glance Sam's way confirmed she had the promise of the Messina beauty.

As the ugly duckling, Brittany was out of place here. And…to top it all off, there was a rip in her leggings from her shin to her knee. Brilliant.

Joe moved past Brit toward the kitchen with the stiff air of put-upon male that plucked at Brit's patience. She was in the wrong, but somehow he managed to make her forget it. He sighed as if being put-upon was his lot in life, as if reminding himself not to complain about dingy apartments, small judgmental towns or persistent, trespassing, auto-part pickers.

Try staying mad at the man when you were the trespassing, persistent, auto-part picker.

Brit couldn't. She could cling to her hurt and anger toward Reggie, but she was going to have to apologize to Joe. Just…not yet.

Sam seemed unaffected by her father's mood. She was in the kitchen, stacking plates and counting out forks. She'd taken off her baseball cap, revealing a bad case of hat hair to go with her lifeless shoulder-length bob.

Brit had a sudden urge to style or cut or at the very least shampoo and blow-dry with a round brush. She forced her gaze toward the source of that tantalizing smell—a Crock-Pot bubbling with beef stew. And there was a package of rolls on the counter. *Hello, carbs!* "Can I help with anything?"

"Guests don't help." Drying his hands on a paper towel, Joe hit Brit with a glance that said she was an unwelcome guest, but it lacked bite now that she'd heard that weary sigh. "Sam will make you a plate. Cups are over the sink. Clean hands are mandatory."

All hands were clean. All plates filled. All three seats occupied. Sam and Joe bookended Brit at the table. The tension was as thick as commuter traffic over the Bay Bridge, just a heck of a lot quieter.

Brit tried to fill the silence. "This is delicious." It really was. The gravy was a rich brown, thick and seasoned with more than salt and pepper.

Sam cast a subtle glance at her father. Joe didn't look up from his plate.

Brit should enjoy her food in silence, give a hearty thank-you and be on her way. That's what her artisan side counseled. Her beautician side whispered that she'd had her fingers in Joe's hair a few hours ago. Right or wrong, that created a bond she couldn't ignore. "I apologize for trying to go behind your back with the BMW." It was the right thing to say, but the words seemed to bounce off Joe and clatter to the floor.

Joe's expression didn't soften to forgiveness or understanding. His eyes—when they found hers—remained as icy blue as a south-facing glacier. "What would you have done if you'd found documentation? Contact the 'real' owner? Make him an offer for the grille?"

"Yes."

"Parting out cars…" His voice was just as gruff as it'd been when they'd first met this morning. But now Brit heard a different growl beneath the boundary-marking bark—the weary rumble of trying to do what was right. "You and me…we don't see eye to eye. And we never will."

"Dad restores cars to their former glory," Sam said staunchly. "Chromed-out engines. Metal-flake paint jobs. Racing wheels." She turned her gaze to the ceiling and sighed dreamily. "We had the best garage in all of Beverly Hills."

Brit squelched the urge to pry about the loss of their garage. "That doesn't sound like resto-ration," she pointed out, trying to be diplomatic for Sam's sake. "You're taking the bones of a car and making it into something more mod-ern, more attractive and more functional for today's world. That's the same as what I do."

Joe sat back and held up his hands in near

eye-rolling incredulity. "How does welding a mermaid to an antique motorbike make it more functional?"

For the first time since they'd met, Brit smiled. And all because of his misplaced passion. "Oh, come on. Guys with big bank accounts buy up automotive antiques, pay guys like you to 'restore' them and then lock them away in their man caves where no one else can see them. I call that hoarding." She tore apart her roll and shook a piece in his direction. "I take car parts and turn them into lamps and tables and—*yes*—gates. But also sculptures that can make a business or event or even a town more memorable. Keira is a calling card for me, both for my art and my beautician business." Brit mopped up some brown gravy with a chunk of dinner roll. "Now, that's functionality, and restoration, *and* social responsibility." *Boo-yah!* She popped the soggy bread in her mouth.

Her soapbox must not have been as high as she thought it was, because Joe was looking down at his food and shaking his head.

If he laughed at her art or called her a stripper in front of Sam, Brit might have to go back to completely disliking him.

"We aren't the same." Joe lifted his head and leaned forward, speaking directly to his daughter in a tone that sent a message. "Messinas respect cars. We fix cars. And we do it honestly for a cash profit. Not for friends and not for barter."

Brit frowned. Joe apparently didn't do anything for free, not even for friends. "When we find a classic car, we feel a responsibility to restore it to its former self, even if it's a modern take on its heyday." His gaze hit Brit's with enough chill to frost the field of cars by morning. "I'll research the vehicles in my possession to make sure there are no questions about ownership."

Hello, boundary setting. Goodbye, jump start to the gate project. Brit couldn't contain a sigh just as weary as Joe's earlier one.

A crease appeared between Joe's black brows, as if her sigh had thrown him off his stride. But that didn't stop him from adding, "Until then, don't sneak onto our property. Or I will call the sheriff."

CHAPTER SIX

"W‌HY DON'T YOU like her?" Sam climbed into her twin bed and slid her legs beneath the denim quilt Athena's mom had made for her. "I think she's cool."

"Who?" Joe feigned ignorance, picking up Sam's dirty clothes and stuffing them into her blue wicker hamper.

When he scowled in Turo's shop, guys backed off. When he scowled at Brittany, she came forward. When he threatened dire consequences at Turo's shop, guys gave his threats credence. When he threatened Brittany, she came to dinner. He was trying to rebuild order in his life. She was chaos.

"Dad." Sam wasn't buying his act. "Brittany? The lady who cut your hair? The lady who ate dinner here?"

"Oh, her." Joe picked up an empty cardboard box and broke it down, wishing he could flatten the unsettling feelings Brittany gave rise to. Because despite her blatant disrespect for his rules, for the law, and despite the pandemonium she caused, a part of him wanted to like her.

That streak of purple in her hair said she was a rebel. Her black polka-dotted fingernails said she was independent. The sparkle in her clothes matched the sparkle in her eyes. And as much as he wanted to hate her mermaid sculpture, the craftsmanship was top-notch.

"Oh, wow," Sam said after several moments of silence. "You like her. I was thinking Regina was more your speed."

"Don't start." He looked around Sam's room, forcing himself not to think of Brittany or her passionate ideas about junk. He should be thinking about how to return Sam to the standard of living she was used to. Her room didn't have a fold-out couch loaded with stuffed animals. Or a flat-screen television mounted on the wall. It didn't have a walk-in closet or its own bathroom. God love her, she hadn't complained beyond the initial hit of *ew*. "We should get you a lamp in here." She liked to read at night and there was only the overhead light.

Sam grinned. "Oh, you like her, all right."

"Quit with the matchmaking. You're no

good at it." There'd been the painfully awkward time she'd asked Joe to pick her up at Holly Prichard's house and Holly's single mom had expected him to take her to dinner. And the painfully awkward situation she'd put him in during a parent-teacher conference when Sam told Miss Carson that Joe had a crush on her. And...well...he'd rather avoid round three of painfully awkward.

No matter how intriguing Brittany's unexpected smile was. He'd been trash-talking and *bam*! There came her smile. He'd nearly smiled back...but he had nothing to smile about.

Sam snuggled deeper in her bed, yawned and closed her eyes. "I'm as good a matchmaker as I am a mechanic." She looked small and fragile, her dark eyelashes thick against her cheeks.

So like her mother, yet so different.

Athena had been tough. She'd managed mixed martial arts fighters and was on the road three to four days a week, accompanying her clients to matches, meeting promoters, recruiting new fighters and making deals. Athena's style had been boots, blue jeans and a black motorcycle jacket. The first time Joe had seen her, she'd been riding her motorcycle on the freeway as if an angel rode shotgun on her shoulder. She'd been gutsy, but she hadn't been careful.

He was trying to raise Sam to be careful. He should have been more careful about his own life. If he had been, he would've seen the signs at Uncle Turo's shop that something wasn't right. He would've left sooner, like day one.

"Good night, baby." He kissed her forehead, flicked off the light and closed the door.

He went to stand at the living room window, staring out into the night, trying not to look at the house where he'd grown up, at the weathered swing set in the backyard or the pile of bald tires stacked next to the garage. But he focused on them anyway and found himself wondering how Brittany would make those things functional.

"HALLOO!"

Joe slid out from under the tow truck Sunday afternoon and sat up. "Hey, Irwin." With the music on, neither he nor Sam had heard Irwin drive up. "You're not here for the tune-up, are you? That's not until Monday."

"No." The older man unzipped his red leather jacket. He had a red bandanna tied around his head, but it'd slipped to one side. He sat on a stool near the main workbench. "What is that racket?" He turned off the radio, silencing the boy band. "There. That's better."

Sam didn't slide out. She kept working on installing the oil pan, leaving Joe to entertain their customer. They'd bought gaskets that morning and spent hours putting the engine back together. A little more lube, several quarts of oil, and the tow truck would be ready for a test drive.

"Can I help you with something?" Joe asked Irwin.

"No. Just thought I'd stop by and hang out with the other bikers." His brow creased. "Where are the other bikers?"

Joe felt his own brow crease. "What other bikers?"

"The ones in your club."

The man thought Joe was in a motorcycle gang? Worse, he wanted to hang out with Joe because of it?

Joe opened his mouth to tell him to get out and Sam coughed. She knew they needed Irwin's money more than Joe's pride.

"I'm not in a club." Joe rolled back under the tow truck. The muffler had a rusty spot from years of condensation. It wouldn't last much longer than Joe's patience.

Sam chuckled. "You must have been hell on wheels as a teenager, Dad. A real punk."

"There were worse kids." Maybe not in Harmony Valley. But he'd make sure his daughter didn't follow in the Messina footsteps.

Irwin got down from his stool and walked toward them, boots clumping on the concrete. "I don't see your hog either."

"I don't have a motorcycle." Joe's eye twitched.

"I must not have heard you right." The boots stopped, possibly rooted in disbelief. "You say you *don't* have a motorcycle?"

"I don't have a motorcycle!" Joe applied pressure to the bone over his eye.

"Dad," Sam whispered. "He's just an old man. Go easy on him." She patted Joe's arm. "I've got the oil pan. You take care of our customer. Our *one* customer."

Joe wasn't cut out to be the front man for a business. That's why he'd loved working for Turo. All he'd had to do was fix cars.

And look where that got you.

He rolled out from under the tow truck.

Irwin paced the perimeter of the empty service bay. "You don't have any calendars up."

"I've got a calendar upstairs." Eager to please, Sam slid free of the truck and ran upstairs before Joe could stop her.

"We don't have what you're looking for," Joe said, feeling the words curl in his chest like a fist. Irwin expected Joe to have a racy car calendar, the kind with bikini-clad women. The ones that were politically incorrect for upstanding businessmen and inappropriate for little girls.

"I like to know what date it is." If Joe looked past Irwin's wrinkles and his white chin stubble, the old man's disappointment with Joe looked surprisingly similar to Sam's—same thin downturned mouth; same disenchanted slant to the eyes.

Sam returned with a calendar Joe had given her for Christmas, one with cartoony smiling unicorns that glowed with the promise of happily-ever-afters and dreams that came true.

Irwin frowned at the unicorn for April, despite it sliding gracefully down a rainbow onto a green grassy field. "This isn't what I was expecting from the Messina Garage."

"We're the Messina *Family* Garage." Sam hung the calendar from a hook in the pegboard.

Irwin pretended not to hear her. He waved

a hand toward the radio. "Where's the hard rock? The pictures of na—"

"Watch it," Joe warned, feeling his anger press against his ribs.

"Where are the pictures of nice women?" Irwin crossed his arms over his out-of-shape chest. "The tattoos? The chains on your wallet? You don't even have a bandanna around your head!" He swiped the one off his noggin', crumpling it in his hand. "This isn't the Messina Garage that I remember." He clomped out into the crisp afternoon sunshine.

"I've got a chain on my utility knife." Inside his pocket. Joe held up the knife.

Sam looked from Irwin to Joe and back. "What's wrong with him?"

"He doesn't believe in unicorns."

"Barbara won't start!" Irwin shouted, his face red as he stomped back into the service bay. "Unbelievable."

Joe and Sam exchanged a glance and then went for the case of oil on the workbench. Who knew how long it'd take to get Irwin's motorcycle running. It would be easier to give him a lift home. It was as good a time as any to test the tow truck. And maybe he'd convince Irwin that he was no longer the hoodlum of his youth.

Grandpa Phil was having a yard sale.

Good. Maybe he'd cleaned out his over-stuffed garage.

Brittany had to park in front of the house next door because there were cars double-parked in front of Phil's gray-and-white ranch home. She'd spent most of the day in Santa Rosa stocking up on hair products and trying to find chair hair dryers. The only units she found were bank-breaking new. She had appointments for wet sets starting Tuesday and no dryers to put her clients under. When she'd envisioned coming to Harmony Valley, she hadn't considered that there'd be a high demand for her services and therefore a high demand on her time to be able to deliver said services efficiently and properly.

Phil sat in a webbed folding chair on the lawn, legs crossed at the knee, lanky elbows propped on aluminum armrests as two women wrestled with a wheelbarrow in a truck bed.

It wasn't until Brit got out of her own truck that she realized they weren't loading the wheel-barrow. They were unloading it! Adding to the clutter in the driveway.

"What's all this?" she asked Phil.

"It's for you." Phil beamed. "I told you I

knew people who had stuff they wanted to give away."

"But…" *It's junk*, she wanted to shout.

There were boxes and bags of heaven only knew what dumped in front of the house. Bicycles and tricycles parked on the side yard. A refrigerator door with a shovel sticking out of it. Four Volkswagen hubcaps. A blue ceramic elephant plant stand with one chipped ear. And that was just what she could see.

Brit turned to the ladies and their cement-caked wheelbarrow. "Ladies, please don't hurt yourselves. I can't take that."

Their sweaty, wrinkled faces fell.

"There's more coming," Phil said stubbornly, his face shiny from too much sun.

"More?" Brit considered sitting on the elephant plant stand and burying her face in her hands. Instead, she moved forward to help the ladies push the wheelbarrow back onto the truck.

A bright red Thunderbird convertible zipped around the corner, Rose at the wheel. She parked it cockeyed in the street. A tall metal floor lamp was strapped into the passenger seat. The lamp shade was pink and had elephants marching around it. "I've always hated this lamp." Rose glided around the car, smooth as silk. "When Phil said you were looking for junk, I rushed right over."

"Unbelievable," Brit muttered.

"It's great, isn't it?" Grandpa's smile practically lifted him out of his webbed chair.

Brit was so overwhelmed, she didn't reject the women's second attempt to remove the wheelbarrow. "I can't use 99 percent of this stuff." She nudged a box of mismatched serving bowls with her toe. "What are we going to do with it all?" She had yet to clean out a space in the garage for her worktable.

"You can't use…" Phil sank back in his chair. "Shoot and darn."

"You can't use any of it?" Rose gazed sorrowfully at her lamp.

"What were you looking for?" The yearning to be a help was palpable on Grandpa's face. "If you tell me, I can find it for you."

Brit shrugged. "I look for things that speak to me." Like Joe's hair and the BMW grille, soft-spoken as the latter was in comparison to mermaids that whispered in her ear, urging she bring them to life.

Phil and Rose made disgruntled sounds as if

her answer had boiled down to belittling their attempts to help her.

"Maybe I'm too tired to see a diamond in the rough." Worn-out from her argument with Reggie. Perplexed by her reaction to Joe. Stressed about the popularity of her beauty services. Down in the dumps due to her creative block. "Or maybe it's just because I've had my pragmatic hat on today. I've been looking for hair dryers for the barbershop."

"Oh, no," Phil said. "Not that again."

"Hair dryers?" Rose frowned. "The kind you sit under?"

Brit nodded. "If I can't find some, I'll have to reschedule a lot of appointments." And rescheduling meant cutting into the time she needed to get back in the creative saddle.

"I might be able to help with that, but—" Rose did a shuffle step across the driveway "—I might not. I need to check with Agnes."

A faded red truck trundled around the corner and came to a slow stop next to Rose's car. An old woman slid out of the driver's seat. She didn't carry anything and she didn't unload anything from her pickup. She moved in between the piles of donations with the slow deliberation of a tugboat working against the tide.

And then she turned to Phil. "This is the worst yard sale ever. All this stuff should go to the dump."

"It's not a yard sale," Phil grumbled. "It's my granddaughter's art supply."

The wheelbarrow ladies hightailed it out of there.

"That's it." Brit tilted her face skyward. "I'm going on a dump run."

"Hey," Phil protested. "I spent hours on the phone arranging this. Why, I practically had to beg!"

If Brit didn't at least look through the piles, she'd be the most ungrateful grandchild ever. She dutifully scanned the detritus and then met her grandfather's stubborn gaze. He seemed as hurt as when she'd suggested she cut Joe's hair. "I suppose there might be something here I could save."

Brit worked her way through the paraphernalia while Rose did the same. Brit held on to a fire poker set, a garden fountain with a black faux marble ball, a metal trash can, rusted metal fence posts with knots of barbed wire and a box of old screws and bolts.

Rose picked up a flour sifter and sifted the driveway with residual flour. "Do you need this, Brittany? I used to have one just like it. Can't remember where I put mine."

"It's yours." Brit considered the bicycles next. Most were too new to interest her. She preferred rust, not paint. But perhaps if she left them outside for a year or two…

"That's it?" Phil sat up in his chair, taking stock of her pile. "You should at least keep this…this…" He cast about for something near him. His hand landed on a large wooden magazine stand. "This! And what about Rose's lamp?"

A large engine rumbled from a nearby street, coming closer.

"Normally, I recycle the electronics from lamps, but that lamp is really old." A fire hazard. And really, that lamp shade…

The engine rumbled closer. A banana-yellow tow truck came around the corner.

"Look at that, Dad. It's either a yard sale or a whole lotta cars broke down." Sam leaned around Irwin to grin. She'd called shotgun, leaving Irwin the center seat in the tow truck.

Joe hadn't been in the mood to argue about respecting your elders and giving them the best seat, considering Irwin thought Joe was a biker thug. Maybe it was time to get his hair cut shorter. The memory of Brittany's fingers in his hair had him downshifting with an epic gear grind.

"Hey, that's Phil. My next-door neighbor." Irwin, who'd been pouty since having to leave Barbara at the shop, perked up. "And he's got friends over. They'll see me in my street gear and with you. This is great."

"Irwin, I don't want to tell you again. I'm just a mechanic. I'm not in a motorcycle club." Joe registered the cars, the stacked boxes in Phil's driveway and a woman with long brown hair with a purple streak. His pulse shifted into high gear, making Joe brake too hard. "Let's just drop Irwin off. We still have to inventory the vehicles in the field." Pulse pounding aside, the last thing he wanted was his impressionable daughter getting more exposure to Brittany.

"Please, Dad. They might have clothes."

"Polyester pants, maybe," Joe mumbled.

"Please…"

The road was blocked. Joe had to relent, pulling behind Brittany's truck and parking in front of what Irwin said was his house.

Sam hopped out before Joe could set the

parking brake. She ran to the edge of Phil's driveway and then skidded to a stop, asking Rose, "Are there any clothes?"

"Only hard goods." Rose stopped digging through a large lopsided box long enough to look up and say, "How are you today, Samantha?"

"Fine." Sam's shoulders slumped, but she didn't return to their rig.

What was the big deal about clothes lately? Joe came around to help Irwin out of the truck.

It was a big step for an old man, made more difficult by the tightness of his leathers, which creaked louder than his deep, wheezy breaths. "Is she—" *wheeze* "—looking at me?"

"Who?"

"Rose," Irwin whispered. With his back to the yard sale, the old man rearranged his leathers. "She's got spunk. Heard she's going to go red."

An older woman Joe didn't recognize, the one wearing faded overalls, caught sight of Joe and scurried toward her truck as if afraid he might mug her.

Joe's head pounded. Maybe they should relocate somewhere else, someplace where Messinas didn't have a checkered past.

Irwin thrust out his chest, sucked in his stomach—no small feat—and turned. "Rose would look mighty fine on the back of Barbara."

"Barbara isn't a two-person bike." Joe drew Irwin aside and shut the door.

"Did you bring anything, Samantha?" Rose was lucky to be oblivious to Irwin's fantasy. "This is something of a swap meet. I left a lamp and got a flour sifter."

"We should have brought Barbara to trade," Joe muttered.

"I should find Barbara a proper mechanic," Irwin grouched in return. "You're ruining all my street cred."

"Oh, I don't know." Joe watched the old woman he'd scared off turn the corner sharply toward Main Street. "Some people still think I'm a badass."

Brittany had noticed the old woman leaving. She gave Joe a sympathetic smile.

And some people think I'm pitiful. Joe didn't want Brittany's pity.

Irwin's phone beeped. "It's time for my meds. I've got to take them with food." He fixed Joe with a hard stare. "Keep Phil away from Rose while I'm gone."

"Aye-aye, Captain." Joe saluted.

The breeze rustled the leaves overhead, sounding like polite laughter.

Irwin didn't laugh. He looked at Joe as if he was a tremendous disappointment. "Don't salute, man. A simple grunt goes a long way."

"I'll remember that." The next time the FBI called. Thankfully, he'd had no calls today from anyone.

"This isn't a yard sale?" Disappointment darkened Sam's words like gathering storm clouds.

"This is a repository for Brit's art." Phil leaned forward in a rickety lawn chair, intent on imparting important news. "A veritable well of inspiration."

Brittany clapped a hand over her eyes, which Joe took to mean she'd found the well dry.

Joe joined Sam on the driveway, pausing to appreciate Brittany's legs and the red Thunderbird convertible. In that order.

"Why this—" Phil tapped a wooden magazine stand with his hand "—this could be a...a...a rocket platform." He got to his feet with a huge wobble. "You could make a merman rising out of it, shooting to the stars." He raised a foot as if about to try standing on the piece of furniture.

"No acrobatics," Brittany warned, hurrying over to steady Phil and lead him back to his lawn chair.

"I love this lamp." Sam gripped a cast-iron floor lamp with a pink lamp shade. "Look, Dad. It has monkeys dancing around the base and elephants on the lamp shade. How cool is that?"

Joe withheld judgment. It looked like something you plugged in if you wanted to start an electrical fire.

"Can I have it?" Sam carried the lamp to the beautician-artist-trespasser-thief. "Or do you want it for one of your projects, Brittany?"

"Call me Brit." She put her fingers in the fringe of Sam's hair.

Brit. The nickname didn't do her justice. It was too short. Brittany had layers. A three-syllable name suited her. A woman like her could've handled a fourth syllable.

Not that she had admirable layers.

Not that you're completely admirable either. The voice in his head sounded too much like Athena's.

Not that Messinas are ones to judge. The voice switched to Uncle Turo's.

"It's all yours." Brittany fluffed his daughter's short locks beneath her cap.

Next thing you knew, Brittany would want to cut and curl Sam's hair. She'd be having Sam in makeup and heels. She'd be encouraging Sam to ride a motorcycle and it wouldn't be Barbara.

"Sam." Joe didn't know what else to say.

"Yeah, Dad?" There was hesitation in Sam's eyes. She expected him to reject the lamp. His concern wasn't about a hand-me-down.

Step away from the bad influence.

He wanted his little girl to stay sweet and innocent and unpolished awhile longer, but that statement wouldn't go over well. "I'll need to rewire that lamp before you use it."

That earned him a smile from Brittany that put his pulse back in high gear. What was going on here? He had to remind himself he didn't like her.

"Thanks, Dad." Sam's eyes lit up. She hurried back to the piles of junk in the driveway. "Oh, wow. This is great." She sat on a three-foot-high blue ceramic elephant. "There's only one chip in him and you can barely see it. Maybe I can use this to sit on in front of a computer desk." Her gaze turned wistfully manipulative. "If I had a computer desk."

"You have a tablet, not a computer." Their laptops had come from Turo. Also confiscated by the FBI.

"That's actually a plant stand," Brittany said. "If you want it, I have some nail polish that might cover that chip."

"Okay." Brittany's gaze wandered again and before Joe could say anything, she caught sight of the wooden magazine rack at Phil's feet. "And that. That would be great to store my books."

"It's yours," Brittany said.

Joe collected the magazine rack and the plant stand and put them by the lamp. "Time to go, Sam."

"But…what about this?" Sam held up a plastic shoe rack.

He got the impression she was picking indiscriminately just to fill up the truck. "You only have three pairs of shoes." That's all a kid needed.

"Oh, yeah." Sam's expression crumpled.

Brittany draped her arm around Sam and said in a scolding tone, "She only has three pairs now. That'll change. Soon she'll have flats and sandals and slides and killer boots."

"No killer boots," Joe said reflexively. "She's not that kind of girl. Don't put ideas in her head."

Sam leaned into Brittany and made her little-girl pouty face.

"I mean—" Joe regrouped "—Sam's not into clothes and shoes and stuff. She likes engines and cars."

"I'm into engines and welding," Brittany said in a voice that suggested Joe should have seen this coming. "And I like pretty clothes and fancy shoes *and* makeup." She high-fived Sam.

Phil chuckled. "She's got you there, son. And usually when a woman has you, you owe her a favor." He gave his granddaughter a sly look and gestured to the spread of items before them. "You need a favor from someone with strong arms and a truck, don't you, Brit?"

"Why, yes. Yes, I do." Brittany hugged Sam before releasing her to focus on Joe. "The town has politely donated things they don't need in the hopes that I can use some of it in my art. But it's slim pickings."

Joe looked around at the collection of junk, agreeing. "And so…"

"I need help getting it off Grandpa Phil's driveway." There was a contagious twinkle to Brittany's eyes.

Joe had been inoculated against twinkles. Still, he could almost feel her sparkliness soothe the anger inside.

"And she needs help transporting it to the dump," Rose added, squeezing the squeaky handle of a dented flour sifter.

"Who's going to pay for the dumping fee?" Money matters were the best way to squelch sparkliness.

"You are." Phil's tone was definitive. "You owe the family for joyriding with Leona's car."

Joe's eyes narrowed. "That was over a decade ago."

"People in Harmony Valley have long memories," Phil continued.

True that.

Phil wasn't done. "And if you do this dump run, I'll recommend your garage to others in town."

"We'll help," Sam blurted. "But only if I can pick through things first." And then she added softly, trying to only let Brittany hear, "Are you sure there aren't any clothes?"

"Sam, you have clothes," Joe said firmly.

"New school, Dad," Sam said in her *duh* tone of voice. "Everybody gets new clothes when they go to a new school."

"Dads never understand." Brittany's mouth curled up on one side, threatening to burst into that smile that had slipped past Joe's defenses a number of times.

Beautician-artist-trespasser-thief. If he said it often enough, he'd be okay.

"Oh, I almost forgot." Rose snapped her fingers. "Mildred thought you'd like some car parts. I've got them in my trunk."

"Car parts?" Joe perked up.

"She brought them for me, Shaggy Joe." Brittany hurried over to the trunk of the T-bird.

"Watch out, Rose." Joe followed them to the convertible. "Brittany might take a liking to your car and steal your fender in the middle of the night for some funky art project she has in mind."

"Well, if she did—" Rose unlocked the trunk "—I'm sure it would turn into something beautiful. That mermaid sculpture is exquisite."

Rose pointed a finger at Brittany. "But don't you dare think about it."

"Never fear. I prefer rusty fenders, Rose." Brittany turned to Joe. "And since you're nosy, you can help carry my gift over to my house."

There were two boxes filled with clean car parts—a camshaft, two pistons, a small manifold cover and some O-rings.

"Dibs," Joe whispered reverently. "These aren't rusted."

"Clean car parts work better in my smaller pieces, like man-cave lamps made from camshafts. You can have what I don't use," Brittany added magnanimously.

Joe leaned closer, running a finger over the name of the manufacturer stamped into the manifold. "This is German made."

"Well, Mildred has a fondness for Volkswagens, so that makes sense." Rose waited until they'd each taken a box before slamming the trunk. "If you like rust, Brittany, there used to be an abandoned Volkswagen out by the north bridge and the highway by the Messina Garage. I don't know what happened to it. It could have been hauled away or overrun by those wild blackberry bushes."

"Dibs." Brittany grinned at Joe as they

walked back to Phil's. "I'm smiling, but I mean it. *That car* is mine."

That smile of hers brought forth a lot of things Joe didn't want to feel, including a competitive streak Joe had almost forgotten he had.

CHAPTER SEVEN

BRIT WAS FREE.

The driveway was clear. Joe and Sam had brought their truck over, filled it and left for the dump, as well as taking some of the better bicycles to a shelter in Cloverdale. Brit had begun work on organizing the garage, but Grandpa Phil had accumulated a lot of junk in twenty years and it wasn't stuff she could go through without him.

Tired from his day of socializing, Phil was sprawled on the couch snoring in a casket-worthy pose that unexpectedly squeezed her heart. They hadn't been close before she moved in, but he was growing on her. She nudged his shoulder until he rolled onto his side.

Responsibilities taken care of, it was time to fill her creative well.

She'd make a lamp out of the camshaft Mildred had donated, using the innards from a cracked ceramic lamp someone had dropped off. And the old tricycle intrigued her…or per-haps Grandpa Phil's merman idea had inspired her. Could she sell a merchild on a tricycle?

The business side of her art gnawed near where her self-confidence lived. True artists didn't make choices based on profitability. But the reality was, she needed to sell her work to justify spending money to create more.

Brit frowned. That was Reggie talking.

Dressed in tan coveralls, a red T-shirt and work boots, Brit slipped out of the house, in-tent on finding the abandoned Volkswagen Rose had mentioned. With any luck, Joe had forgotten about the car or was busy preparing his garage for its grand reopening tomorrow.

Procrastinating, her pragmatic inner voice said.

Prospecting, her fearful creative side re-plied.

"Hey. Wait up." It was Reggie, no doubt fresh from making beds, booking rooms and being deceitful to Leona. The B and B was just a few blocks over.

They hadn't talked since last night. Brit had no desire to talk now.

She waved and walked faster in the other

direction, toward the river. "No time to talk." No time to be her sister's accomplice.

"Wait up." Reggie jogged after her, sandals slapping on the sidewalk.

"I've got to be somewhere." She could see the break in the roadside brush next to the river. It led to a path along the bank, which eventually reached the highway near Joe's garage. She'd used it last night in her failed attempt at reconnaissance. "Come by the house after dinner."

"You'll only find another excuse later. Talk to me now."

Talk to me. Not *I'm sorry.* Not *I didn't mean to hurt your feelings.*

Brit turned. Planted her booted feet. Dug in her heels. And sprouted her most determined expression.

"You don't have to put in any money." Reggie held up her hands. Unlike Brit, she had callous-free palms. Unlike Brit, she looked well rested.

For a moment, Brit doubted her choice to take a stand. Maybe working at the B and B would be easier than cutting hair. "The money isn't the issue." It was a moot point since Brit had none. "Grandmother loves that house and when you present her with plans, she expects you to honor your word that we're in this together."

Reggie shrugged. "Please, Brit. Just a signature. Nothing more."

The path to the river beckoned. Was she missing out on a good thing? Brit didn't think so. A contract was legally binding and Brit no longer trusted what Reggie said. The wounds made by her twin's words were still fresh and raw. If she said yes, she'd be validating Reggie's opinion. If she said yes, she'd be pushing her creative bent to the back burner where it would slowly fizzle out.

"I recognize that look," Reggie was quick to say. "Don't turn me down. Not yet."

Brit pressed her lips together.

"I'll come up with a different solution. Just…for now, can you not say anything to Leona or Grandpa Phil?"

"You mean lie?" How could Reggie ask her that? She knew how Brit felt about being honest.

"No lying," Reggie said firmly. "Just…don't say anything."

"You have to tell me why you want this so badly." *Tell me why you want me to compro-*

mise who I am. Tell me why you want this so much you'd ask me to be someone I'm not.

Reggie's face closed off.

Brit turned away. She didn't want to acknowledge her twin was trying to use her. But what else could this be? She pushed through the overgrown brush, rushing down the dirt path toward the river. The tepid warmth of spring was blocked beneath the thick canopy of leaves. The minty scent of eucalyptus and the pungent smell of rich wet soil filled her lungs. The river passed by with eddies and silent swirls, tugging at Brit's frustration and worry for her twin. She tried to replace it with a feeling of anticipation for new beginnings. A car. What would she do if she found an abandoned car?

Her footfalls changed from an angry march to a purposeful step as she bobbed and weaved along the path. Birds swooped along the water. Leaves rustled in the breeze. She stopped at a bend in the river about fifty feet from the highway bridge, which rose from gray pillars out of the gray-green water. But here at the bend, the water was clearer. It swept out beneath the steep bank, seeming to ripple over rocks on the bottom, around a large trout making lazy circles in the shadows from a fallen tree trunk and a...bicycle tire?

She bent down, pulse quickening with excitement. Was it just the tire or the entire bicycle?

Brit couldn't tell.

"THIS INVENTORY IS a waste of time." Sam banged the clipboard against her leg. "We've only found a few cars with ID numbers. There are weeds coming out of this truck's gas tank where the cap should be. Something ate through the convertible's top on the little MG over there." She glared at the sports car from beneath the rim of her ball cap. "And I don't think we have the equipment to dig that BMW out of the mud."

Despite coming back from their trip to the dump with a child's wooden chair and a garden gnome, both in need of a fresh coat of paint, Sam was back to prickly preteen mood.

Joe figured the best way to get past it was to ignore it. "Since when did you shy away from a challenge? Do you know what midcentury modern cars are going for nowadays?"

"No." She slapped the clipboard against her coveralls once more and gave him a dark look. "But I suppose you're going to tell me."

"Four to five times what they sold for new."

He worked the latch on the truck hood of a Ford Falcon station wagon until it popped free. "We need to pick one or two with identification numbers and the best moneymaking potential." As of yet, they hadn't found anything about the BMW's ownership.

Sam made a strangled noise as she glanced in the engine compartment. "And just how do we do that?"

Good question. The Ford's engine was surrounded by a tangle of weeds that seemed to be dragging it downward. Might just as well have been yanking down Joe's hopes. "We take that inventory you're making and do an internet search to see what an equivalent car in prime condition sold for recently."

"By we, you mean me?"

"Yep."

"And then we'll order parts and fix it up."

"Yep."

"So…" Her lips flattened resentfully. "We have money to spend, but we're spending it on car parts?"

They had little money to spend. He'd have to charge parts on his credit card. "You've got to spend money to make money."

"Dad, look at my shoes." Sam enunciated

each word as if Joe was missing an obvious point. "I need new shoes."

He looked. They were almost the same bright blue they'd been when they'd bought them last fall. The soles were good. He'd made sure to buy good lugs. The laces clean. "Sam, new clothes won't make us money."

She scoffed and walked away. "I need a break."

Joe slammed the hood of the station wagon and leaned on it, waging an internal boxing match between Sam's short-term happiness and the need to put food on the table. His cell phone rang, ending the round with no decision.

For a moment as he scrambled for the phone, his heart pounding. *A customer!*

And then he recognized the notes of "Jailhouse Rock." It was Uncle Turo.

Why was he calling again? Was he angry with Joe? Did he need help? Would he tell Joe where he'd stashed the stolen goods if he asked?

Joe debated so long, the call rolled to voicemail.

He stood in the field, held immobile by the forces around him—Sam's disappointment, Turo's bad decisions, the town's suspicions, the FBI's threats. All he wanted was to make an honest living working on engines. Was that too much to ask?

Movement by the river caught his eye. A woman with long brown hair and tan coveralls made her way down the opposite bank.

Suddenly, he could move again.

BRIT NEGOTIATED THE steep slope, slipping and sliding until she landed on the thin lip of mud making up the bank. She peered into the water.

"Definitely a bike," she said to the fleeing fish. She could see the frame prongs on either side of the wheel spokes, covered in bright green algae. Here was a bike deserving of a mermaid. Or maybe a merman. One with unruly blue-black hair and a superior gleam in his eyes. Her pulse quickened with artistic enthusiasm. He'd never be as perfect as Keira, but he'd be beautiful in his own right.

But how to get the bike out of the water?

Fishing pole? Small boat anchor? Grappling hook? She had none of those things. All she had was her hands and the passion to create.

The river gurgled past, uncaring that Brit had found something that made her feel so alive.

She was a decent swimmer, but wasn't foolish enough to go in the water wearing all her clothes. She glanced around. She could shuck her coveralls, T-shirt and shoes, and dive in. Her boy-shorts underpants and sports bra covered more than most bikinis nowadays. This was the north end of town and the highway wasn't frequently traveled. She was alone. And the bike was waiting.

Decision made, Brit stripped down to her skivvies. Her toes sank into cold mud. She took a step into the water. "Oh, mama." The frigid temp bit into her skin.

"Jump in. Drag it out. Get on your way." She gave herself a murmured pep talk. This salvage would make for a good story if she used the bike. It'd be a solid reason to turn Reggie down.

I'm too busy, Brit would say. *My so-called art career is taking off.*

She took a farther step out on the ledge before the drop-off. The water was ice-cold, fed from the mountains. The current was strong enough to challenge her balance. It was too late to back out now. Besides, she couldn't wait to see what the algae hid on the frame. Rust? Battered metal?

Drawing a deep breath, she crouched and launched herself into the bracing water, swimming a few feet until she saw the bicycle beneath her. Her efforts to tread water kept her afloat, but not near her goal. The river pushed her downstream. She swam back and tried to touch the tire with her foot.

Nada. Not so much as a slime of algae met her big toe.

It was deep here, the clear water deceptive. She didn't want to dive beneath the surface. Her fingers and toes were already stinging with cold. This was worse than the time she'd discovered Keira's ride in the Sierras—in a muddy field on a side road. It hadn't been easy then either. She'd never gotten all the mud out of her boots.

She could do this.

If she ignored her shivering and the niggle of doubt.

She ignored both and dove under. It took her several strokes to reach the tire. The green algae was slick beneath her fingers. The wheel rotated back and forth when she pulled on it, but the bike didn't budge. She tugged and tried not to think about fish nibbling her toes or being swept downstream into the rocks at the next bend in the river.

She swam forward, yanking the tire from

a different direction. The current pushed her hair in front of her face, tried to push her away from the bike.

Tug-tug-tug.

It wasn't budging and she needed air. She let go, kicking upward.

Something yanked her hair and held her back.

Her heart raced with fear. *A merman?*

But it wasn't something dark and mythical that held her. It was the bike wheel. Her hair was wrapped around the hub and spokes.

Yank-yank-yank!

Her hair wouldn't come free.

She was going to drown and be fish food unless she could untangle her hair or wrench the bike free.

Her lungs burned.

Drown. She was going to drown.

Reggie would never get to buy the B and B. Rose would never get her red hair. And—

She swallowed water.

JOE WOULD NEVER classify himself as a Peeping Tom. But when he'd seen Brittany slide down the slope to the riverbank, he had to know what she was doing. Something in the water had caught her eye, because she kept staring into the depths of his old fishing hole.

Had she found the Volkswagen? If Rose had seen the car on his side of the river, it seemed unlikely it'd be underwater on the other side.

And then she'd taken off most of her clothes— quickly, as if she was regretting showing the world all those subtle curves and her pink underpants.

Joe had no regrets.

And then after standing and looking in for what seemed like a long time, she'd done a motorboat launch on her belly into the water, letting out a gasp that Joe took as *Oh, crap. It's cold!*

Just the sight of her limbs flailing had set Joe's pulse pounding. Her strokes weren't confident. He'd slid a few feet down the slope, catching himself on a tree limb in case she needed help. But she righted herself and swam farther into the fishing hole. He'd watched her from behind the tree—*okay, kind of like a Peeping Tom*—but he only planned to do it until he'd reassured himself she was okay. He'd even taken a step upslope, prepared to give her some privacy.

And then she'd dove underwater.

He couldn't leave then. She was just eccentric enough to start performing water ballet. And if she was going to point her toes and lift her long legs out of the water…

Well, that wasn't a performance a sports-minded man wanted to miss.

But her legs hadn't come out of the water and neither had her head. In fact, she hadn't resurfaced at all and where she'd gone in seemed to be churning, kind of like the National Geographic special he'd seen where crocodiles dragged their prey underwater and rolled.

Stuck on the image of the jaws of death, Joe slid the rest of the way down the slope. He kicked off his shoes, tugged off his shirt and dove in.

The river was just the way he remembered it from growing up here—cold with a strong current you never expected since the surface was so smooth. He had to work hard to stay even with where he'd last seen Brittany.

He reached the middle of the fishing hole, and looked down on Brittany floating ethereally like that mermaid of hers. Only Brittany's face was pale, her eyes wide-open and pleading, and her hair was tethered to what looked like a submerged bicycle.

For the love of Mike!

There was no time to think about her foolishness. As he watched, the light seemed to go out of her eyes.

Adrenaline gave him gooseflesh. He dove down, reaching for the chain at his belt and the utility knife there. It seemed to take forever to pry open the blade, to grab hold, to cut her hair free. Almost immediately, the current pushed her body clear. He had to swim quickly to latch on to her arm before she was swept away. He dragged her to the surface, floating on his back, holding her against his chest so her face was out of the water.

Was she breathing? He couldn't tell. Her face was as blank as Athena's had been when she'd bled out. Her body cold.

Joe cursed as he swam to the thin strip of shore where she'd gone in, his movements slowed by the cold water and the fear that she was dead. He prayed to whatever higher power watched over fools as he tried to remember CPR. Was it two chest compressions, one breath? Or five chest compressions, two breaths?

He'd barely dragged Brittany out of the river when she began to cough up water.

She was alive.

Joe was suddenly furious, suddenly energized. "Are you kidding me? You dove down there for a bicycle? You're lucky I was around, because you nearly died." He swallowed, his throat clogged with fear—past and present. "No. Oh, no. You didn't nearly die. You died. You were dead."

She sat up, wrapping her arms around her chest, staring at him with huge emotionless eyes.

Dead eyes.

Athena's eyes.

Anger had to be blazing in his. "That was stupid. You should have thought it through. You should have slowed down. You should have remembered who you'd leave behind."

Brittany's expression returned to normal and she blinked, seemingly surprised. "Who'd. I. Leave. Behind?" She croaked, louder than any bullfrog he'd heard the last couple of nights.

His mouth snapped shut and his brain fog suddenly cleared. *"Athena."* Oh, God. Athena.

"It's. Brittany." Her teeth chattered around the syllables like maracas. "And. I. Did. Think." She got to her feet, as unsteady as Phil.

Joe stood with her, balancing on the rocks,

grabbing hold of her arm, which was just as cold as his hand.

She stared at their clammy flesh and shivered. "I need…my clothes."

"You need to go to a doctor."

She drew a shuddering breath. "If you say psychiatrist, I may have to push you in the river." Her words were coming smoother now. Her shivers more like small tremors. She stepped away from him toward the bush a few feet above them where she'd left her clothes, but her foot slipped.

He stopped her downward slide by placing his palm on the delicate pearls that made up her spine. "Slow down. I just fished you half dead out of the river."

"I wasn't in that long. And I wasn't dead." She scrambled behind the bush, pulled on her shirt and stepped into her coveralls. A lock of purple-tinted hair inches shorter than the rest swung past her chin. "I saw you swim toward me and then everything went kind of…"

"Black? That's death." He crossed his arms over his chest, not feeling as cold as he should have. She'd triggered his anger once more.

"I didn't see a light. I didn't see my departed great-aunt Edna." She zipped the coveralls.

They were thin and instantly soaked. "I saw you." And then softer. "I saw you."

Now he was cold.

"I was never so grateful to see anyone in my life," Brittany said in her softest voice yet.

Joe contemplated the watery depths that had almost been her grave. Algae floated like supple green fingers from the tire where he'd gripped it as he'd cut her free. His pocket knife was swinging at his side. He snapped the blade closed and returned it to his wet jeans pocket.

"Who's Athena?"

He glanced at Brittany over his shoulder, staring into eyes that were warm and alive. "My wife. She died in a motorcycle accident after we had an argument."

"'She should have slowed down,'" Brittany murmured, repeating his words. "Thank you for saving me. I'll make sure I braid my hair when I come back for it."

"Back?" The misstep was all but forgotten. "You can't be serious."

"I can." She twisted her hair and wrung it out. The snap was back in her whiskey-brown eyes. "Upcycle artist, remember? I'll get a hook and a rope, and bring my sister." She began the steep climb to the top of the bank on all fours.

"If you couldn't drag it out, there's a reason." Dead bodies and cement shoes came to mind, but he'd always liked those mobster shows. That is, until recently.

"Years of mud. That's the reason." She'd almost made it to the safety of the upper bank, but she was just as reckless as Athena had been. She'd never learn from this.

He scaled the slope on two feet after Brittany. "There could be something you can't see down there. Something keeping the bike where it is."

"Shaggy Joe." That tone. So like Athena's. It said she was pretending everything was all right.

In addition to being a beautician-artist-trespasser-thief, she was a stubborn-scavenging-risk-taker. Defeat wouldn't stop her.

She was the same as Athena and Uncle Turo.

The anger was gone, and with it the guilt. In its place was pure sweat-popping dread. The kind he'd felt when he'd gone after Athena because he'd known she was too angry to drive safely. The kind he'd felt when Uncle Turo made a joke about the law in the hours before his arrest.

He'd tried to be there for those he loved when he saw trouble ahead. It hadn't protected them from slick turns or sharp FBI agents. It hadn't saved them at all. He couldn't stand by and watch this time. He couldn't, even if it was a beautician-artist-trespassing-thief.

"Shaggy Joe," Brittany said again.

"Don't call me that." *Don't make a joke out of this.*

"Heroic Joe." She gave him a crooked grin that acknowledged her mistake and her self-consciousness in thin, wet coveralls that clung to her curves. "Thank you again for saving me." Her grin flatlined. "But I'm not Athena. I'll go slow and figure this out. And I'll be okay." With a small wave, she headed off down the path.

He reached the top of the bank, muttering, "Don't make promises you can't keep."

CHAPTER EIGHT

JOE SLOGGED ACROSS the apartment's living room in wet, muddy jeans.

Sam sat up and set aside her out-of-date tablet. "What happened to you?"

"Your friend Brittany nearly drowned in the river trying to salvage a bicycle." He closed his bedroom door behind him and shucked off his jeans, grateful that the flooring in the entire apartment was linoleum. He rummaged through his drawers until he found his bathing suit.

"She's all right?" Sam's voice sounded her age. "Dad? Say she's all right."

In his haste to live up to Brittany's nickname for him—*Heroic Joe*—he'd forgotten Sam was just a kid, one who'd lost a mother to a motorcycle accident. "She's all right." Nothing a hot shower and a stiff drink wouldn't fix.

"Oh. Okay." She still sounded eleven and small for such a big, heartless world. She was standing on the other side of the door when he opened it.

What if that had been Sam? What if she'd seen a bike and gone under, trying to help the sparkly, determined woman they both barely knew? He felt the cold of the river, the cold of the fear, all over again. He'd have wanted whoever rescued Sam to take her home, to make sure that when the shock wore off she was safe in her own bed surrounded by those who loved her. "I made a mistake."

"Dad?" Sam's eyes were huge.

"She's fine. It's not that." He pulled Sam into his arms, hugging her tight. "In some ways, she reminds me of your mother—strong and brave. But she's also human. Same as Mom. Same as me." Same as Uncle Turo. "Brittany nearly drowned and I let her walk home alone. I should have followed her. I shouldn't have left her until her grandfather or her sister was by her side." There to soothe the horrifying what-ifs that would inevitably come after a brush with death.

"Can we go see her?" Sam's voice was muffled against his chest. "Maybe she'd like a hot chocolate from the bakery?"

Joe swallowed back the need to preserve both

his bank account and his defenses against Brittany's appeal. "Sure we can, honey. But first, are you up for a salvage mission? I need someone to operate the winch on the tow truck."

Sam nodded, still not letting him go.

Soon thereafter, Joe drove the tow truck off the highway on the north side of the river. He parked as close to the bend above the fishing hole as he could and then got out. "If we're going to live with a river practically in our backyard, you need to know how dangerous it can be." A memory returned. His father standing on the other side of the river, telling Joe about water safety. "Look at the bank. Here it's steep and high, but that doesn't mean the water is shallow. I'm over six feet tall and that bike is at least ten feet under."

Sam nodded. Not joking. Not making light of his lecture.

"Look how smooth the river is on the surface. It looks slow-moving. But it's not." He gestured upstream to the bridge. "There's a sharp bend before the river goes under that bridge. And another one right before this spot. Water moves faster downhill and after sharp turns."

"Just like cars," she murmured.

"Just like cars." And motorcycles. Joe unhooked the winch. "I'm going to attach this to the bike tire. When I give you the signal, you turn on the winch and pull it out."

Sam was suddenly hugging him again. "You're going to be okay, right?"

"Right." His throat felt as if King Kong was gripping it. "The bike is right there. And my cell phone..."

His cell phone was wet and in his jeans pocket at the apartment. Ruined. He wouldn't be getting any calls. Not from Agent Haas and not from Uncle Turo. There was gut-sinking relief in the thought. *No calls.*

And then he realized there wouldn't be calls from potential customers either.

"Is it raining?" Grandpa Phil asked when Brit came in the front door, hair still dripping. "You're wet, but..." He took in the wet patches and mud on her coveralls. "Did you go skinny-dipping in the river? Bad form, girlie. It's too early in the season. The current can be strong this time of year."

"I fell in." Kinda-sorta. "I'm going to shower and then I'll make dinner." Normalcy, that's what she needed. And hot water. Lots of hot, healing water. Brit had to wash off the feeling of failure, wash away the memory of Joe's strong touch and fight off the shuddering fear and sudden, sobbing bursts of panic that things could have gone much, much worse.

Brit hurried down the hall.

She remembered it all with breath-stopping clarity. She remembered the blackness. And then seeing Joe swim toward her with urgent strokes. She recalled his frantic efforts to cut her free, his strong arms around her, his big hands on her shoulder as she floated on his chest, and then his palm on her back when she slid going up the slope.

She closed the bathroom door behind her and shivered.

Joe was right. She'd been reckless. But she was no dummy. She'd learned her lesson.

It was too bad she'd learned how deeply his wife's death had hurt him, how passionately he could feel. Because now he was no longer a man she could make fun of with the moniker Shaggy Joe. Now he was a man with a heart and feelings, who'd loved deeply and suffered a profound loss, a brave man who'd risked his life for someone he barely knew and didn't like.

The loved-deeply part bothered her, because she doubted she'd ever experience such passion. She didn't like the hurt part either, because she longed to have someone like Joe call her a friend.

She curled into a crumpled heap in the tub-shower and let the fear come, the tears flow and the pity burn them away.

Showered, warm and dry, equilibrium temporarily restored, she emerged from the bathroom with a section of hair snipped on the other side of her face so it matched the lock Joe had cut to set her free. She wore jeans and a pink sleeveless sweater.

"Look, Brit," Grandpa said unhappily. "We've got company."

It was the three ladies from the town council—Rose, Agnes and Mildred.

Had they heard she'd nearly drowned? Brit froze, reliving the heart-pounding fear of being trapped, submerged, her lungs on fire.

"We have something to show you." Agnes dispelled her fears immediately. Her gray sweatshirt with its hand-painted Easter eggs comforted.

"You're going to love it," Mildred said from

her walker. The smooth state of her teased curls comforted.

"It was my idea." Rose sitting on the couch and tapping her feet heel-to-toe comforted.

Brit drew a deep breath as the panic receded. "What is it?"

"Get your shoes on and come with us." Agnes waved her hand to Mildred, who pushed to standing and pointed her walker toward the front door.

Rose bounced to her feet.

"I think I know where this is heading." Phil extended his long legs across the couch cushion Rose had vacated. "I've already collected your rent and let you hang a bicycle on my wall. Just remember that, girlie. You're committed to operating your business at Phil's."

His words stumped Brit. She resisted the tide of the town council as it moved toward the door. "What's going on? Where are we going?"

"To Minna's." Rose had a light dusting of flour on her cargo pants. "It's just a few blocks over."

"The woman who used to have a hair salon?" At Rose's nod, Brit added, "I thought she was dead."

"She is." Agnes opened the door for Mildred. "But her family never cleared out her salon equipment."

"We think." Mildred trundled over the threshold.

Brit looked at her grandfather. How could Leona have left him? He was predictable and steady. He was the type of guy who'd jump in the river to save a stranger. "I'm not interested in renting other space."

Phil tipped his head in acknowledgment of her loyalty.

"We're not saying you should reopen Minna's." Agnes gave Brit's shoulder a squeeze. "I talked to Minna's son today and he said they never cleared out her equipment. He'll accept whatever offer you think is fair for the dryers."

Equipment. Chair dryers. Something to accomplish that was safe. Brit eagerly slipped into a pair of tennis shoes she'd left by the door and told Phil she'd be right back.

Minna's house was a short drive away, a faded brown ranch home with hedges so high they blocked the front windows, tops nearly touching the rain gutters. The garage door had been replaced with a wall, and a regular door was smack-dab in the center.

Agnes opened a lockbox, revealing a set of

keys to the house. "We created a system so we could access the abandoned homes in town. That way, we can show them to potential buyers or renters more quickly."

"I'm not interested in buying or renting." Brit felt the need to repeat herself as she followed the town council inside.

There were posters of Marilyn Monroe and Elizabeth Taylor on the pink walls. Two stations stood empty, waiting for stylists, mirrors streaked as if they'd been cleaned without enough water. A layer of dust covered the floor thick enough to show footprints.

And there was Brit's salvation. Two chair hair dryers stood ready for customers. Brit turned on the timer on the unit closest to her. Nothing happened. She tried the second unit. Also nothing.

"I forgot there's no electricity." Agnes frowned.

"I can't make an offer until I know they work." Which Brit couldn't verify without electricity. And they weren't exactly easy to lift.

Unless you were Joe.

He probably never wanted to see her again, much less come to her rescue once more.

"Let me phone someone." Agnes stepped outside.

A few minutes later, the cavalry arrived—two broad-shouldered men in a blue truck with a star on it.

"We heard there were damsels in distress at this location." Sheriff Nate was tall, with a wry grin and matching tone of voice.

He was handsome, but when Brit looked at him, all she could think of was how she preferred Joe's stoic expression.

"Welcome to Harmony Valley." His passenger was one of the winery owners, Will Jackson. He was blond and clean-cut, definitely all-American in the looks department. "Call anyone at the winery if you need help."

He was handsome, too, but when Brit looked at him, all she could think of was Joe's unruly midnight hair.

Within thirty minutes, they had the chair units at the barbershop. Brit turned one on. It hummed steadily right away, blowing out lots of hot air, although it made the room smell like burning dust. She turned it off and tried the other one. It sounded as if it'd been wound too tight, it barely put out any heat and it didn't smell at all.

The sheriff turned both on at the same time and everything in the shop shut off—the lights, the dryers, the barber pole out front. "I wouldn't recommend having these run on the same wire."

Will found the fuse box. "It's only flipped the circuit off. Nothing was blown."

"The electrician is coming on Monday," Brit said, hoping he was willing to work on hair appliances.

Used dryer units were hard to come by. Brit gave Agnes a figure to relay to Minna's son. The pixie-sized town councilwoman stepped outside to do so just as Joe's truck parked in front of the barbershop.

Sam ran in carrying a hot to-go cup from the bakery. She snuggled against Brit's side. "I brought you a hot chocolate. Dad says Mom used to drink it when something bad happened."

"Something bad happened?" Rose asked. And not of Brit.

While Sam relayed the details of Brit's near-death experience, Brit lifted her gaze to Joe's. Two sheets of glass separated them—the barbershop window and his windshield. It didn't matter. He cared. He cared enough to allow his daughter to bring her a hot chocolate. His caring eased the tightness in her chest, and partly erased the memories of deep water and death.

She may have lost her twin to selfish ambition, but maybe—*a slim maybe*—there was a relationship to be had with Joe. Not an altar-heading relationship, but an understanding relationship, a friendship. One bound by her knowing the extent of his loss and him seeing her nearly dead.

Brit lifted her cup in salute and took a sip. Joe gave a brief, simple nod in return and Brit felt the rich warmth of hot chocolate spread.

The crowd in the barbershop hovered and fussed and marveled. Brit appreciated their friendship, but despite their help, she didn't feel as connected to them as she did to Joe.

Who'd probably regret telling anyone about his heroics come morning.

He hit the horn once.

Like a well-trained puppy, Sam dutifully sprinted toward the door. "Dad's cell phone wasn't as lucky as Brit. We've got to get a new one." She skipped out the door and hopped into the pickup.

Just like that, Heroic Joe was gone. Brit felt disoriented, almost dizzy. She sat down beneath Keira, head buzzing with too many thoughts. She needed to reimburse Joe for his phone. She needed to send him some type of thank-you gift. She needed to ask the sheriff and Will if they'd help her recover the bike.

Agnes came back inside. "The dryers are yours. What's all the excitement about?"

There was another round of retelling Brit's misfortune, all done without Brit's input.

The sheriff sat in a chair next to her and took her hand in both of his. They were strong hands, dependable hands. They just weren't Joe's hands. "You okay?"

Brit blinked back tears, completely blanking on asking for a favor. "I should go home now." Back to the safety of Grandpa Phil's before the fear returned full force along with those powerful, uncontrollable sobs.

Nate sprang into action. The barbershop was cleared and locked up. Brit was hustled into the backseat of Agnes's faded green Buick.

And Brit was fine. She really was.

Until Agnes parked in front of Phil's house and she saw an algae-covered bike on the porch.

"SAM! YOU'RE GOING to be late for the first day of school." Joe shoved an apple in a brown bag next to a bottle of water and a cheese-and-jelly sandwich. Not only did he want Sam to be on time, Joe wanted to open the garage for business as soon as possible.

Sam emerged from the bedroom wearing coveralls and her baseball cap.

"Hold it. That doesn't look like school attire." In LA County, she'd be violating the gang code. "Turn around and change. You know what to wear."

"But, *Dad.*"

"Turn around. And change." Joe said it harder this time, like his mother used to say before she'd decided motherhood wasn't for her. He stuffed Sam's lunch into her backpack.

She huffed and puffed all the way back to her room, slammed the door and gave a defeated war cry.

"Five minutes." It occurred to him that Sam hadn't worn anything but coveralls since they'd left LA. Was she trying to make a statement of solidarity with Uncle Turo?

"I'm seriously considering putting myself up for adoption." Sam's muffled complaint was designed to make Joe feel like crap. The worship from yesterday's heroics had long since been worn away by Sam's dissatisfaction with her wardrobe and nerves regarding starting a new school.

"Four minutes." Joe stood by the door holding her backpack.

Drawers opened and closed. The closet door slammed. "Maybe Brittany will adopt me as thanks for salvaging that bike."

Joe would drown before he let that happen. "Three minutes."

"I hate my clothes."

"Two." He didn't care that he wasn't keeping accurate time. They needed to hustle.

Sam ran out of her room and into the bathroom wearing blue jeans and a gray zippered hoodie. Not much better, but it'd have to do.

"Lose the hat."

Another feral groan.

The water ran. Stopped. Sam ran to the door with wet hair slicked back. She snatched her backpack from him and raced down the stairs. "Let's go or we'll be late."

"No kidding." Joe hurried after her, waiting until he was backing the pickup past the tow truck to say, "Be nice to everyone."

"Dad. No lectures." The know-it-all was back.

Joe missed the little girl who'd clung to his leg on her first day of kindergarten and flung her arms around him when she came home. "I know first days can be rough, but it's only six hours."

"Six hours and forty-five minutes."

"You can't count lunch and recess."

She thunked her forehead against the window. "New clothes would give me patience."

"Your clothes are fine." At least the ones back in her room that weren't coveralls. He turned down the street to the school. "I'll expect a full report when I pick you up. We'll get a cookie or something from the bakery." Maybe splurge for nachos at El Rosal if enough customers came by today. He pulled into the lot.

"Dad. No goodbye kiss." Sam pushed her hair back from her face and turned to him. "I need my space." She hopped out of the truck and slammed the door.

Since it was an old door, it was a hard, hollow slam.

Joe watched her walk away, wondering when his eleven-year-old had turned into a brooding teenager. The sun glinted off his windshield and he recalled a different time in this parking lot.

The afternoon sun had been beating down

on Joe as he waited for Mom to pick him up after school. Some of the kids were headed to the field for middle school track practice, the one sport Joe didn't participate in. The family's old Ford truck barreled too fast around a corner. Mom must be mad at Dad again.

The crossing guard frowned as it approached.

The Ford lurched to a halt in front of Joe. Gabe was at the wheel.

"Get in." Vince slid to the center of the bench seat. "Don't say a word."

"Why?" Joe slung his tattered backpack to the floor and climbed in. He had to slam the door twice to get it to latch properly. Gabe punched the accelerator before Joe got his lap belt on. "Slow down or I'm telling Mom."

"I said don't talk." Vince slapped Joe upside the head. "We were told to bring you back. No talking."

"Why? What's wrong?"

"We're up a creek, that's what," Vince said, discounting everything he'd just said about silence.

Only last week the boys had had a conversation about what would happen if their father was arrested again. "Is it…Dad? Is he gone?" Mom would be upset. But Mom was always upset lately. There were no more hugs. And for Joe, no whispered *you're my favorite*. Sometimes Joe wished Dad would go away. Then everything would be better.

"Mom's gone," Vince blurted, his words bleeding with damnation and disbelief. "Dad doesn't want us to say a word to anyone."

Dad. With his sometimes scary mood swings and his sometimes violent behavior. His fists had landed him in jail twice since Christmas. And their one defense against him—*Mom*—was gone.

"She left us?" Joe couldn't believe it. He wanted to throw up.

"When we get home, don't say anything," Vince warned. "Not another word about her. Not ever."

Joe took that order to heart. He didn't speak of his mother, of the feeling of betrayal or the hurt of abandonment. He didn't say a word to his brothers or to his friends, including Will Jackson. When folks in town asked about Mom, Joe turned a deaf ear. But being deaf didn't mean he wasn't angry. And for a teenager with an unpredictable home life, anger was often expressed on the school yard. Or the football field.

It wouldn't be like that for Sam. He'd make sure of it. She may have lost one parent, but she wouldn't be losing another.

Joe drove around the block to the town square, which fed into Main Street.

The mayor stood at the corner, wearing a tie-dyed yellow-and-green hoodie. Standing next to him was a tall man with golden-blond hair. Both men turned as he drove by. Only then did Joe recognize his childhood friend Will Jackson. He'd heard Will was a millionaire now.

He passed the bakery and then the barbershop. Brittany juggled an armload of bags as she opened the door. He had the strongest urge to stop and help her. But helping implied things he wasn't interested in giving.

Come to think of it, he shouldn't have dragged the bicycle out of the river for her. He'd done it for purely selfish reasons. His chest couldn't stand another knot of guilt if anything happened to her while she salvaged the bike.

So he drove on, feeling a heaviness in his chest.

When Joe arrived back at the shop, Irwin was waiting for him. He had a thermos of coffee, a pastry bag from Martin's, and he wasn't wearing his red riding leathers. "I'm ready to start."

"Start?" Joe unlocked the waiting room door and held it open for Irwin.

"Yep. I'm here to watch and learn."

Joe no longer worried about Sam or Brittany. "I can't let you in the shop while I'm working."

"Can't or won't?"

"Won't." Joe turned on the office lights and unlocked the door to the service bays, one of which was occupied by Betty or Bertha or whatever it was Irwin called his motorcycle.

Irwin sat down, making himself at home by arranging his things on top of the blue elephant plant stand. "Your uncle used to let people hang out here."

Joe winced. "That was my uncle." Things had changed after Mom left. Uncle Turo had come to town, moving into the apartment over the garage. "He had…friends." The wrong kind of friends.

"I wanted to be his friend, but back then I was working and married." Irwin's stringy hair framed his round face in innocence. "Now things are different."

Understatement of the year. "Listen, Irwin." This was hard. Joe needed the money. But it was Monday morning and they'd canvassed the town with flyers. Surely there was other business to be had. "I don't think your bike needs a tune-up. I checked it last night and it was out of gas."

Irwin shrugged. "I don't care. I want a tune-up, anyway."

"Why?"

"Because I have no place else to go today." Irwin's words told Joe more about the state of Irwin's life than Joe wanted to know.

Joe was afraid Irwin would have no place else to go tomorrow, too.

CHAPTER NINE

THE MORNING AFTER the bike incident, Brit thought she was doing fine.

She looked no different in the steamy mirror after her morning shower.

Grandpa Phil said nothing about it as he patted her shoulder and went for his morning checker match at Martin's Bakery. No one waved to her from the patio of the Mexican restaurant where they were serving breakfast as she drove past. No one ran out of Martin's Bakery as she unloaded her truck with things for the shop. No one demanded details of her near drowning. It was as if it'd never happened.

It wasn't until she was unlocking the barbershop door that she felt the hitch in her breath. And that was only because she caught sight of Joe's truck trundling down Main Street. And if the hitch turned into full-on can't-breathe-itis when he drove past without stopping…well, the worst thing was she nearly dropped some bags.

She didn't have time for the aftereffects of foolish endeavors. This was her last day to prep the shop before she took on paying clients. She had to restock the supply cabinet. And there were a few finishing touches she wanted to make—most of which would probably upset Phil. Pretty spring-themed hand towels for the bathroom. A jar of mints on the table in the waiting area. A coffeepot, canister of coffee and set of mugs with fun sayings.

Only when she had the place in good order did Keira's reflection in the mirror snag her attention. She understood the peacefulness of hair floating on the current now. She understood the release of giving in to the river's cold embrace. But thoughts of creating another mermaid made Brit feel worse than ever before.

She couldn't do it. Not yet.

Maybe not ever.

And not for lack of materials.

Brit had enough bicycles to make a school of mermaids. But there was only one bike worthy of a mermaid like Keira—the bike Joe had brought her. He'd saved it from the river without being asked or asking for anything in return. He hadn't even left her a note. So typical of the iceman.

Still, she felt as warm inside as if he'd given her a bouquet of flowers with a card that read "Get well soon, friend."

"Good morning." A petite blonde about Brit's age pushed through the door and introduced herself. "I…saw your mermaid yesterday when I walked past. I…had to come by and ask about it."

Take that, Heroic Joe.

"It's not for sale."

"I mean," Tracy said with an infectious smile. "I have a proposal for you. I work at the bakery. I also do marketing on the side." She checked out the barbershop with an approving nod. "Harmony Valley…needs any PR angle it can find. Hooks to interest visitors. I was wondering…if you'd be interested in some cross-promotion."

Brit hesitated, trying to get a handle on Tracy. She seemed sincere, but her speech was halting and it sounded like a sales pitch.

Tracy must have sensed the reason for Brit's hesitation. Her fingers fluttered near the right side of her head. "I had a car accident. My speech…" She shrugged. "It falters on long sentences."

"I wondered," Brit said, not one to pretend she hadn't.

"No worries." Tracy had a smile as brilliant as the diamond on her left ring finger. "Jessica—my boss—can bake some mermaid cupcakes or cookies. We'd give you samples. A few times a week." She pointed to the coffeepot. "As long as you…don't mind us selling them in the bakery, too."

"Of course." Quid pro quo didn't require Brit to go all Reggie in this situation and complain about licensing or rights to protect Keira's image.

"Thanks." Tracy rushed forward to hug her, which Brit took as her way of sealing the deal instead of a handshake. "I'll bring a box tomorrow. For your grand opening."

"Actually," Brit felt compelled to say. "Phil's has never been closed."

"Tell that to the town." Tracy waved and left.

She would. Grandpa Phil was being great to her.

The electrician arrived next and spent an hour rewiring the shop so that her hair dryers wouldn't blow a transformer and put half the town in the dark. He didn't have time to look at the underperforming hair dryer, although she got the feeling he'd prefer never to look under that hood.

"Yoo-hoo." An older woman with black readers perched atop her teased purplish-gray bangs entered. "Everyone at the bakery has been talking about this mermaid." Her penciled-in eyebrows lifted at the sight of Keira. "Oh, she's quite large. I didn't need to bring my glasses." She gave Brit's sculpture a critical look-see. "This could be harder than I thought. I don't do bicycles. Frankly, I've never done mermaids before either."

"Are you Jessica?" The baker?

"No, dear. I'm Eunice, godmother to Jessica's baby." She said this proudly, as if it was an accomplishment rather than an honor. "I make baby quilts for the boutique across the road? Mae's Pretty Things?" She pointed to the small shop with sweaters, appliquéd dish towels and baby quilts hanging artfully from tree limbs in the display window. "Tracy thinks your mermaid is the cat's meow. She wants me to create a mermaid baby quilt." Eunice removed her glasses, folded them and tapped her chin with the frame. "But the bicycle…That's a challenge." Eunice's reflection in Phil's mirror distracted her. She fluffed her bangs higher.

What had seemed an easy exchange of services with Tracy was turning into something Reggie would certainly caution against—several people using an image Brit had created for their own profit. Brit needed advice. Truth be told, she missed talking to Reggie. If only her twin had apologized yesterday.

"Not that I can't create a mermaid," Eunice was saying. "But it won't be easy. And the Spring Festival will be here sooner than any of us think."

Brit had no idea what the significance of the Spring Festival was on anything, but she was intrigued by Eunice's attitude: *creating a mermaid wouldn't be easy, but she was willing to try.*

More willing than Brit?

BARBARA WAS TUNED sharper than a piano in the philharmonic. Had been for hours.

Irwin didn't care. He seemed to have no plans to leave Joe's waiting room. He'd brought a couple of motorcycle magazines and was reading them cover to cover. As for other customers, there were none.

None! All those flyers...

Since the old man had paid in cash, Joe didn't want to be totally rude. He brought Sam's antique lamp to the waiting room and was working on removing the old wiring and cord. But he was nearly done and it was almost lunchtime. "I suppose you'll be heading home soon."

"No rush." Irwin slurped what had to be the last of his coffee.

A heavyset old man wearing plaid golf shorts and a blue Hawaiian shirt pulled into the lot in a golf cart. He got out, wielding a cane in one hand and carrying a large white paper bag in the other.

"Can I help you?" Joe asked, figuring the man was lost.

"I'm delivering." The big man handed Irwin the bag and sat down heavily in a plastic chair.

"Ah, super nachos." Irwin passed him a twenty. "The lunch of champions. Thanks, Rex."

"Call me old-fashioned," Joe said, because his patience was wearing thin, "but donuts for breakfast and nachos for lunch don't seem very healthy."

"When you reach the end of the road, that doesn't matter anymore." Irwin high-fived Rex. "Want some, Joe?"

"No, thanks." Joe had made a peanut-butter sandwich when he'd put together Sam's lunch. He removed it from the plastic sandwich bag and took a bite, swallowing down the urge for nachos.

"Had a doctor's appointment this morning." Rex dug into the nacho tray with hands as large as oven mitts. "Did I miss anything over here?"

"Nope," Irwin said around a mouthful of chips and cheese. "Maybe this afternoon, though. You in?"

"I'm in." Rex glanced at the small counter, the large round clock on the wall and the blue elephant plant stand between his and Irwin's chairs. "Where's the soda machine?"

"We don't have one." Soda machines required large deposits to distributors.

"I brought sodas in the cooler." Irwin nudged it with his foot. He'd brought it in from his car an hour earlier.

"Also not healthy," Joe muttered.

The clock on the wall ticked off a minute.

Sam wasn't the only one counting down the hours to the end of the school day. That clock couldn't move fast enough for Joe.

"Are you sure about this place?" Rex gestured with a big hand toward Joe. "He's about as exciting as paint drying."

The two old dudes chuckled.

Something moved by the bridge. He spotted Brittany's pickup slowing and stopping. She got out of the truck, pulled black coveralls over her leggings, rolled up the sleeves and then took a rake from the back of the truck.

She was going to look for that Volkswagen Rose had spoken of. The one Joe had forgotten about.

She had little chance of finding it. The blackberry bushes had taken over the bank on his side of the river. Fifteen feet wide and nearly one hundred feet in length. The thorns alone were a deterrent to uncovering what was underneath. She was wasting her time.

Joe took a bite of sandwich. The clock ticked off another minute.

On his side of the service counter, his new cell phone began playing "Jailhouse Rock."

"Aren't you going to answer that?" Irwin asked.

"No." He'd decided he wasn't ready to talk to Turo, to hear the disappointment in his voice when he yelled at Joe for selling him out. He'd decided not to ask where he'd hidden the stolen vehicles. Was it too much to hope that Agent Haas would get lucky and find them on his own?

Luck hadn't been with Joe lately.

Joe stared at his white-bread sandwich. He stared at the men scarfing down nachos. His phone beeped to indicate he had a voicemail. "Gentlemen, can you watch the shop while I take care of something outside?"

"Now we're talking." Irwin rubbed his hands. "We've got your back, dude."

MOST DAYS, WHEN Brit was poking around in the weeds for discarded junk and heard footsteps behind her, she got up quickly and put on her friendliest smile.

But this wasn't most days and she knew whose booted steps were nearby.

"This isn't your property, Heroic Joe."

He stopped walking.

Maybe she should have been at the house clearing out the garage. But Phil had been napping and a treasure hunt was more appealing than tackling her grandfather's stuff and setting up an art studio.

Brit was on her hands and knees, crawling along the edge of the blackberry patch. Judging by the inch-long thorns, the bushes were very old. Every few feet she carefully lifted the vines, letting them poke her skin through her coverall sleeves while she peered into the gloom. When she saw something—she'd only seen something inorganic once so far—she stuck the handle of the rake through the shrub to see if she could hit metal.

So, yeah, she was on her knees, crawling along like a hound dog trying to find a scent. And there was an attractive, heroic guy standing behind her. If her father were alive, he'd want to kick the snot out of Joe for standing there, presumably watching her, certainly not offering to help. Her mother, who'd remarried and was living comfortably in Southern California, would encourage Brit to stand up and smile as if Joe was the most attractive man on earth. But Brit had an agenda and too many obstacles in her path. She couldn't afford a fight or a smile.

"Save your knees. There's no car under there." The tone of voice Joe used was different today. Not the volume of anger. Not the bite of annoyance. Not the rumble of frustration. Would his eyes be more sky blue than arctic?

She didn't dare look. "Not your knees, Heroic Joe. Or your expedition."

"I suppose." He had a nice voice when he wasn't yelling at her.

"Which means you can leave." Watching her crawl around couldn't be that interesting. And having an audience made her self-conscious about her love of carbs.

"I'll give it a few more minutes. In case you get lucky."

Brit inched forward, trying not to think about Stoic Joe teasing her, because that just seemed impossible. Something caught the light when she moved the branches in the next section. She edged closer, thorns pricking her side. And then she stuck her rake in between the vines, deeper and deeper until she held it by the tines.

Thunk.

A thorn bit into the back of her hand making her drop the rake. She lifted the vines with more care so she could probe once more.

Thunk. Thunk.

Definitely solid. Glory hallelujah! "Did you hear that?"

"Nope."

She got to her feet, removed a pair of clippers from her pocket and began snipping the vines a few painful feet at a time.

"Is this a public service? Hedge trimming?"

Brit spared him a quick glance to see if he was smiling. He wasn't. How like him to deadpan a tease. "There's a car in there." She cut a vine, held it with two fingers to avoid being skewered by two-inch-long thorns and tossed it behind her. "I'm not going to drown. You don't need to watch over me." But didn't it feel nice that he was? Brit glanced over her shoulder again. "I don't mean to sound ungrateful. You saved my life. You rescued the bike from the river. But this is going to take a long time and you have a business to run."

Translation: *please go.*

Left unsaid: *you make me nervous.*

He glanced back at the garage.

"Ouch." A thorn penetrated the skin on her arm. She turned back to her task at hand. "At this rate, it'll take me all afternoon to see what's under there."

Perhaps realizing she wasn't putting on much of a show, Joe left.

The task should have been better alone.

It wasn't.

It was a painstaking process without the distraction of Joe. Emphasis on *pain*. Her hands and arms were getting a free acupuncture treatment. She now knew what it felt like to be a voodoo doll.

A strong hand landed on her shoulder. She yelped and skittered free before she realized it was Joe.

"This might speed up the process." Without apology, Joe eased her away from the vines. He was holding a chain saw and wearing goggles. "Your problem is, you're approaching this the old-school way." He started up the chain saw.

Brit stumbled back as bits of vine flew about. Joe was no stranger to the chain saw or using it against thick ropey vines. Brit gave him space, breathing in the fresh smell of green vines and exposed earth.

In no time, Joe had cleared a wide path into the brambles. He shut off the chain saw. "I wouldn't have bet money on it, but you're right." He stepped to one side so she could see.

A bubble hood and cracked headlights peered at her from beneath a thin layer of vines.

"It's roached," Joe said. "Rusted clear through."

The vegetation and weather had worked the body into rusted metal lace. It was beautiful.

Brit grinned with unabashed relief. "I guess you won't be fighting me for this one."

"I don't know." He knelt for a better look. "If the chassis and floorboards are intact, it's still worth something."

She gave a faux gasp. "You'd part it out?"

His mouth worked as if struggling to hold back a smile. Instead, he shook the black hair from his laughing eyes. "Sure. If it wasn't salvageable. Why not part it out?"

"Ha!" She couldn't resist teasing him. "You'll be making money off the parts in your field in no time, just like me."

The ice returned to his gaze.

A beige sedan drove over the bridge. Brit waved. The driver, an elderly woman, raised her hand as if to return the greeting, saw Joe and sped up.

"Why does everyone give you a wide berth?" Brit asked. "From what my grandfather has said, which is very little, you were a wild teenager, but this…" She gestured toward the fast-retreating car. "I've seen you at night. You don't have fangs." And he'd rescued her. She couldn't discount that.

"Not everyone avoids me." Joe's attention drifted from the repair shop to her. The ice in his eyes had melted to a minor frost. "You certainly don't."

"You can't call this avoiding. You keep showing up to save me."

"Maybe you should stop taking risks." His voice was getting louder.

She'd struck a nerve somehow, but Brit wouldn't back off the teasing. She wanted to reclaim that moment from last night—a connection made through glass. Although she would kind of miss his stormy bluster.

"And then you give me those bossy, territorial glares," Brit continued as if he hadn't said a word, because they'd fallen silent and it was her turn to speak. "Like this." She lowered her brows and tried to show him her best glower. "Maybe that's why people avoid you."

"My glares are overrated." The frost had thawed. A rare blue sky had appeared. The man had the most expressive eyes. Who needed smiles with eyes like that? "They don't work on you."

Oh, they worked. Just not how he might like. "What did you do? Besides joyriding? You can tell me."

Something rustled in the vines, but other than that they were alone. She wasn't going to let this opportunity to know something else about him—something as intimate as the story of how he'd lost his wife—get away.

His voice started low. "My brothers and I were the wild ones in town."

"Big deal. It's a small town. Wild could have meant staying out late with the mayor's daughter." That had been her first impression of him. Wild with women. Now that she knew him better—*ha! Just a smidge*—she knew he'd have no patience for most women. And most women would have no patience for his brooding nature.

"My older brother was the ladies' man." Joe's mouth quirked to one side, but almost immediately fell. "We were just like any other boys in town. That is, until my mom left us. Not that we fell apart or anything."

The way he said the last part—all monotone— she recognized it as a lie, the same as any lie she'd been told from people who didn't understand her junk creations were art. And so she kept up the teasing. "Careful, you might become a cliché. Bad boy raised by a single dad."

He studied her the way a scientist does a new species. "It's not that simple. We weren't bad when Mom was around. More like a handful. My father was…" There was nothing on Joe's face even resembling a smile. Nothing in his eyes either. This was serious stuff. "My dad struggled with mental health issues. Schizophrenia. We were teenagers. We didn't understand. So we avoided him after Mom left because it was… He was…" A deep crease formed between his bladed brows and he turned away.

She hadn't imagined him being abused or abandoned as a child. He presented himself as invincible. "I'm sorry."

"Don't be." He gestured with his hand, but his fingers were fisted as if clenched around memories he couldn't let go of. "It wasn't all bad. Uncle Turo came to live above the garage. He got Dad on some good meds." He picked up the chain saw, looked at it, set it down again. "Dad had force-fed us the basics of mechanics—how to change oil, how to clean a carburetor, which electrical wires not to cross." He knelt in front of the Volkswagen and pushed on the rusted metal bumper. "It was my uncle who gave us motorcycles and made fixing things fun."

There was a trick to interacting with Joe, she realized. When he blustered, you had to weather the storm and blow back. When he shared something personal, you had to do much the same, but with no visible sympathy, no pity. She'd given him exactly that kind of look in Phil's driveway when the woman ran away from him and he'd blasted her with a frozen glare.

This time, even though her heart was breaking for him, she put on her poker face and sent some breezy humor his way. "Tsk-tsk. Again, you turned into a cliché. Black leather jacket and a Harley. I bet you had a lady-killer glint in your eye and enjoyed every minute of it."

He pivoted so he could look at her. She could swear he almost smiled. She could swear her heart nearly skipped a beat.

For the first time, she realized this connection they were building was dangerous. Not physically dangerous. It was her heart that was at risk of injury.

"I could've convinced you to take a ride on my Harley."

If her heart had been skipping before, his words had it sprinting. She needed to remember who she was. The ugly duckling. The wallflower. She needed to backpedal. "You wouldn't have offered me a ride. You would've asked Reggie."

He frowned. "Reggie wouldn't want her hairdo ruined by the wind."

Yep.

The frown softened. "You would've laughed when I went fast."

Brit smiled. She didn't mean to. But she suspected he was right.

And then a miracle of sorts happened. He smiled back. Not a big smile. Certainly not a flirtatious smile. It was the smile of a boy inviting a girl to take a secret, forbidden ride on the back of a Harley.

Be still my heart.

It was beating so hard her ears were ringing.

Joe stopped smiling and checked his cell phone, silencing a beeping alarm. "I can cut you some space around this junker and then I've got to pick up Sam from school."

Without waiting for her to answer, he re-started the chain saw and went to work as if he hadn't just made an ugly duckling's day.

CHAPTER TEN

SAM RACED TO the truck almost the instant after the bell rang, flipping up her hood as she ran.

"How was your day?" Joe asked when she'd slammed the door.

"I didn't die."

"Sam," Joe said wearily.

"Can we just not talk about school?" She gave him the once-over. "You smell like you've been to a gym and mowed the lawn."

Eau de Women Repellant. It hadn't worked on Brittany. If anything, it'd jimmied the locks he had on his past. "I trimmed the blackberry bushes by the road."

"Why?"

Here was a conversation he wanted to avoid. Any time he told his daughter he was helping a woman, she got ideas. He put the truck in gear and headed home. "Do you have homework?"

"Math. Vocabulary. Reading in my science

book." Sam slumped in her seat. "I can't wait to be done with school."

"You've got about ten to twelve years left."

"How do you figure? I've got seven years to graduation." Leave it to Sam to have counted out her time as if it was a jail sentence.

"College. You're going to college."

"You didn't go to college. Mom didn't go to college. And Uncle Turo—"

"Should have gone to college. We all should have gone." Maybe then Uncle Turo would have learned his letters—the letters of the law.

A few minutes later, Joe turned onto their street.

"Is that Brit's truck?"

"Yes." Gray body filler had been used to smooth damage to the fender, but had been left unpainted. It was the gray color of Brittany's skin when he'd fished her out of the water. Since then he'd been doing all the wrong things—giving her a glimpse into his past, letting himself smile.

And where had that gotten him? Nowhere. There were still no customers at the garage. Irwin's small white sedan and Rex's golf cart were exactly where they'd left them in the parking lot. He hadn't gotten Agent Haas the answers he was looking for. And the cars in the field were still a potential, if questionable, source of income waiting to be dealt with.

Sam was still fixated on Brittany. "Is that a car in the bushes?"

"Yes."

"So...those are the bushes you trimmed?" A smile split her cheeks. "I want to say hello."

More likely, she wanted to arrange a date. "Go sit behind the desk and do your homework. If you have any questions, you can ask Irwin or Rex."

"Dad, you left Irwin in charge of the garage?" Her smile vanished. "I don't think he's qualified to handle clients."

"Luckily, he's been the only client all day."

"Oh." He could see her realizing she wasn't going to get new clothes. She tugged her hood forward.

"Run along and get your homework done. Take my things so I won't lose them in the bushes." He handed her his wallet, keys and phone. He waited for her to go inside and then sat in the truck, watching Brittany, delaying the inevitable.

She was clipping a path through the brush behind the car. She'd pulled her hair back into a ponytail. The lock he'd had to cut to release Brit from the bike spoke swung free every time she bent to chop a low vine, as did a matching lock on the other side of her face. Had she found something else buried beneath the brambles? Or was she just prospecting?

Curiosity won over common sense. He got out and crossed the field to join her. "You should be doing someone's hair. Time is money."

"It's Monday. Shop's closed." Brittany wiped her forehead. She'd rolled up her sleeves. The marks on her arms looked like she'd been in a cat fight. "You should be fixing someone's car. Time is money."

They stared at each other for a moment and an understanding passed between them. Life was hard. Money was tight. But cars...cars and engines made a tough life interesting.

She and her curves and her sparkly clothing were hidden beneath plain black coveralls. It didn't matter. She still sparkled with energy. "I found something else."

"And you waited this long to tell me?"

Her dark brown eyes were hidden beneath her long lashes. "I didn't think you'd want to know."

He'd counseled himself against it, too. "Should I get my chain saw?"

"Could you?" She smiled sheepishly, not telling him what she'd found. On purpose, he'd bet. "I'll reimburse you for gas."

They both knew he wouldn't accept.

It was hard work and took a long time. Irwin and Rex came by when it was almost five.

"What have you got there?" Irwin scanned their finds. "A lawn mower. What used to be a couch. An empty rum bottle."

"Yo-ho-ho." Rex leaned on his walker. "Hardly seems worth the effort."

Had Joe been clearing the vines for anyone else, he might have agreed. But Brittany was fascinated with each treasure and after Sam completed her homework, she'd joined them with just as much enthusiasm.

Brittany remained calm under their fire. "But look at this bumper. Isn't it a beauty?" It'd been what she'd found behind the Volkswagen.

"That's a 1930s Packard bumper guard," Sam piped up. "Worth hundreds of dollars. I looked it up on Dad's phone." The enthusiasm drained from her voice. "It's Brit's."

"But this is a bottle of soda that was discontinued in 1980." Brittany held up the bottle, which was labeled Orange Soda, although the liquid was now brown. "Sam found it."

"I'm going to sell that online." Sam practically danced like Rose. That alone was worth the sweat and thorny piercings. "Forty or fifty bucks."

"What's that?" Irwin pointed to what Joe was holding.

"It's a motorcycle engine." The size of a deflated basketball, it was rusted like one of the old girders beneath the bridge, but who knew what it was like inside. Joe hadn't been able to put it down since he'd tripped over it twenty minutes before.

"Antique." Brittany nodded. Her smile was as soft as a rose petal. "Joe's going to use it to restore a motorcycle."

He hadn't said what he was going to do with it, but her idea resonated with him. Talk about putting the chicken before the egg. He'd always started with a car body and looked for an engine, not the other way around.

"What motorcycle?" Irwin elbowed Rex and forced out a hearty guffaw. "He doesn't have a motorcycle."

"I'm going to look for one that needs this."

He held it up to eye level, checking for some indication of make or model, but the rust was too thick. "An Indian maybe."

"Don't you mean Harley?" Irwin's question confirmed he knew nothing about motorcycles. "My next bike is going to be a Harley."

"Whatever makes you smile." Brittany's smile wasn't going unnoticed by Sam. "I might be willing to make a trade, Joe. My Packard bumper for the BMW grille."

Joe nearly dropped the engine. To be safe, he put it down. Finders keepers and all.

"I'm up for that." Sam handed Joe his phone. "Check out the price, Dad. Then shake on it before Brit changes her mind."

"She can't have it." He met Brittany's gaze squarely, and didn't look away when her smile crumpled. "I don't know who that car belongs to. Legally."

"I know where this is going." Clearly disappointed in him again, Sam wandered over to the riverbank.

"I understand." Brittany mustered a smile for Irwin and Rex. "I don't suppose either of you remember who owned the BMW over there."

The two older men shook their heads.

"That kind of car isn't par for the course around here." Rex moved at a slow pace toward his golf cart. "Sorry to break up the party, but I've got to get on home for my shows."

Irwin's phone beeped. "And it's time for my meds."

At least the circus was leaving town.

"Maybe we shouldn't come back tomorrow," Rex said, plodding ahead with his cane. "Nothing happened here."

"But he's a Messina," Irwin protested. "Don't you remember what it used to be like when they lived here before?"

"I suppose it wouldn't hurt to give it another day." Rex collapsed onto the golf-cart seat.

"You'd see more action if you recommended the garage to your friends." Brittany sounded more like a schoolteacher reprimanding boys on the playground than a beautician-artist-trespasser-thief. She rounded on Joe. "You should always ask for referrals."

"Ask? Is that what you call it?" She hadn't just asked. Joe received a scowl for his attempt to lighten the mood.

"You need to put yourself out there when you start a business." Brittany unzipped her coveralls to her waist. The blue top beneath it had lost its sparkle. She tied the arms of her coveralls around her hips. "Work the few clients you have."

"Client. I have one client." And he'd left his motorcycle. Of course, he'd be back tomorrow. "Rex is a bystander."

"He didn't sound like a happy bystander." She gathered her clippers, rake and bumper, then dragged them toward her truck. "Did you at least give him free coffee?"

"Bystanders don't deserve free anything."

She dropped the rake and clippers so she could lift the bumper into the truck. "I'm giving out free coffee and cookies. And you can bet I'm not going to ask if they're having a service or if the only reason they're in my shop is because they've offered someone a ride."

They'd never had free coffee for the customers at Messina Family Garage. At Turo's shop in Beverly Hills, they'd had free espresso and scones. Joe hadn't known what a scone was before then.

She loaded the rake and clippers in the truck bed. "We made good progress on the vines today."

How quickly it'd come to this. Discussing mundane things like the weather. It was as if they'd broken up, when they hadn't so much as started being friends.

There were some long, thick vines still in the ground, but he'd cut down all the others to stubble. Not that it improved anything. In fact, the bank looked worse. The cut vines were piled high. Nearest the highway there were now chunks of concrete exposed, as if someone had broken up a sidewalk. The frame of the couch was an eyesore. And the Volkswagen... Sadly, its floorboards were riddled with holes. There was so little metal, it wasn't even worth hauling to the scrap yard.

"I'm not taking the debris to the dump." Joe had to draw a line somewhere.

"I'll put Agnes onto finding someone to get rid of the vines and couch." Brittany had a distant look in her eye, even though she was staring right at the Volkswagen. "I might have some use for the concrete. But I don't think the car would survive a move."

The car had no visible identification number either. "So...what? You're just going to leave the car here to rot some more?"

"No. I'm going to..." She gave him a polite smile, like the kind doctors' receptionists gave to patients who were troublesome. "Well, I'm beginning to see what I might want to do with it. I need to find out whose property this is."

"If you don't move it, the vines will be back in a few weeks."

"I know. I'll keep it clear."

He doubted that. Not wanting to stand there just looking at her, Joe moved to the top of the bank. "Sam, what are you doing?"

She'd stacked river rock into two piles on the sandy shore. "I was trying to make Parish Hill." She gestured to the looming mountain above the treetops to the east. "But the rocks kept tumbling down. So now I have two hills."

"Hey. That's awesome." Brittany moved past Joe, carefully going down the slope. "It looks like you made two dinosaurs."

Leave it to the "artist" to see something in a pile of rocks.

"Two brontosauruses." Brittany sank to her knees in front of Sam's work.

"Their tails are too round for that." Sam pushed a rock out of the way. It clacked against other rocks on the bank.

"Round." Brittany stood and hugged Sam. She laughed and looked up at Joe, sparkling once more. "Round."

It made no sense. But when she smiled at Joe, it made no difference.

Brittany chose a rock and climbed back up the hill. "Round," she said when she reached the top. She drove away and Joe still had no idea what she was excited about.

Shaking his head, Joe checked the time on his cell phone. "Sam, we need to get cleaned up for dinner." And then he checked his call log for the number of missed calls, since there were no messages.

No calls had been missed, but an hour ago, one had been answered.

"Sam?"

CHAPTER ELEVEN

"*SAMANTHA ELLEN*, GET up here now." Joe paced the crest of the bank, dodging tree roots and scrub brush.

"Why?" Sam stared up at him from the river's edge with the wide eyes of the guilty.

The river flowed past, as deceptive as Uncle Turo.

Why? "Because I said so." Joe stifled a groan. *Because I said so?* That was the worst response an adult could give a child. "I want to talk to you about the call you took on my phone."

Sam wasn't making the climb. She picked up a stone and heaved it into the river, creating a fat splash. "It was just someone asking about the price of an oil change." She didn't look at him when she lied.

"Try again."

"Dad."

"I know the number originated from Uncle

Turo." Agent Haas had probably listened in on her conversation. It would be just like Turo to tell Sam something she thought meant nothing, but was the key to the location of the stolen cars. Joe's mouth had gone dry. He had to swallow twice to ask, "What did you two talk about?"

"Nothing."

"Sam, this is important. You need to tell me the truth." He was nearly shouting now. He never shouted at Sam. Unlike Brittany, Sam couldn't take it.

She started to cry.

He sailed down that slippery slope faster than was safe, kneeling in the mud at the bottom and wrapping his arms around her. "I'm sorry. I'm sorry, but I need to know."

He let her cry it out—she'd lost a favorite great-uncle, after all. And while he waited, he forced himself to breathe, to clamp down the anger and guilt, and counseled himself on the proper tone to use with children.

"Uncle Turo…" Sam hiccuped. "I knew it was him." She shuddered on an intake of breath. "The jail song ringtone…"

So much for the passive use of irony. Choosing the ringtone had made Joe feel better, but look at the trouble it caused.

"No one answer-er-er-ed when I said hello." Sam wiped her nose on her sleeve. "But no one hung u-u-up either."

Three minutes. The call had lasted three minutes. "Did you say anything else?" *Please say no.* He brushed the short dark hair from her face.

She nodded. "I told Uncle Turo we loved him. I told him we had to leave Beverly Hills. I told him I'd sleep on the couch if he came to live with us."

"That can't be all you told him." *Three minutes!*

Sam nodded, wiping at the tears on her cheeks. "I told him over and over again. Until he hung up."

Joe sat back on his heels. The calls had to stop. He'd block the number from his phone. Erase it from his contact list.

"He didn't say a word." She blinked fat tears. "Is Uncle Turo mad at me?"

"Oh, no, honey." Joe held on to her small shoulders. "Turo could never be mad at you. He probably didn't know what to say." Joe had gotten lucky there.

And then her voice rose to a high-pitched, fragile thread. "Are *you* mad at me?"

"No, honey." Joe rose to his knees and hugged her once more. "I love you. You're my favorite person in the whole world."

That calmed her. She drew a shaky breath, patted his back and whispered, "Everything will be all right when Uncle Turo comes home."

But it wouldn't be all right. Uncle Turo would never forgive Joe for turning state's evidence, for betraying family, for helping to put him behind bars.

Although if Turo never forgave Joe, what harm would it do to ask him where the stolen cars were hidden?

"MAYOR LARRY OWNS that land." Agnes cradled a cup of tea at Martin's Bakery Tuesday morning. A bacon and horseradish scone sat on a small plate in front of her. "I say we ask him to pay for its cleanup."

"Seconded." Rose blew at the foam on her latte.

"It's a discussion, Rose." Mildred eyed the scone she'd been about to eat and dropped it back on her plate. "We're not voting."

"Force of habit." Rose drank deeply from her latte, giving her a foam mustache. She dabbed at it with a paper napkin.

"Ladies." Brit set down her mug of plain black coffee, trying to call order to the town council without seeming to lose her cool. All she'd wanted to know was who owned the land where she'd found the Volkswagen. The next thing she knew, they were prying out the reason behind her curiosity and taking charge of a project that Brit hadn't fully committed to. "One step at a time."

The bakery was bustling, heedless of the doubt wrapped around Brit's chest. The photographs of previous generations of bakers hung on the walls. Out of habit, Brit's mind wandered to mermaids. These would be cast in plaster and mounted in the corners like the cupid frescoes she'd seen in an Italian art textbook.

"Yes. Focus, ladies." Tracy delivered a steaming egg sandwich to Brittany. "Brit has a great idea. A free outdoor art display. It's like the Sundial Bridge in Redding. Or the CowParade in Chicago. People will drive here to see it. They'll arrive for breakfast. Stay for lunch. Visit the boutique. And the winery. And enjoy Harmony

Valley's charm." Her enthusiasm had everyone at the table smiling back and nodding. Everyone but Brit.

At the next table, Grandpa Phil played checkers against a short, frail Asian man with a walker, who kept sliding an appreciative eye toward Mildred. Word had it they were an "item."

"My granddaughter is one smart sugar cookie," Phil said. "Can't wait to see what she'll do with the Volkswagen. I bet there's a mermaid involved."

"Her mermaid is awesome," Tracy said as she hurried back to the register for the next customer.

"I just need to know—" Brit jumped back into the fray, unwilling to commit to mermaids. The bar had been set high with Keira and she wasn't sure she could bring her beloved merman vision to life. That was the rub. Mermaids blocked her. Rock sculptures did not. "—if Mayor Larry will donate the use of the land and clean it up."

"Never fear," Agnes said. "We're on the case."

Brit wasn't finished with her questions. "I'd

also love to know who owns the cars in the field by the Messina Family Garage."

"We'll head out that way today," Mildred promised.

"I'll clean your glasses before you go, dear," her beau said.

The conversation deteriorated to how best to get rid of smudges from eyewear, the impact of a morning scone on a person's cholesterol level, and the pros and cons of elastic waistbands.

Brit's cell phone rang. It was Reggie, so she sent it to voicemail. She made short work of her egg sandwich, accepted the box of frosted mermaid-shaped cookies Tracy brought over and asked Grandpa Phil if he was ready to leave.

Phil blinked at her in surprise. "I'm in the middle of a game."

"But it's almost time to open."

He blinked again.

She didn't want to tell him she'd never run a shop alone. She was certainly capable. It was just…every client scheduled for the day was new to her.

A barrel-chested senior wearing a navy blue

firefighter's T-shirt came to stand beside Phil. "Next game."

"You can take over for me, Felix," Phil grumbled. "My granddaughter needs me at the shop."

Felix turned to look at Brit. "It strikes me, young lady, that you don't have a cat."

This statement was met with groans from the room.

Phil stood up quicker than Brit had ever seen him move. "She's living with me. You know I'm allergic to cat hair."

"So you say," Felix countered. "I rescued some calico kittens last night behind the bowling alley in Cloverdale."

Phil grabbed a newspaper from an empty table and then took Brit by the arm. "Come along. We can't open late."

Brit waited until they were outside the bakery in the bright sunshine. "I didn't know you were allergic to cats."

"I'm not. Your grandmother is." Typical Phil. Wanting nothing to stand in the way of Leona's possible return.

"I've always wanted a shop cat," Brit said, only half joking. She tugged her jean jacket tighter around her. It may have been sunny, but the morning still had a chill.

"You can wait until I'm dead and gone."

His statement seemed to throw a shadow over the sky. "Can you use another analogy?" Brit asked.

He glanced down at her, which made him weave as if he'd been drinking.

A lot.

She smiled. "Specifically, one without death?" She was sensitive to the subject since her near-drowning experience and his coffin-like nap habits.

Grandpa Phil gave a brief nod, righted his steps and said, "You can wait until I retire. Which, by the way, will be when I'm dead."

Brit sighed.

A group of old women were bunched up outside Phil's. The crowd was thicker than one waiting on a Black Friday door-buster sale.

"They never lined up for me," Phil grumbled.

"There shouldn't be that many." Brit felt an anxious flutter in her stomach.

"In this town, women are like rabbits. They find something they like and all of a sudden they're everywhere." Phil told the ladies to step aside, and considering the wobble to his gait, they must have cleared a path for safety reasons. "Let us get things set up, ladies. Then you can come in."

Brit wasted no time turning things on— lights, coffeemaker, music, barbershop pole. She set out the coffee creamer, checked the bathroom, the supply cabinet, the cookies.

"It looks fine, girl." Phil lifted his newspaper in front of his face and pretended to ignore her anxiety. "Put them out of their misery and let them in."

Brit did, barely getting her feet out of the way of the walkers, canes and slip-on sneakers that marched inside. The throng cooed over the changes Brit had made and the uniqueness of Keira.

Brit was stumped. "Why are there so many of you? I only have one appointment at nine."

"That's me. Sandra." A woman with frizzy, gray, shoulder-length hair raised her hand.

Brit invited Sandra to sit in her chair. "For the rest of you, I'm sorry. My appointment book is filled."

"We know." A woman with shoe-polish-black hair and a widow's peak poured herself a cup of coffee. "I'm your ten forty-five."

"Eleven thirty," said another, selecting a cookie.

Two other women sat in the waiting area chairs, mentioning afternoon times.

"Why are you all here so early?"

Phil lowered his paper. "Polly and Dierdre don't have cars. Georgia and Violet don't drive." He shook his paper more violently than usual.

"So you carpooled with Sandra?"

"We don't mind waiting." The black-haired woman poured an unhealthy dose of creamer into her coffee.

And they didn't. They talked at a volume louder than the music Brit played.

Rose stopped by for her nine-thirty hair color. She sidled up to Brit, frowning. "I need some privacy for my color."

"We can reschedule." Brit was relieved Rose was canceling. There were plenty of women willing to fill Rose's spot.

"Good. Mildred wants to get started on car identification right away." Rose glided out.

Brit was hopeful they'd find the BMW's owner. Then she could buy the grille outright and be done with it.

A young woman entered holding a sheet of

paper. "I'm Becca Harris. I run a caregiver service in town. I have a list of clients who'd like appointments."

A list? Brit tried not to cringe. How many women lived in Harmony Valley? "I'm busy until next Tuesday."

Phil opened Brit's appointment book and flipped a page, looking startled. "She is."

"I only have one hair emergency." Becca smiled hopefully. "Mary is going in for a hip replacement and wants to look good for her surgery. It's next Wednesday."

"I could do her hair," Phil said hopefully. "It's not like I haven't done it before."

"The last time Phil cut a woman's hair," Sandra said in a sharp tone, "he tried for a wedge and it looked like a Mohawk."

Phil's cheeks got some much-needed color for all the wrong reasons.

"I guess that means she gets an early slot on Tuesday." Brit rubbed Phil's shoulder. It wasn't bad enough that Leona was tough on him, but the rest of the women in town were, too? "Give me your number, Becca, and I can call you back tonight for the rest."

"I can book your appointments." Phil picked

up her pencil, regaining his paleness. "I've got nothing better to do."

"Thank you, Grandpa." Brit placed Sandra's final pin curl and stretched on her toes to kiss his cheek. "I'll cook dinner tonight."

Sandra went under the good chair dryer with a book, a coffee and a cookie.

"I'm Georgia." The woman with the black widow's peak slid into Brit's chair and Rose's appointment. "I'm down for a haircut, but I need help with my color."

Did she ever. Brit ran her fingers through Georgia's hair. It was overprocessed and brittle. "How often do you color?"

"Every other week. I have so much gray."

Brit suspected she was coloring every week. There wasn't a gray hair on the woman's head. "I have a product that will strip a lot of the color away, but your hair is fragile. I'm afraid we'll do more damage to it than good." Brit splayed her hand so Georgia could see the amount of hair that had broken off. "I can cut it today and send you home with some natural hair lightener products."

"But then I'll be gray." She cast a sideways glance at Phil and lowered her voice. "I can't go gray. I just can't."

"I understand. But once you go black or dark red, you can't make a color correction. You have to let it grow out. If I apply color to your hair today, I can't guarantee your hair won't fall out tomorrow."

Georgia jerked upright. "How about highlights at the roots?"

Brit shook her head. "I know you prefer some hair to none."

The peanut gallery laughed. The shop was too small for any type of privacy. Georgia pursed her lips. Embarrassing a customer wasn't the way Brit wanted to start her time here.

"Ladies, I know you all have a lot of experience at salons." Brit felt the need to make an announcement. "I'm afraid I'm not the kind of stylist who'll lie to you about what style or color looks good on you. And I'll be brutally honest about protecting the health of your hair." She put her hands on Georgia's shoulders. "I'll understand if I'm not the stylist for you."

"I'd color her hair," Phil muttered, having finished setting up appointments with Becca. He lifted the newspaper in front of his face as if taking on a client was no big deal.

"Not without my permission," Brit snapped,

feeling as brittle as Georgia's hair. "A bald client is bad for business."

Phil closed his newspaper, which fought returning to its neat folds. "I know when I'm not appreciated." He left.

His seat was quickly filled by a waiting client, but nothing was able to fill the void stretching between Brit and her grandfather.

"Given the alternative, a cut it is." Georgia gave in graciously. "You should sell hats. I could wear one until my hair got healthier."

"I'll take that under advisement." She fastened a drape around Georgia's neck and then directed her to the shampoo bowl a few steps away. "Does anyone have car trouble? Or know somebody who needs a tune-up? There's a new garage in town." She owed Joe a mention for his heroism.

She must have imagined the sudden silence. She couldn't really tell above the hum of the hair dryer.

Georgia, her most captive audience, was also her least quiet customer. "The garage run by the Messina boy?"

"Yes. That's the one." Although Brit wouldn't call the iceman a boy.

"I don't feel comfortable taking my car

there," Sandra shouted above the dryer. "Tony Messina got in a fight with my son once."

"He probably deserved it," Georgia said for Brit's ears only. "Her son is a drunk."

"Tony was the dad or the uncle?" Brit rinsed the shampoo from Georgia's hair.

"They were all bad seeds, just as likely to overcharge as to fix the problem," a woman with an afternoon appointment said over her gossip magazine.

The need to defend Joe was as necessary to Brit as breathing. "Joe isn't like that. He pulled me out of the river on Sunday when I would have drowned."

"That really happened?" Georgia raised her brows.

"Yes." Brit raised her voice. "Joe Messina saved my life."

There were murmurs and whispered comments Brit couldn't catch over the music, dryer and running water.

"And he has the sweetest little girl." Might just as well play that card. Brit shut the water off and reached for a towel, beginning to understand the obstacles Joe faced while trying to open a business here. "He's a single dad. A widower."

That elicited lots of sympathy.

"I'll wait to see what other people say about his service," Sandra yelled to the room.

There was a consensus of head nods.

Before noon, Tracy dropped by with small bags of cookies, scones and bread. She sold every bit of her inventory. "And, ladies. I know…once Brittany makes you beautiful. You won't want to go home. Giordano's is running a lunch special. Buy one entrée…get one half off. Tell them Tracy sent you."

Four ladies decided lunch was in order. While they were gone, another carload of women arrived. The driver scraped bumpers with the Lincoln it was trying to park next to. Pandemonium erupted. Someone called the sheriff. The mayor made an appearance. Phil stood outside, complaining bitterly about poor drivers.

The day was crazy. Brit was ready to collapse as soon as she got home that night. She was now booked solid for the next three weeks. And the mantra of the day—*I'm going to tell all my friends*—was still ringing in her ears. She was too tired to go out to the garage and create some space to work in. She was too tired to think of anything other than the fact that at this pace, she'd never have the energy to do anything artistic.

"What's for dinner?" Phil asked.

She made cereal and frozen burritos.

CHAPTER TWELVE

"I TOLD YOU something would happen today," Irwin said to Rex. They'd been playing gin rummy on the blue elephant plant stand.

A faded green Buick had pulled into the parking lot.

Joe stopped playing solitaire on his phone and checked out the Buick in the hopes of a reversal of fortune. Good tires. No squeaking brakes. The engine sounded okay. Maybe an oil change?

Agnes got out from behind the driver's seat. She hurried around to the trunk and removed a walker for Mildred, who had the shotgun door open. Rose had exited from the backseat and was walking toward the garage as if she was performing a tap routine from one of those black-and-white musical films his mother used to watch. Toe-heel, toe-heel. Arms swinging in tandem to her steps.

"Rose is coming this way," Irwin said in a strangled voice. "How do I look?"

"You have a little powdered sugar here." Rex tapped a finger to the corner of his mouth. "No. The other side. Here." He reached out to take care of it, but Irwin brushed his hand aside.

"I can do it," Irwin insisted. "Otherwise she'll think I'm quirky."

"I think Rose is quirky," Joe said. In a good way. But Rex and Irwin hanging out all day was not as endearingly quirky.

Irwin ignored him, having closed his eyes. He began rocking back and forth and chanting under his breath, *"Be cool. Be cool. Be cool."*

If Joe had been the eye-rolling type, now would be the time. "You didn't date much before you got married, did you?"

"He married his elementary school sweetheart." Rex winked. Or maybe he had something in his eye, because he blinked a couple of extra times.

"Good morning, Joe." Rose entered with a grand stage voice and a hand flourish. She cast a gaze to Rex and Irwin. "Gentlemen."

Irwin's lips were moving: *be cool. Be cool. Be cool.*

"Brittany suggested we come by and attempt to solve the mystery of ownership regarding several cars on your property." Rose turned to look out the window at the field spotted with vehicles. "I hadn't realized there were so many. My apologies for my constituents. I think I see Lloyd Peterson's minivan. His wife made him drive it even after their kids left for college. Such an emasculating vehicle for a man. I prefer a car with some power myself."

"Wh-wh-what about a m-m-motorcycle?" Irwin asked, blushing like a fifth grader.

"Terrible things. Death traps." Rose did a graceful pivot turn and smiled at Joe. "Do you perhaps have a clipboard, paper and a pen? We've come ill prepared."

"I can do better than that. Sam and I started a list. I'll bring it out and help you."

"Wonderful." Rose glided toward the door. "Catch up to us. We're headed into the fray."

Joe retrieved the list from a folder on his desk and put it on a clipboard.

Irwin had wilted in the plastic chair. "She doesn't like motorcycles. What am I going to do?"

"Watch the shop while I'm inventorying

cars?" Joe found a pen that worked and walked determinedly to the exit.

"Have another game of gin?" Rex patted his friend on his bent shoulders. "Maybe later you can come to my house and watch *The Lords of Flatbush*. You know that always cheers you up."

"I like *Oklahoma!* too." Irwin sniffed, picking up his cards.

The two began humming the famous song.

Joe hurried after the town council, feeling lighter than he had since yesterday when he'd been cutting those vines with Brittany.

"Joe." Agnes waved him over. She'd stopped by the green MG Roadster. "Mildred is sure this one belonged to Hubert Sweeney. He died without any next of kin. His property is owned by the state."

"Would the 'possession is nine-tenths of the law' rule apply?" It might be worth the trouble to find out. Other than the torn convertible top and the weather-beaten interior, the car was in fixable shape.

"You'd have to wrestle with the department of motor vehicles." Mildred's tone indicated she had no desire to do so.

Joe made a note on his inventory list. "What about the BMW?"

"That's the one Brit was asking about?" Rose waded through the knee-high grass to the front fender. "It's a brilliant piece of machinery. This grille will make a fine gate."

At least Joe knew whose corner Rose was in.

Mildred shuffled slowly through the grass with her walker. "I can't remember anyone driving a car like this. Is there a license plate frame? Sometimes it has the dealer's name stamped on it."

"No," Joe said. "We checked. The plates are gone and the vehicle identification number is missing on the dash." Along with half the car's interior.

Agnes tilted her head this way and that, and then huffed in frustration. "No idea who drove that about town. But that Ford station wagon." She marched toward the old beast. "That used to be Crandall's."

"He's dead." Rose made a neck-cutting motion. "His wife is still in town. Although I can't imagine why Bev would leave his car here."

Agnes peered in the window. "I believe she mentioned having trouble paying for her medicine last time I saw her. The canceled car insurance and licensing fees probably saved her much-needed money."

"Why didn't she sell it?" Joe asked.

"To who? There's no market for an old car like that." Rose crinkled her nose at Joe. "Is there?"

"There is." If he ever got a steady stream of paying customers, he'd offer Crandall's widow a fair price for the Ford.

"I had no idea there were so many cars out here," Mildred said. "I suppose it makes sense. This location is a perfect dumping ground. No one lives out this way. Traffic only rarely goes by on the highway this far north."

"What about this one?" Rose had moved on, uninterested in Mildred's theories about the graveyard's reason for being.

But Joe was interested. And as they went through the field, he looked back at the BMW more than once.

"So you're going to ignore my calls?" Reggie swept into the barbershop with style, confidence and an air of outrage. "You weren't even going to tell me you practically drowned?"

Brit closed the supply cabinet doors and met her twin's glare with her chin up.

It was Thursday morning, day three of her part-time operation in Harmony Valley. Nothing was going as Brit wanted. Cutting hair wasn't part-time. Her garage workspace had yet to be set up. And facing the person who was supposed to be the closet soul to her in life and reliving the river's cold embrace made her throat want to close up. "Yes, I'm ignoring your calls. And you. Which means I choose not to share the accidents in my life either."

Reggie held a thick stack of papers in her hand. Brit was glad to see the stack trembled. "I brought you the contract."

"And…" Brit said, finding a bead of annoyance among the lumps in her throat, "I'm especially going to ignore any contract that legally binds me to working and paying money into a venture I'm not a part of."

Reggie grimaced. "I'm not here for your signature." Her sentence ended awkwardly, as if she'd bit back *yet* at the end.

"Then you won't be disappointed when I don't sign." Finished with inventory, Brit moved on to making the first pot of coffee. Tracy would be arriving soon with the day's complimentary treats. The small blonde had increased sales at the bakery and Giordano's across the street. Was Tracy also drumming up business for Brit? She'd have to find a polite way to tell her not to. Otherwise she'd never get back to her art.

"It's a draft." Reggie continued to hold the contract out to her. "I thought you might want to read it."

"Wrong again." Brit wasn't usually such a hard-liner. Blame it on her overbooked schedule.

"You want to know why I'm buying the B and B?" Reggie dropped the contract onto Phil's chair and gripped the worn leather back.

"Yes."

"It's because of Dad." Reggie's words fell like a thick curtain between them. "Do you remember how Dad used to say he wanted to retire here and run a B and B?"

"Yes, but…" Brit shook her head and pressed the brew button on the coffeemaker. Reggie had no right to bring Dad into this. "Dad only said that to tease Mom, because he'd joke that they could never afford to retire, that she'd work here and he'd run the B and B until death forced their retirement." *A hairstylist who never retired.* The words sent an extrasharp spike down Brit's spine. "And you used to say you wanted to run it with him."

"It wasn't a joke. This was Dad's dream," Reggie said, firmer this time. "And I'm going to make it happen."

All very noble, but… "He's dead, Reggie. And Mom remarried." Six months after they'd laid him to rest. Brit banged around the drawers beneath the coffeemaker, feeling for napkins. "You don't want to run a B and B. You love big luxury hotels."

Reggie didn't deny it. "Dad wanted this. And do you know what else?" Reggie's voice had turned rough, as if she was forcing her words past jagged glass. "The night before he died, he asked me to take care of you."

Brit's fingers clutched a wad of napkins, curling them into an unusable ball.

"Dad said, 'Brit's going to struggle to make ends meet unless you help her.'"

Brit's eyes burned with tears.

Not Dad. He always believed in me. He was the only person who believed in me.

She didn't realize she'd said the words out loud until Reggie replied.

"Don't say that. Don't ever say that. I believe in you." Reggie faltered and shook Phil's chair.

"But I made Dad a promise and I quit my job for this. *For you.* You can't let this be a waste of my time."

Frustration left a sour taste at the back of her throat. "I didn't ask you to quit your job." And Brit doubted Dad had either. "I don't need you to take care of me."

"You do. I can see this place is wearing you down." Oh, her sister was good. Perceptive. Persuasive. "I know you're afraid you're never going to create anything as good as Keira again."

Deep down, where she was the most vulnerable, a small voice whispered, *Never again.* She swallowed, refusing to be diverted by artistic doubt. "I won't lie to Leona about what I want and who I am." Brit moved to stand beneath Keira. "I'm busy, Reggie. You need to go."

"I'll leave the contract with you." Reggie tossed her hair. "I'll come by again tomorrow and see what you think. You don't need to be afraid anymore, Brit. Not when you run the B and B."

Brit didn't have time to consider Reggie's misplaced sense of protection, much less the contract or Brit's own fears. She shoved the thick stack of papers into the back of the supply cupboard and went to clean yesterday's coffee cups, which had been soaking all night in the bathroom sink.

There were things that needed her immediate attention. If she didn't spend more time with clients, she'd never have enough money to do anything artistic.

The trouble with being able to spot a liar was you could too easily spot the lies you told yourself.

"SLOW DAY TODAY," Irwin noted midmorning on Thursday. He'd shown up every day since Joe restarted the business.

"Slow week," his sidekick Rex said. He'd driven them to the garage in his golf cart, which allowed them to pack a cooler with food and bring reading material.

Joe couldn't believe he'd had no customers all week. He couldn't believe he hadn't seen Brittany around either. He'd almost run out of things to do around the place that didn't cost money. Among other chores, he'd patched the hole in the wall the snake had been using and fixed the soft stair tread. "What did you two do before I opened?"

"I sold insurance." The sun through the window glinted off Irwin's scalp between the thin strands of his gray hair. "And after I retired, my wife and I took vacations. I laid her to rest last year." He blinked watery eyes.

"I was a golf pro." Rex glanced out the window at his main method of transportation. "Been hanging out with Irwin since I got laid off in '05. Lost my Amelia two years ago."

Great. Three widowers marking time by shooting the breeze.

But they hadn't answered the real meaning of his question. Joe tried again. "What did you two do *during the day* before I opened?"

"Oh. We watched game shows," Rex said. "There's a whole network that shows them, hour after hour."

"And we played cards," Irwin pointed out.

"March Madness." Rex sighed. "That was something."

Basically, they'd done the same thing they were doing here, except for watching television. "Well, if you're going to use this as your second home, you need to do me a solid."

Irwin leaned forward, suddenly eager. "What?"

"Recommend me to your friends."

Irwin gave a sarcastic snort. "I can't do that."

"Why not?"

"I told you. Because of my street cred. I want Rose to think I can chill with the toughest of dudes."

"I can't recommend you." At least Rex looked sorry. "I don't own a car."

Joe's eye twitched. "You both need to leave."

"But…" Irwin pointed with his thumb toward the highway. "Your gang hasn't come by yet."

"I'm not in a gang." He didn't care that he was using his outdoor voice. "The only group I belong to is the parent-teacher association."

"The PTA?" Rex tossed the back of his big hand against Irwin's chest. "Come on, Irwin. We're missing an *Oprah* rerun marathon for this."

Irwin's face flushed red. "I do *not* watch *Oprah*."

"I watch *Oprah*," Joe lied with a straight face.

"This is wrong." Irwin stumbled to his feet. "You're supposed to be hard-core. You're supposed to be living on the edge. You're supposed to be villainous." He struggled to get the door open.

"Rose doesn't want any of that," Joe called after him.

"Don't worry, Joe," Rex said with that slow, friendly smile of his. "He'll get over it. We'll be back."

Joe wondered if he and Sam were too old to run away.

CHAPTER THIRTEEN

SHOW ME A bored man, and I'll show you a slacker, Uncle Turo used to say.

Joe wasn't a slacker. The garage tools gleamed. The tow truck gleamed. The waiting room floor gleamed. Not because Joe wanted to spend his time scrubbing and waxing and washing, but because he had no customers.

Agent Haas had returned Joe's call last night. "I need your cooperation," he'd said with unsettling heat, and then hung up. That destroyed what might have been a good night's sleep.

And then there was Sam. She'd slicked her hair back and worn a hoodie to school every day this week, changing back to coveralls and a ball cap when she got home. She alternated between the sweet daughter he loved and the sulky teenager he was dreading her becoming.

Joe dropped Sam off at school on Friday and opted for his usual route back down Main Street. He needed something to take his mind off things. He needed a car to work on. He was wound up tighter than a bandage in a first-timers first-aid class.

Once again, he passed Will and the mayor standing in front of El Rosal. Will's golden hair looked as if Brittany had just given him a trim.

The barbershop pole was spinning. That meant Brit was at work early. He hadn't seen her in days.

On impulse, Joe angled his truck into a parking space and went inside, sitting in the chair at Brit's station. "Cut my hair like that millionaire's." If he had to go shorter to achieve respectability like Will Jackson, so be it.

Brittany emerged from the bathroom wearing plastic gloves and holding a toilet scrub brush. She'd tinged the tips of her brown hair orange. She wore a shiny red blouse over a short denim skirt and black cable knit stockings. Just the sight of her made Joe feel better.

"Joe." She lowered the brush. "Did we have an appointment?"

"No." It struck him that he'd thought theirs was a relationship without need for appointments. He'd trimmed back brambles for her and saved her from drowning.

"Huh." She disappeared into the bathroom.

The sound of an actively used scrub brush drifted to him, followed by a loud flush. Brittany reappeared without gloves or brush. "I'm not cutting your hair. I told you, that won't make you respectable."

His frustration multiplied by ten. "Where have you been all week? The vines are beginning to come back." Not as urgently as his tone implied, but he hadn't seen her since they'd discovered the Volkswagen.

"There are legalities involved with the car and I wanted to get them cleared up."

"Since when do you care about the law?"

"Since…" She glanced up at the mermaid.

The sculpture's flowing hair reminded him of Brittany underwater, before the light went out of her eyes, before hope dimmed in her body.

"Since…" she tried again, "you threatened to call the sheriff on me?"

He liked that she hadn't said it with certainty. "I wouldn't have done that."

She arched a brow.

He'd missed sparring with her. "Okay, I would have done that. But now…" His gaze drifted to the short ends of her hair where he'd cut her free. She'd turned that lemon of near death into lemonade. Why couldn't he do the same with the mess Uncle Turo had made?

The mayor and Will entered the shop, nodding a greeting to Joe. The pair was the ultimate odd couple. Will with his classic good looks and red polo. The mayor with his boho chic throwback ponytail and purple tie-dyed T-shirt.

Mayor Larry flopped into Phil's chair, next to Joe. "Brittany, this place is becoming the most popular destination in town. I've had several shut-ins call me for a ride here over the past few days."

"Me, too." Will took up a position by the door, his expression inscrutable.

"I'm glad you two are together, since we've got business with both." The mayor leaned back in the chair, tilting his face to the ceiling. "Joe, don't bother having Brit cut your hair. No matter what you do, it'll still be thick and black, the mark of the Messinas for those who remember."

The sudden pressure to Joe's chest made it hard to breathe. For years, he'd been grateful that Uncle Turo had come to town. That he and his brothers made it through high school with a roof over their heads. How ironic that Uncle Turo was the biggest obstacle to his making a living now that he was back.

"Let's be honest," Mayor Larry said with an easy smile that didn't fool Joe. "Your dad and uncle were a caution."

Joe tensed. Were they throwing him out of town? Could they do that? He wouldn't let them do that.

Brittany's light touch on Joe's shoulder kept him from leaping out of the chair and leaving.

"Let's not hold Joe responsible for the sins of his father." Brittany's voice was a quiet shelter in the storm that was Joe's life. "Or those of his uncle."

Will refused to meet Joe's gaze.

There'd been a time that summer after Joe's uncle had arrived when Turo was the pied piper for the boys, Will among them. They'd all hung out at the garage, soaking up Turo's unlikely brand of rebellion. *Don't pay for that—if they aren't looking, it's their loss. Don't cut your hair—what, you want to be like your parents? Do you always do what someone tells you to do? Like that'll get you ahead.*

Will had walked out after a week.

Joe followed him down to the river. Most kids traversed the town along the river. It was quicker than taking the streets. "Will, where are you going?"

"Away from that." Will gestured back to the garage. "He wants us to steal and lie."

Joe couldn't quite refute that statement, seeing as it was true. "At least he tries to spend time with us. Dad doesn't do anything."

"My mom says your dad is mentally ill. My mom says your uncle is a crook. My mom says you're halfway to being a crook, too."

His friend's words hit harder than any punch. "Shut up!"

"Come home with me, Joe. You can stay at our house."

Joe shook his head. He couldn't. He couldn't leave his brothers. Even back then, he'd known about loyalty and family. Maybe he'd even understood that by going to the Jackson house he'd be ruining Will, future millionaire.

A car backfired as it passed, returning Joe to the pretty crappy here and now. Anger strained against his chest. "You're talking about my family." His hands fisted on his knees.

Brittany laid her warm palm over his clenched fingers.

"I'm talking about a family led by a violent father and an uncle who was a petty thief," Mayor Larry went on before Joe could. "They didn't do you boys any favors."

"I'm not like my father or my uncle." This comment Joe directed at Will, who stared at Joe with a neutral expression. So much for childhood ties. "I'm here for my daughter." Only Sam kept him from bolting out the door.

"Maybe you are different," the mayor allowed. "I'd like to think so. I'd like for you to succeed here."

Joe felt numb. In the mirror, the mermaid went with the flow, a talent Joe didn't have. But he did have Brittany's hand on his, her strength at his disposal should he need it.

"The majority of our populace is frail," the mayor went on. "They don't want to give you the benefit of the doubt like we're going to do." Mayor Larry gestured to himself and Will.

"We?" Joe couldn't believe Will was part of this.

The mayor nodded. "Will and I have been talking. We might be able to help you. Can you bring your tow truck to my house first thing tomorrow morning? I finish yoga around seven. We can talk more then."

Joe was desperate enough to try anything. For Sam.

He glanced up at Brittany once before leaving. For Sam.

"BRIT, WE'VE STUDIED your proposal regarding the art display by the river." The mayor spun in Phil's chair after Joe left.

"And?" Brit was almost afraid to hear what the mayor thought after how stern he'd been with Joe. It'd been hard not to follow Joe out the door. Her heart was pounding. What if they refused her proposal? Should she argue? She pulled her sketchbook from a drawer, but was too nervous to open it.

The mayor stopped spinning. "The property is mine and I have no immediate plans for it." Mayor Larry's grin was layer upon layer of thin wrinkles, which made it hard to tell if he was being sincere or not. "I'm willing to write up an agreement for free use of the land."

Brit couldn't move. There was no *but* in his speech. No catch. No price tag. "You don't want to see my sketches?"

"If your ideas are anything like that mermaid, I'll be happy." The mayor kept on grinning.

Brit experienced a twinge of disappointment. She didn't plan on incorporating mermaids into her feature.

"Can we help with anything?" Will was smiling, his demeanor ten times warmer than it'd been when Joe was in the room.

"I still haven't confirmed the use of river rock, other than being allowed to remove fourteen rocks a day from shoals and banks that aren't part of the public park system."

"I'll have my lawyer look into it." Will tapped something in his phone.

"I'm glad my art will help the community." Brittany was. Harmony Valley was a nice place. "And with exposure like that, I'll be getting something out of it, as well." If her vision of the Volkswagen could be executed. If she could create other pieces to sell.

The mayor stood and looked at Keira. "Your mermaid is special. We're happy to have more."

Brittany felt the need to control expectations, but couldn't quite say *no more mermaids*! "I want to work on things I'm passionate about." If only she had the time and energy to be passionate. "I'll start with the Beetle and see where it takes me."

Will nodded. "My winery would be willing to pay you for a mermaid sculpture. Perhaps even the rights to use her image on a wine label." He stared at Keira the way Brit did when no one was looking—awestruck. "Our logo is a running horse on a weathervane. Maybe you could consider incorporating your mermaid into our logo."

"Commissioned sculptures and licensing images is a big deal," the mayor said, as if she'd be foolish to consider turning them down. "What do you say?"

"I'm not ready," Brit blurted. "I mean, I'm so busy with the shop, I need time to slow down and think about what to work on and when." She needed to recapture the leap-off-the-edge courage that had guided her hand when she'd created Keira. She hadn't feared failure back then.

"Take as much time as you need." Will gave Keira one last look before heading toward the door. "We can talk numbers if you're interested."

"Don't wait too long," the mayor warned, rising from the chair. "That's how opportunities pass you by."

Brit sank into her chair.

The mayor was wrong. Opportunities weren't lost when you didn't pounce on them. They were also lost when your creative juices were constipated.

OUT OF NECESSITY Joe walked into town to pick up Sam from school. He needed to conserve gas in both the truck and tow truck. He had no idea what the mayor wanted with the latter, but he didn't want to lose out because he couldn't afford to fill up the tank.

He came around the corner in time to see two younger girls skip out the school door. And then a boy about Sam's age exited the building, got into a car and left.

Sam ran out with her hood up and her eyes red. "Where's the truck?"

"It's a beautiful day. I thought we'd walk." He shouldered her backpack.

She grunted and hurried along the way he'd come.

"I thought there were only girls at school. Who's that boy?"

"Brad Hendricks. He's a sixth grader. His first day was today." Sam shoved her hands in her hoodie pockets.

"What's wrong?" Joe slung his arm over her shoulders.

She shrugged him off. "Nothing."

He let her cling to that belief, but his mind was racing. Was Brad a bully? Had Sam failed a test? Was she feeling sick? Fighting a fever?

When they finally finished walking the length of the vineyard and turned down their street, Joe said, "You know you can tell me anything."

Sam couldn't hold on to her secret any longer. "Brad thought I was a *boy*," she wailed. And then the waterworks came.

"I'm sorry, Sam." He draped an arm around her shoulders. "Boys can be stupid."

"He called me dude. He asked me if I'd ever played football. He asked me—" Sam couldn't catch her breath; her hood slipped off, revealing her too-stiff, slicked back hair "—if I had a *girlfriend*!"

This was sounding less like an initial misimpression and more like something that had gone on all day. "How long did this last?" She wasn't shy. Why hadn't she stood up for herself?

"Until lunch." Sam snuffled. "Until Miss Bernard corrected him. He…he…he *argued* with her." The tears returned.

"About you being a boy?" Joe didn't know whether to hunt down the kid's family and have a few words about good manners or to accept the mantle of blame. He should force Sam to wear dresses to school. He should learn how to braid hair.

"I need...I need new clothes."

"You have plenty of pretty things in your closet." And yet she'd chosen to wear that hoodie to school every day this week.

"I can't wait for new clothes until September, Dad." The panic was back in her voice. "I can't." She sprinted to the garage.

Joe's cell phone began the opening notes of "Jailhouse Rock." He answered, releasing all the sharp frustration he'd been feeling for weeks. "You are so lucky you're in jail right now. Sam is a wreck. No one will give me business because of what you did in Harmony Valley before. And the FBI is going to arrest me if you don't tell them what you did with those cars." Joe couldn't halt the words. He was on a short track and had the pedal to the metal. "We're paying for your mistakes and guess what? We aren't going to be able to pay much longer." He wished he could take back the words. They let slip too much weakness. "So don't waste your time calling anymore unless you're ready to help. And by help, I mean tell the truth."

The line went dead.

CHAPTER FOURTEEN

BRITTANY OPENED THE door to the Messina Family Garage a few minutes before five on Friday night.

Having received Mayor Larry's permission to use the land, she'd spent the day holding on to the idea of her own outdoor art exhibition with equal parts joy and fear. Joy because she didn't have to hope that someone other than Reggie would see what she'd created. Fear because she hadn't created anything good in nearly a year. What if she couldn't come up with something the town would be proud of? They all wanted mermaids!

And alternating with the joy and fear had been worry for Joe. Will and the mayor hadn't told him what they had in mind. How was Joe handling the uncertainty? Would he be happy when he heard her news?

Would Reggie?

Brit didn't know.

She'd finished her last client early, because her client's hair had only grown back an inch after chemotherapy and was too short to handle a pin curl. She'd left her truck at the shop and taken the river path, needing time to clear her head. She'd ended up near the highway bridge, careful not to look at the bend in the river that had almost been her watery grave. And while she was careful to not look down, she looked up and saw the field dotted with abandoned cars and anchored by the Messina Family Garage. It was then she realized she'd been heading here the whole time.

She'd expected the garage to be run-down. After all, apart from the winery, there had been no new construction in town. She hadn't expected run-down to the extent of falling down. Warped dark wood paneling and cracked particleboard counters painted black. Orange plastic chairs that made airport seats look comfortable. The blue elephant was the cheeriest thing in the waiting room.

Joe sat behind the customer service desk. His gaze was as cool as a losing blackjack dealer's.

"I like what you've done with the place." Brit retrieved a bottle of blue nail polish from her bag. She'd been carrying it around for days with the intent of coming here. She shook it, and then brushed some color over the chip in the elephant's ear. "And when I say I like what you've done, I mostly mean this guy." She capped the polish and tucked it away in her bag. "FYI. Once you've received a house-warming gift, you can't move for at least five years or it's bad luck."

He looked ill and he hadn't even said *hello*, much less *what can I do for you*.

Somewhere behind him a cricket chirped.

"I've just proven why I'd never make it as a stand-up comedienne," she said instead of turning tail and running. "I'm actually here to schedule an oil change." That sounded better than admitting she'd been worried about him and let her feet take her here. "I didn't get a flyer the other day so I couldn't call."

"Careful," Joe said, his voice so rough she almost felt it scrape along her skin. "I may take you up on your offer."

"You think I'm joking? That this is a pity purchase?" Would that she'd thought that far ahead of her motormouth. "I haven't changed my oil in over a year."

The worrisome crease appeared between his dark brows.

"I swear I'm not joking. I lived in San Francisco and paid to store my dad's truck in a garage. I just got it out last week when I moved."

The crease didn't go away. "Why do I get the feeling you know how to change your own oil?"

"I can." Thanks to Dad and her ugly ducklingness. "But I'm too busy. How about Monday? I can work on the Volkswagen while you work on my pickup."

The round clock on the wall ticked.

The feeling that this had been a mistake tocked.

"Let me check my schedule." He flipped a page in a weekly appointment book and ran his finger down the blank entries. "You're in luck. We have an opening at eight fifteen. Shall I pencil you in, Miss…"

Joe was playing with her. His eyes had warmed to the shade of a summer blue sky.

Finally.

Brit's smile bloomed. "Miss Lambridge."

"See you Monday, Miss Lambridge." He wrote her name in his book.

She should leave—Grandpa Phil would be

expecting her to cook dinner. She stayed right where she was. She was enjoying those warm blue eyes too much. And then her stomach growled. "Would you...would you and Sam like to have dinner with me and my grandfather? My treat." She'd had a very good week at the shop. She'd tell him about the art exhibition over dinner. She was certain he'd respond better than Reggie. "My refrigerator has nothing much left in it. And I'm tired of cereal and frozen burritos."

His gaze cooled. He lifted it toward the ceiling. "Thanks for the offer, but tonight isn't a good night."

She took a step back over the friendship boundary. And then another, mumbling, "Some other time."

She should have swallowed the impulse to share with him. She'd go home and tell Grandpa the mayor approved of her idea. That would be enough.

Her feet carried her quickly to the bridge, and swiftly across it.

"Miss Lambridge!" It was Joe. "*Brittany.* Wait."

Brit turned, one step away from the path leading to the river.

Joe's blue shirt with his name stitched over the pocket, navy pants and dark brown boots reminded her of Dad. Her father had a strong work ethic, a love of metal and a friar's bald spot. Dad had been satisfied with a home and a family that was less than perfect because he'd loved his wife and his daughters and he'd been a loyal man.

Brit wanted a man like that. A man who didn't pay her empty compliments to be nice. A man who didn't care that she wasn't a fragile flower. A man who could see past the ugly duckling to the beautiful woman she sometimes felt she was.

A man like Joe.

She gripped the bridge railing, watching him approach, her heart pounding against her sternum as if trying to reach for him.

A man like Joe.

No. This was so not happening to her. She wasn't falling for him.

She bent her gaze to the river, hoping he wouldn't see the longing in her eyes. Hoping she could erase it before he saw the yearning for love there.

She'd averted her eyes, but she'd forgotten to seal her lips. "I'm sorry." She seemed to be apologizing a lot lately. "My news this morning from the mayor was good and I wanted to share it with someone who wasn't my sister or a client. And then I got here and remembered the truck had been sounding a little parched, but also that several of my clients were saying how they couldn't use your services until someone they knew had. And then my stomach growled and I didn't want to cook because this is a really big day for me and so I asked you to dinner when I shouldn't have and..." Her gaze floundered and flopped around until it met his. "Now I've made you feel uncomfortable. I'm sorry."

He stared at her as if she'd just told him she'd heard elephants trumpeting in her muffler. "Why are you so..."

"Annoying?"

He shook his head.

This was it. The end of their not-quite so-called friendship. It'd make it easier to bury her awareness of him if he told her right here, right now that she could change her own oil.

"The reason I can't go to dinner with you tonight..."

Brit gripped the railing tighter and tried to smile like an acquaintance would, someone who hadn't just realized that Joe could be The One and was receiving the *all I can ever be to you is a friend* speech.

"…is because there's a new boy in Sam's school."

It took a moment for his words to sink in. She let go of the railing. "What?"

"This new boy…he thought Sam was a boy, too."

"Oh, poor Sam."

"She was shocked into silence." He shook his head. "I thought my daughter didn't have a mute button."

"Mortification will do that to a child."

"And that's why we can't go to dinner. Sam's not in the mood to go anywhere in public."

"I understand." She tried not to grin at the rejection that wasn't really a rejection. If she grinned, Joe would think she was reading too much into things.

"We'll take a rain check. And…I'll even let you pay." Oh, those words cost him. Joe had a reluctant set to his mouth. "Because I know it'll make you feel better."

"I look forward to torturing your male ego when I pay the bill."

She was rewarded with a smile that lit up his

face. "I came out here to bring you this." He took her hand in his larger one and pressed a slip of paper against her palm, holding it there with his other hand. He closed his eyes and gave an almost imperceptible head shake. "I don't know what I'm doing anymore. My life feels like I'm standing on a ledge during an earthquake while juggling eggs." He opened his eyes and stared down at her.

The wanting slammed into Brit again. She wanted to wrap her arms around him and tell him everything would be all right. But who was she to make promises? She could ruin the Volkswagen and destroy her hopes of being a legitimate artist. Her future hinged on one thing—creating something as good or better than Keira—while his was balanced in an egg basket.

Besides, this was Joe. He might have calmed to a rumbly spring storm instead of a frigid blizzard, but he wasn't looking for her sympathy.

"Don't be afraid," Brit said softly and with a straight face. "I'm hard-boiled."

He wanted, too. She could see it in those wonderful, expressive eyes. He wanted to laugh. He wanted to hold her close. He wanted to…

Her heart pounded and she waited for his laugh, his embrace, his kiss.

None of it came.

"You're a good egg, Brittany Lambridge." He let go of her hand and stepped back. "I'll see you around."

Brit watched him walk across the bridge, across the car-strewn field and into one of the open service bays at the garage. She watched him work the chains to close the big door. She watched him shut himself away, and once again she felt like the rejected wallflower at the sixth-grade Promotion Dance. The girl whose own mother couldn't see her as beautiful. Why would she imagine Joe would see her any differently?

And then she remembered the slip of paper beneath her curled fingers.

It was his phone number.

DRAWN LIKE A donkey to the promise of a carrot, Joe knocked on the mayor's door at seven fifteen Saturday morning.

Tendrils of morning fog still clung to the road and the gables of Mayor Larry's rambling ranch home. It made him think of Brittany's hand lingering in his last night. Joe had no right to bring her into his life when it was such a mess. Maybe he shouldn't have given his phone number to her.

The mayor was well-off and could afford to play God with Joe's life. He'd made a fortune during the early days of internet commerce selling tie-dyed apparel. His home had the most waterfront in town and was one of the few houses with a pool.

But Joe had been taken in before by wealth and favors and "I'll scratch yours." He wasn't going to be so gullible this time around.

Mayor Larry opened the front door. He had on running tights and a red-and-yellow tie-dyed tank top that hit him midthigh. "Perfect. You brought the tow truck."

On its last few gallons of gas. Joe hoped this wasn't a waste of time.

There was a Volkswagen van in the driveway. It was in cherry condition. Pristine. Not a spot of rust anywhere. Brittany wouldn't give it a second look.

"So? What's wrong with the VW?" Joe gestured to the van.

"Nothing." The old man chuckled. "It runs like it just came off the assembly line. That's not what you're fixing."

There was relief in knowing he was being asked to fix something. It countered the stress that the mayor didn't want to tell him something.

Mayor Larry led Joe to the side yard and a view of the lower Harmony Valley River. He stopped by a used pink party bus parked next to a long RV. "It's this." He patted the pink fender.

"Why do you need a party bus?" It wasn't as if there was a lot of prom business out here.

"Opportunity, dear boy. Opportunity." He placed a bony hand on Joe's shoulder and turned him squarely toward the bus. "I want to offer a shuttle service from downtown, to the winery's tasting room, to the view atop Parish Hill. Tourists won't have to worry about drinking and driving. Why, the trip to Parish Hill is long enough to be sobering."

Joe said nothing about the ten switchbacks on the route or the likelihood of car sickness after a glass or two of wine.

"But given the popularity of Phil's and a few new businesses on Main Street, I'm also considering a dial-a-ride service. I just need the bus to run." He eyed Joe speculatively. "And a driver."

Something plopped into the river. It might have been Joe's hopes sinking.

"I can help you get it running," Joe allowed, seeing where this was going.

The mayor's broad politician smile appeared and his fingers might have dug a little harder into Joe's shoulder. "And be my driver for a few weeks? I'll pay you."

"I'm trying to start a business myself." One the mayor was supposed to help. Joe shrugged off his hand. "I can't be on call."

"Don't be so quick to decide. You need friends in order to get more customers." The mayor was slick. His smile never faltered. "I assure you, this is the answer to both our problems. My lumbago means I can't drive." He touched his lower back. "And your family's reputation means you need a reintroduction to the townspeople. What better way to do that than by driving them around?"

"To Phil's?"

"To everywhere."

There was one flaw with the mayor's plan. "What happens when people don't get in the bus with me?" He remembered the woman in overalls at Phil's house hurrying away from him.

"Will and I will make sure that doesn't happen." He patted Joe's shoulder again. "We want your business to succeed. Showing citizens how different you are from the Messinas of the past is the answer."

It might not have been the answer, but it was the only option before Joe. He sighed.

"Atta boy." The mayor's pat became a hearty backslap. "How quickly can you fix it?"

CHAPTER FIFTEEN

"I DON'T LIKE sorting through my life. Feels like I died and no one told me." Phil sat in a chair in the middle of the garage, surrounded by boxes Brit wanted him to go through. "Why not just put these things in the attic?"

"You don't have an attic. You have a crawl space." Brit opened a box filled with dog bowls and toys. "When did you have a dog?"

"Nearly twenty years ago. We're not getting rid of that. Sparky meant a lot to me." He pointed to the opening in the ceiling above him. "Crawl space."

Brit was beginning to agree that she should stuff everything in the crawl space because he couldn't let go of anything.

"Leona seems to think you and Reggie are fighting." Phil sounded chipper at the news, most likely because Leona was talking to him. "You should make up. Arguments with family shouldn't sit and fester. What are you bickering about?"

This was why Brit wasn't talking to Reggie. She couldn't tell him.

Brit opened the next box, which was filled with unopened packages of socks. "Was there a sale?"

"There was. And I can always use some new ones. Give me a pack before you put them upstairs." He clutched the plastic bag she gave him in a shaky hand. "This ought to help mend fences then."

"Socks?"

Phil nodded toward the driveway.

Reggie was approaching, dark hair down and swinging with each step. She wore jeans and a black button-down. She almost looked in uniform, ready to clean toilets, except for her shoes. Her shoes were marvelous—four-inch heels with crisscrossing suede straps and a tiny silver charm at the ankle. The swan had arrived.

"Good morning." Reggie's words were flat and she smiled without showing any teeth. "Cleaning house?"

"We're making room for Brit's workshop." Phil held a trembling hand toward Reggie, an invitation to come closer. "She's booked full up. Busy, busy, busy."

Reggie kissed Grandpa Phil's leathery cheek and then looked down her nose at things. "You're setting up a beauty station here? Can't you take all your appointments at the beauty salon?" She paused and gave a little laugh. "Oh, did I say salon? I meant barbershop."

Nothing like a little punch below the belt to welcome the morning.

But this time, Brit was more worried about what Grandpa Phil would think than her own feelings. He was touchy about his shop.

"You've misunderstood me. Your sister is busy with commissions for her art." Phil's brows lowered under the weight of frown wrinkles. "She's going to have a permanent outdoor art display over by the highway bridge. And the winery is interested in using her mermaid on a label. Not to mention Arlie asked me if Brit would consider making mermaid lapel pins or whatever it is you females stick in scarves. She thinks she can sell them at the boutique in town."

Brit wanted to kiss Phil for coming to her defense, and then rejected the idea of pins of any sort involving mermaids.

"Let's hope she's not giving her images away like those free cookies I saw at the bakery. There's a lot of money to be had in licensing Keira's image." Reggie's smile was stiffer than the meringue on the mini custards Tracy had been pedaling at the shop yesterday.

"I know how to make a business deal," Brit said, finally feeling her patience fray. "And when to pass up a bad one. I'm not going to be your partner in the B and B."

"Leona told me about your offer." Phil tsked. "Now, there's a bad deal in the making."

"Why would you say that?" Reggie asked. "We have a chance to get in on the ground floor of something huge."

"We?" Phil cut his glance to Brit.

"When Reggie says *we*, she'd really like it to mean me." Brit closed the flaps on the sock box and shoved it toward the rest destined for the crawl space. "I'm not interested."

"Dad wanted to run a B and B here," Reggie said stiffly. "And we feel…" Finally, Reggie stumbled over the truth. But when she continued, her voice had hardened as if it was Brit who was in the wrong. "*I* feel Brit would be making a better choice for her financial future by taking the reins."

"Brit run the B and B?" Phil laughed once, a short, loud sound like a burst balloon. "That's ridiculous. She can't even keep my refrigerator stocked."

"Hey, I've been busy."

"My point exactly." Phil threw up his hands and in the process tossed the sock package over his head. "Brit has more than enough on her plate." He pushed to his feet, shaking so badly he nearly tripped over a box of Christmas lights at his feet. When Brit would have steadied him, he waved her off. "Robert hated it. And to tell you the truth, so do I."

Reggie jerked back a step on her killer heels.

"Hear, hear." Brit applauded.

Exhausted by his tirade, Phil plopped back down in his chair. "Leona was raised in the Victorian. She has memories and an attachment to it unlike anything the rest of us can feel. She loves that house more than she loved me or your father. And trust me, your father was smart. He knew it. That's why he joked about it."

Brit's breath caught in her throat.

Reggie looked as if her swan-like wings had been clipped.

"Don't shackle yourself to the Victorian."

Phil shook his head. "Robert never meant for either one of you to run that place."

Brit took one of his hands in hers. "If you hate the house so much, why are you still pining for Leona? She'll never choose you."

"If that house is her one true love, she's mine." His eyes brimmed with unshed tears. "You can't choose who your heart wants, girlie." He squeezed her hand. "Enough of being maudlin. Who's up for coffee and checkers at Martin's?"

Brit was the only taker, because Reggie had gone.

"BARBIE CALLED." SAM STOOD in the parking lot of the garage, watching Joe reverse park the towed party bus into a service bay. She wore flannel pajama bottoms and Joe's high school football jersey, which fit her like a large, shapeless dress. "She wants her pink bus back."

"No can do." Joe hopped out of the tow truck. "It doesn't run and we've been hired to make it work."

"Seriously?" At his nod, she grinned. "My Saturday just got a whole lot better." She ran upstairs to change. A good night's sleep and an engine to fix were just what the doctor ordered to cure her funk.

"Shouldn't we have more customers by now?" Sam asked hours later when they'd diagnosed the party bus with a bad starter. Despite it being a warm spring afternoon, Sam wore a hoodie over her baggy blue coveralls.

"Sometimes it takes a while for a business to take off." Joe had called around and found the part they needed in Santa Rosa. They could pick it up later. "Why don't we go into town and be sociable?"

Her bangs fell forward over one eye. No wonder she'd been slicking her hair back. "You mean show people you don't bite and hit them up for business?"

"That, too."

"Can we go see Brit? Lisa went there with her grandma after school on Thursday and said she had free cookies."

Joe agreed, glad of an excuse to see her.

They parked in front of Mae's Pretty Things boutique. Sam paused in front of the window, staring at a thin pink sweater with silver threads, very similar to the one Brittany had been wearing the first day they'd met.

Dad Failure struck Joe square in the chest.

Sam wouldn't be mistaken for a girl in that sweater. But even the promise of a paycheck and driving gig weren't enough to change Joe's mind about spending money on clothes when she already had a closetful. Or make promises he couldn't keep if the mayor's plan didn't work.

"Come on, Sam," he said gruffly.

"Hey, that's the sheriff." Sam pointed to a tall man leaving bills on a table across the street at El Rosal's outdoor dining patio. "He and the old fire chief gave us a safety lesson at school."

The law. Joe hoped the man hadn't been contacted by the FBI to watch him.

The sheriff looked up, noticed Sam and waved.

Muted laughter reached them from the barbershop. An elderly woman with shiny silver curls stepped carefully onto the sidewalk. Her blue polyester slacks and shamrock sweatshirt hung from her too-thin frame. She put a hand on the fender of a white 1970s sedan for balance as she moved off the curb. She did a shallow shuffle to get the door open and then sat daintily behind the wheel. The engine turned over and caught rougher than sandpaper on tree bark.

Joe jogged across the street as the driver cranked down her window. "Excuse me." He tried to catch her attention without sticking his head in her face and scaring her with all his tainted Messina black hair. "It sounds like your car needs a tune-up."

On cue, Sam appeared at his side with her salesman smile and handed the woman a flyer. "We fix cars."

The woman's eyes were a wide, faded blue. Her gaze fixed on Joe's long hair, making him glad she couldn't see the tattoo on his bicep. "My car runs fine."

The sedan backfired and died, refuting her statement.

Another old woman, sporting pink rollers, came out onto the sidewalk. She clutched her cell phone as if prepared to dial 911.

"No need," Joe told her, raising his hands in the surrender position. "The sheriff is headed this way."

The sheriff walked with the disciplined steps and posture of former military. But he was still halfway up the block.

"What do you think, Dad?" Sam said eagerly. "Gunky carburetor? Timing off?"

"Clogged air filter?" Joe added, because the woman seemed as if she could barely breathe. "Bring it down to the garage tomorrow and we'll have a look. Free of charge."

The driver stared at Joe's hair again. "I'll... um...ask my husband." She started the car again. This time it didn't die.

Sam and Joe moved to the safety of the sidewalk, waving goodbye as if the driver was leaving on a cruise and they were wishing her bon voyage.

The woman with curlers scurried back into the barbershop. Neither woman's reactions boded well for Joe being the front man of the mayor's dial-a-ride service.

"That's promising," Joe said for Sam's benefit. "Maybe our luck is turning."

"Not likely." The sheriff had reached them. He was as tall as Joe, but there the similarities ended. His hair wasn't black as motor oil and he probably had never made a bad decision in his life, considering he was sheriff. "Her husband is dead."

"But she said she'd ask him." Sam blinked up at the lawman. "Is she psychic?"

"Nope. Just suspicious." The sheriff ruffled Sam's hair, possibly to distract her from the steam coming out of Joe's ears. "Did you learn your emergency phone numbers? Did you make sure your outbuildings are secure so no critters or stray cats could get in?"

"Uh...we're doing that today." Sam glanced at Joe and then quickly away. She hadn't mentioned that assignment.

"I hear you're trying to identify owners of those cars on your property," the sheriff said to Joe. He produced a business card from his wallet. "Give me a call to arrange an appointment at the jail."

"At the jail? Can I come?" Sam grabbed Joe's hand. "I know someone in jail. My uncle—"

"Sam." Joe didn't manage to cut too much information off at the pass. "I don't think the sheriff has anyone we know in his jail."

"It's Nate," the sheriff said kindly. "The older residents call me Sheriff Nate, but it's just Nate. And I'm sorry, Samantha, but I don't have anyone in my jail right now." He ruffled her hair once more. "Whoever you want to visit is in a different jail."

"Oh." Sam was crestfallen.

"Doesn't mean I don't like to have visitors."

Nate waved at the women staring at them from inside Phil's. "Let's talk, Joe. I have access to the motor vehicle database. We can enter pieces of information for each vehicle and see what comes up."

"That'd be great," Joe said, meaning it.

Who'd have known that a pink bus and a meeting with the sheriff would give him hope?

JOE AND SAM entered Phil's just as Brit turned on the second hair dryer over Ingrid's pin curls.

The elderly ladies in the room gasped, which seemed silly. They'd all seen Joe outside talking to Patti before she drove off, and then to the sheriff.

But Brit felt like gasping, too, if only for a different reason.

Last night, she'd entered Joe's number into her cell phone. Only that. His name and number. She hadn't added him to Favorites or added a photo to his contact information. She had his number and that was that.

And then she'd seen the shadow cross his face when Patti looked at him as if he was an ax murderer. She'd wanted to put him in her favorites file, fling open the door and shout, *Stop being mean to my friend!*

Joe would've turned icy at a public display of loyalty and probably would've dropped one of those eggs he was trying to juggle.

She didn't want to make things any harder for him. Instead, she gave the Messinas the same welcome as anyone else who crossed Phil's threshold. "Come on in for a cookie. Don't be shy."

The chair hair dryer made a clicking noise, gasped and passed out.

"Holy wet set," Brit muttered.

Carmen, her next customer, had already sat at her station. Laurelyn had returned to the first dryer after charging outside unnecessarily to rescue Patti from Joe. She'd be done in another twenty minutes. Brit needed Ingrid to sit under the second unit for at least thirty minutes or she'd be off schedule. And her schedule required her to be on time.

Stoic Joe stood at the door trying to look invisible, while Sam wandered to the back counter for a cookie.

Brit unplugged the troublesome unit, counted to ten, plugged it in again and turned it on.

Clack-gasp. Clack-gasp. Sudden death.

She turned it back off and counted to ten.

"Is it broken?" Sam came to stand next to

Brit, her hair slicked back beneath her ball cap, her mouth full of sugar cookie. "My dad can fix it. He can fix anything."

Joe took one step forward. "I can take a look."

Every woman in the room, except for Brit, tensed.

Joe wasn't wearing a tool belt, so the chances of him fixing the dryer were slim. But Brit couldn't afford to fiddle with it while Carmen waited in her chair and Ingrid's hair didn't dry. "If you can fix this in fifteen minutes or less, you'll be my hero. Again." She shepherded Ingrid to Phil's chair and hurried to the supply cabinet for Phil's small toolbox while making a public-service announcement. "Ladies, this is Joe Messina, single dad, mechanic and the lifeguard who saved me from drowning in the river. His daughter, Samantha, is a sweetheart." There. That ought to make her clients less tense.

And make sure no one mistook Sam for a boy.

Sam trailed after Brit. "Why is everyone wearing curlers?"

"They like their hair a certain style." Almost all of them. The monotony of pin curls was getting to her.

Sam fingered a large pink roller in a plastic storage box in the cupboard. "Do you roll your hair?"

Brit's hair was down today, knotted in a long, thick mass over her right shoulder. "No. My hair is too heavy." Unlike Sam's, whose hair was fine and straight.

Sam fingered the roller and made moon eyes at the other women.

Brit's heart melted. She delivered Joe the toolbox.

"Sam, you don't need your hair rolled." Joe opened the box. "You're not that kind of girl."

Geez, the man didn't understand girls at all. "Oh, come on. Every kid should play dress-up. It fosters imagination."

He slid the dryer away from the wall. "Imagination doesn't help you later in life."

That gave Brit pause, but only long enough to take in the disappointment in Sam's eyes. The tween didn't have the depth of feeling Joe did in her big brown eyes, but her feelings lived in those eyes all the same. Brit decided then and there that she was going to break some of Joe's eggs. For Sam's sake. "If you help me early tomorrow morning by the river, Sam, I'll roll your hair afterward."

Sam held herself very still. And then she

dropped to her knees next to Joe. "Oh, can I, Dad? Please?"

"We don't have haircuts in our budget."

Sam's lower lip trembled.

Now the other women in the shop were tsking, siding with Sam, too.

Brit knelt next to the pair and lowered her voice. "I made Sam a friendly offer. No charge." The poor kid probably slept in a blue race-car bed. "Just like you're fixing my hair dryer. No charge. Friends don't charge friends for an occasional helping hand."

Joe didn't look up. He frowned. Brit got the feeling he wasn't frowning at the innards of the dryer. He flipped the switch and it began running as smoothly as the other unit. When he met her gaze, it was with an icy, stormy stare, which was why his words surprised her. "I suppose everybody needs a friend sometime."

CHAPTER SIXTEEN

"YOU USED TO live here?" Sam stood outside the main house next to Joe.

They'd returned from picking up the starter for the party bus. Joe had made an executive decision: homework before auto repair. Sam had to learn her emergency phone numbers and check all the outbuildings on their property to make sure there were no unwanted residents. Joe had thought it'd be easy. He hadn't counted on the way his stomach soured just looking at his former home.

"The house didn't look so bad when I lived here." It had only felt bad when Dad was inside.

The ranch house was a faded gray color. The trim had been white once, but was streaked with dirt. The bushes in front had died sometime in the drought years and were barren sticks shooting up from the ground. The windows had a grimy film so thick they didn't glint in the sunlight.

"Let's get this over with." Joe's stomach was beginning to turn.

All the windows were shut and unbroken. The front door locked, although the wood was weathered and a top panel was cracked. The main garage door was padlocked. The side garage door secure.

"Whose tires were these?" Sam stood nearly as tall as the four bald racing tires.

"Vince's. He built a drag racer one summer. Crashed it the next." That hadn't gone over well with Dad. And Mom had put an end to Vince's racing career after that.

They walked into the overgrown backyard. A small mowing tractor rusted in the corner. The swing set used to be white, but the chains were now dark and weathered. He could still remember Mom pushing him on the swing and him shouting, *Higher!*

"Don't even think about playing on that." Joe turned away, following the uneven sidewalk to the back patio. "It's not safe."

The redwood picnic table had survived, but the benches had blown over in the wind and had been eaten by termites. Joe tested the table with one hand. It creaked and a board popped loose.

He knelt next to it and looked underneath. "Still there."

"G.M. loves M.Z." Sam was on her knees next to him. "Why did Uncle Gabe carve that under here?"

"Because M.Z. was dating some other guy at the time." And Gabe had already carved a similar message with half a dozen girls on trees all over town. Joe stood and tested the kitchen door. It and the windows there were all closed up tight.

"What's that over there?" Sam pointed to the large barn beyond the backyard.

"That's where we stored our family vehicles—cars, trucks, motorcycles. Vince built his race car there, too."

"Cool. Is anything left inside?"

"I don't think so."

They walked through the tall grass. When they reached the barn, they stopped and stared. The building was nearly one and a half stories high, but blackberry vines had ascended to the roof. There was a latch beneath the vines somewhere, but Joe couldn't see it.

"That was the front door?" Sam kicked at the ground. "There's no driveway."

"It had a gravel driveway." Some days, they'd raced home on their motorcycles, skidding to a stop just inside the open doors. "Turo poured concrete inside."

They strolled around the perimeter. The vines had claimed nearly everything, but they looked diseased on the south side of the barn. The leaves there weren't as thick as the others. The vines weren't as firmly attached to the wall.

"Did you see that?" Sam ran forward, bending her knees and pointing under the vine. "Something ran in there. I think it was a cat."

"More likely a rat." Joe bent to look, but couldn't see a thing.

"What if there's a hole?"

"What if there isn't?"

"Dad. Get your chain saw and cut the vines back."

"Sam." He didn't relish cutting down the vines out here. His arms still had scratches from helping Brittany cut down the vines by the river. Besides, everything was locked up tight. "That'll take time. We need to put in our hours on the mayor's bus."

She frowned. "You can't sign my paper for the sheriff unless we know for sure."

"I tell you what. When we get paid for fixing the party bus, I'll buy more gas for the chain saw and cut down the vines out here."

Sam stared at the vines at the base of the wall and nodded.

THE TEMPERATURES SATURDAY night had slipped below fifty degrees. That made the fog roll into Harmony Valley and linger like whiffs of perfume in the cosmetics department.

Brit pulled her truck off the highway and parked near the bridge. She hadn't given Sam a time to help her other than "early." For a kid, early could mean 9:00 a.m. That was still hours off. But Sam came running across the field, surprising her.

For once, Sam's short hair wasn't hidden beneath a baseball cap. It looked choppy, as if Joe had given her a home cut. She sported the smile of the enthused. When she reached Brit, she had no qualms about looking inside the cab of the truck. "I'm ready to help. Did you bring the curlers?"

"I did." Hot rollers, styling product and a

flat iron. She'd decided not to go old-school on Sam's hair.

"Sam, calm down." It was Joe, halfway to them.

Brit wasn't the type to dwell on romantic notions. She hadn't been the girl who'd doodled hearts in the margin of her history notes or practiced writing her name over and over in her English notebook as Mrs. I've-Got-a-Crush-on-Him. But in this moment, with the knee-high grass still green and fog-kissed, with rays of soft golden light edging over the treetops, her heart pounded and her knees went weak at the sight of the man striding purposefully toward her.

He wasn't charging to her on his hulking black warhorse. He didn't ride to pick her up on a big Harley. But he came toward her with the same sense of determination and purpose. As if he was claiming her. As if he and Sam and Brit all belonged together.

Mine. Heart and soul. Forever.

She felt warm and cold, heavy and light. She wanted to laugh and cry, to shout and whisper, to hold on to this new feeling, the one where she wasn't the overlooked wallflower. The one where she was the bright and beautiful rose.

Brit shifted her feet, trying to find steadier ground.

She found a gopher hole.

Her booted foot sank. Her stomach lurched. And her sense of the romantic evaporated like a wisp of elusive fog.

"You okay?" Joe was by her side, a steady hand on her arm.

She stared into his eyes, looking for hearts and flowers, the intent to claim. Heck, she'd settle for a warm grin that said he didn't loathe her.

"Are you all right?" he asked, not a grin in sight.

"No, I…I mean yes, I…" She stepped back, extricating her arm, trying to remember why she'd come.

"Are we working on the Volkswagen?" Sam was a bundle of energy. She climbed on the rear bumper of Brit's pickup and examined the contents of the bed. "Are we making mermaids? Why did you bring a sledgehammer?"

"One question at a time." Joe thrust his hands in his jacket pockets.

"You sound like my teacher." Sam perched on top of the tailgate.

"What's the plan?" Joe peered at a still shell-shocked Brit. When she didn't immediately answer, he added, "You said you wanted Sam's help."

The plan. Her project. It all steamrollered back over Brit.

"Mayor Larry has given me permission to establish a semipermanent art display on his strip of land here, one that will attract tourists."

"Yay!" Sam leaped to the ground. "Mermaids!"

Fear tried to elbow its way into Brit's chest. "The first piece is going to be the Volkswagen." She pulled her sketchbook from the truck's passenger seat and flipped to a page with her vision. "The car, as your father so eloquently put it the other day, is roached. But that's perfect for what I want to do with it. I'm going to attempt to take one car and make it into two."

Joe and Sam both looked at the Volkswagen and then back at Brit. She could tell by their expressions that they were stumped. So much for feeling confident.

She showed them the first few sketches.

"I'm going to separate the upper body from the heavy undercarriage. And then use supports to make the rusted metal body appear like it's floating above the grass." She'd taken the idea from the dragons they used in the Chinese New Year parades through San Francisco.

"Cool," Sam said.

Brit flipped to a page with multiple sketches. "And then I'll build a skeleton of the Bug on the chassis and cover it with—"

"Are those rocks?" Joe leaned in closer. "And concrete?"

"Yes. I plan to build a set of bumpers from those pieces of concrete over there. And then cover everything but the windshields and windows with river rock. I got the idea from Sam's brontosauruses."

"The weight of the stone will collapse whatever you build the frame with," Joe said, sounding skeptical.

I will not doubt.

"That's why I need to reinforce it. The chassis is already sitting flush to the ground. The concrete adds a solid foundation. I'll find materials to make the body able to support a layer of rock."

"We're doing all that today?" Sam sounded like she'd just been assigned a ten-page paper due tomorrow. "I thought you were going to do my hair."

"This is a long-term project. Today, you two can help me take measurements, break up some concrete into two-foot chunks and collect fourteen river stones each." Before they could ask, she explained the law and the daily per-person quota for river stone.

"What about inside the cars?" Mollified, Sam climbed into the truck bed and wrestled the sledgehammer up and over, letting it fall to the ground. "I think there should be mermaids driving them."

"But it's dry land," Brit protested.

"You found a bike under the water. I found you underwater. Who's to say what else is below the surface." Joe helped Sam down.

"Oh, my gosh." Sam grabbed Brit's hand and tugged her closer to the Volkswagen. "This could be a whole bunch of stuff that pretends to be below the river."

Brit, who'd been about to pooh-pooh anything to do with mermaids, was momentarily rendered speechless by Sam's enthusiasm. "What a great idea."

She could see the panorama—the original Volkswagen body floating to one side, the rock bug, a mermaid on a bicycle, perhaps one driving the car.

If only she was up to the creative task.

It was a good thing Brittany wasn't a taskmaster, because being an artist was harder than Joe expected.

They'd taken turns swinging the sledgehammer at the concrete after she'd told them of her vision. Sam had been unable to do more than lift the sledge a few inches. Brittany had raised the tool to her shoulders and dropped it on the slabs, barely cracking the surface. It was Joe who'd done the real destruction. After five minutes, he was spent.

Perhaps recognizing this, Brittany had suggested they go over to the car, where Joe and Sam had held the tape measure and called out measurements to Brittany, who scribbled them on her pad.

"At fourteen rocks a day times three people—" Joe handed Brittany the tape measure

"—you'll have enough rocks to make a Volkswagen…"

"Math was never my forte." Brittany put her nose in the air in a way that made Sam giggle and Joe want to smile. "It'll be done when it's done. But speaking of rocks…"

She led them down the bank to the river's edge. Brittany had brought a backpack. First she loaded it with fourteen stones and allowed Joe to lug it to the top. He'd filled the backpack next. Finally, it was Sam's turn.

"I want to find pretty ones." Sam splashed along the edge, having more fun getting her boots wet than paying attention to the task at hand.

"The longer it takes you, the longer you have to wait for those curlers you haven't stopped talking about." Joe may sound like he wanted Sam to hurry, but he was enjoying the camaraderie too much to insist she quit.

The sun was slanting off the water, chasing away the last of the fog. There wasn't a cloud in the sky. It was shaping up to be the kind of day where you were grateful for what you had in life, little though that might be. And right now, Joe was lucky enough to be in the presence of two pretty special ladies.

"Let her have some fun." Brittany brushed the hair from Joe's eyes.

Her touch reminded Joe he was lonely more than an empty bed ever could. He stared into Brittany's brown eyes, wishing—

"Oh, my gosh." Sam rushed into ankle-deep water. "Here's a perfect one for the headlights."

Brittany broke off their connection, smiling. "Those boots are going to take forever to dry."

"I don't care." Sam bent, wrestling with something underwater. And then she lost her balance and tumbled backward. Almost immediately, she leaped to her feet, but she was drenched. Her coveralls already clinging to her slight frame.

She slogged to shore. "It's so cold."

"Are you all right?" Joe asked, but he was trying not to laugh. She was clearly fine.

And then Sam shrieked and crossed her arms over her chest. "Don't look at me."

"Why not?" He shrugged out of his jacket and went to wrap it around her. "It's not like I haven't seen you wet before."

"Not like this." Sam turned pleading, pained eyes toward Brittany.

"Sam, I… Can you tell us what's wrong?" Brittany asked unhelpfully.

"Come here." Joe lifted the jacket toward Sam again.

"Dad, don't." Sam snatched his jacket away and held it in front of her as if she was naked. She began climbing up the slope.

"What did I say?" He looked to Brittany, who drew a deep breath and shook her head, as stumped as he was. "Sam? What's wrong?"

Sam reached the path, gulped air and sobbed, "I need a bra, okay. I've been asking to go clothes shopping thinking I could slip that in at the register. But no-o-o-o." She glared at him, sparing Brittany. "I hate my life!" She spun and ran off.

Joe stared into the sturdy oak tree branches above him, feeling chilled.

"That was really brave." Brittany rubbed his back. "Of her, I mean."

Joe was growing weary of the need for either of them to be brave. "My daughter just had a meltdown and I'm feeling like a bad dad because I didn't even notice…"

Brittany chuckled, the sound blending with the soft gurgle of the river. "The hardest thing in the world for a girl to do is tell her parents she needs a bra, especially a dad. Have fun at the store."

Joe's stomach lurched. "I don't know how to shop for a bra."

Brittany picked up the backpack and began making the climb uphill. To her credit, she didn't collect Sam's quota of stones. "You can do an internet search on what to measure to determine her size. Do you want to borrow my tape measure?"

"No." Not for the first time in the past few weeks, Joe wondered how many more hits he could take. "I'll give you the BMW grille if you go shopping with us." He worried about putting the offer on the table. He still had no idea who owned the car.

Brittany glanced back down at him with the presence of mind he should have had. "You don't barter."

"I'll barter for Sam's sake." The words had trouble breaking free of his throat.

"Going shopping hardly seems fair payment for the grille. I'll throw in a haircut for her, too."

"I thought that was girl time and free."

"Rollers were girl time." She gave him a wry smile. "Haircuts are business."

Joe grimaced. "There are too many rules at play."

"Not so many." Brit resumed her climb. "You'd be doing me a favor. All requests so far have been for pin curls and petal teases."

"You cut my hair."

"I didn't want to. It's too short now." He could tell from the sharp intake of breath after her statement that she regretted sharing that much information.

She liked him. Even if, like him, she didn't really want to like him.

Joe felt something in his chest shift into alignment. His head and his heart. His breath came easier because of this. This woman. This place. This moment, flawed as it was. "Deal. Come back down here and shake on it."

"Careful. I might think that tough-guy image is just an act." Brit grinned, pausing before picking her way back down the slope to him. "Nice guys... Now, nice guys are usually the ones I end up dating. And you aren't nice and I'm not dating you."

Joe liked it when she grinned. The angle of her lips created something warm inside him. Something that made him see her in his arms, wish for the subtle smell of her hair filling his lungs, the soft touch of her lips against his. She didn't think she was beautiful. She didn't think she was worth dating, if their one teasing conversation about motorcycle rides was any indication.

Nice guys? She probably didn't know any. She kept men at arm's length. Until they were in her chair.

Suddenly, he remembered Sheriff Nate had a hair appointment with Brittany. Jealousy pressed in on him.

She stopped a few feet away, holding out her hand to shake.

He ignored it. "You have a…uh…leaf…" Without waiting for permission, Joe plucked an imaginary leaf from over her ear. His fingers brushed the silken softness of her hair. His thumb glanced over the fullness of her cheek.

He wanted more imaginary leaves to be in her hair. He wanted his hands to be in her hair. He wanted…

Their gazes connected.

Brittany frowned. "Hey… Joe…"

He took a step closer.

"Don't look at me like that." Her voice was low and uncertain. "When you look at me like that I see knights in shining armor." She placed her palm against his cheek and gently turned his face away. "Guys look at Reggie like that, not me."

He covered her hand with his and easily angled his head back to her, feigning ignorance. "At who?"

"Reggie. Regina." She swallowed, her voice dropping to a whisper. "The pretty twin."

Oh, man. Brittany had a huge self-confidence issue when it came to men. "I don't know who you mean." Joe moved closer. "To me, you're the beautiful twin."

Her brown eyes were luminous and staring up at him as if she'd never had anyone say anything that nice about her. Ever. She should hear someone tell her she was beautiful every day. It was the truth.

She swallowed, lowering her gaze. "Why, Shaggy Joe. I never expected a compliment from you."

"Stop talking like that." He placed his fingers beneath her chin, tilting her face up to his. "Stop talking and kiss me."

She froze. A deer in his headlights.

And then she laughed, loosening his hold. "You almost had me."

He did have her. He had his arms around her. He tugged her body against his. And kissed her.

A simple act. Four lips. Two hearts. One beat.

It didn't feel simple. It felt complex and intense and terrifying.

He had no right to kiss her. Kissing implied intent. He was broke, with a daughter to provide for. His world was imperfect when she deserved perfection.

He had no right to kiss her. Kissing opened the door to heartbreak. He couldn't stand to be left or betrayed by another person he loved.

He had no right to kiss her. And yet he did.

And for a moment, the promise of perfection seemed within reach.

CHAPTER SEVENTEEN

BRIT WANTED TO float on Joe's kiss forever.

She wanted to stay within the circle of the arms of Harmony Valley's bad boy.

She wanted to linger where she was no longer the overlooked wallflower.

Regardless of what she wanted, his arms unwound. The kiss was ending.

Brit sighed and opened her eyes.

There was a wariness in Joe's eyes. He was having doubts. That must have been one of those accidentally-on-purpose kisses Regina had told her about, the ones between two people caught up in a moment, two people who were only ever supposed to be friends.

Best remember that.

"Moving on," Brit said crisply, her gaze dropping to her feet because she couldn't feel her toes. "Hands down, that was a better way to seal a deal than a handshake." She risked a glance at Joe before she turned back uphill.

His gaze hardened.

Good. She couldn't stand it if he apologized for kissing her.

Brit reached the top of the bank and headed for her pickup, pausing only to dump the few rocks Sam had collected on the pile they'd started.

"Where are you going? I thought we were taking Sam shopping."

"I need to go home and change." She needed distance and the reaffirmation that she was Brittany Lambridge, ugly duckling. To hope for more than that was the path that led to broken hearts.

Or in this case, the crushing of a hard-boiled egg.

BRIT RETURNED TO the Messina Family Garage waiting room an hour later, armor suitably in place. Long jeans, a favorite light blue sweater, a touch more makeup.

"Nope," she said when she saw Sam in a dry pair of coveralls. "We're shopping for a woman. You need to dress like one."

Sam ran back upstairs without argument, leaving Brit alone with Mr. Fantastic Kisser.

"How're you doing?" Brit asked on autopilot, followed by a blushing blurt of "I mean, with Sam and the whole transition to womanhood. Not about the…"

Joe's mouth quirked up on one side. "I'm fine. Firing on all cylinders."

"Try being the egg sometime," Brit mumbled.

Sam skipped back downstairs wearing blue jeans, a simple red T-shirt and a hoodie, which she zipped up to her chin. She ran past Brit and flung open the door. "Shotgun."

Joe gestured that Brit should follow her out the door.

Brit couldn't help but feel that a trap had been sprung. "My father had one rule in his truck. Adults don't ride in the center seat." He would have made a special rule barring her sitting next to fantastic kissers.

"Your dad only had one rule?"

Brit glared at Joe over her shoulder.

"One of my rules is to respect the call of shotgun," he said.

She should feel flattered that Joe didn't mind sitting next to her. And she was flattered to the point her cheeks were burning. She didn't plan on kissing him again or letting him know he flustered her. And yet, she wasn't off to a very good start.

"Hurry," Sam called from the open passenger door. She'd left her ball cap inside. Her dark hair lifted on the breeze, revealing uneven, choppy bangs.

Brit's fingers itched for her scissors.

"You're still going to do my hair later?" Sam didn't succeed in keeping the worry from her voice. Or maybe she wasn't trying to.

"Of course. I promised and I like to keep my word." Brit just might do more than curl and style. She might try a blunt wedge that softened the sharpness of Sam's little chin.

Brit climbed into the old pickup and slid across the cloth seat into the middle. Joe swung up next to her, a lock of thick hair falling over his forehead.

Brit stopped thinking about Sam's hair.

But her fingers didn't stop itching.

THREE BRAS, TWO coffees and one hot chocolate later, Joe sat on the couch in the living room watching Brittany and Sam talk hair at the kitchen table.

Sam was in seventh heaven. Her body insecurities were temporarily taken care of and her hair issues about to be resolved.

Since their kiss, Brittany hadn't been the same. She'd skittered away from his casual touch at the small of her back while he was trying to guide her through crowds at the store. She'd blushed whenever he caught her looking at him. And she'd edged as far away from Joe as she could get in the truck. Hence him sitting as far away from her as he possibly could in the apartment. He wanted to show some respect and give her space.

That wasn't true. Joe wanted to wrap his arms around Brittany and kiss her again. He wanted to hear her sigh and feel her snuggle close. But he'd start with showing her respect and giving her space.

Sam sat in a kitchen chair, swinging her feet happily.

Brittany stood behind Sam, finger combing his daughter's dark, shoulder-length locks. "Has your father been cutting your hair?"

"No," Sam snorted.

Brittany spared Joe a glance.

Joe shook his head.

More finger combing ensued. Joe'd like some finger combing, too. He scratched his head.

"Do you have a favorite celebrity?" Brit asked Sam. "One with hair you wish you had? Or do you have a magazine photo of a hairstyle you like?"

"Why do you ask?" Sam said slowly, lacking her usual enthusiasm.

Joe's Dad Radar went on red alert.

"I want to know how to curl your hair so you like it." Brittany locked eyes on Joe, but not with an invitation for another kiss. She looked at him the way she had in the mirror at Phil's.

This time, Joe had more of an inkling as to Brittany's lingo.

Raised brows and wide eyes: *pay attention.*

Gaze cutting to Sam: *something's not right here.*

Significant gaze to Sam's hair and her fingers holding up Sam's bangs. Sam's *uneven* bangs: *your daughter cut her own hair.*

Apparently, skill with a socket wrench didn't necessarily translate to skill with a pair of scissors.

"I have a picture that I like," Sam said slowly. "I don't think she's famous."

"A picture would help." Brit patted Sam's shoulder.

Sam walked to her room, pausing in the

doorway to glance back at Brittany, and then she closed the door behind her.

What? Joe mouthed.

Brittany shrugged.

Joe knew what they were both thinking: *guilty.*

But of what?

Despite the tattered drapes, the afternoon sun filled the living room with almost-too-warm natural light. They'd need better curtains in another few weeks to keep the place cool.

Sam emerged carrying some kind of thin book. She laid it on the table and opened it to a page with a bent corner. "This one." She snuck a glimpse at Brittany before pointing to another picture. Her shoulders were curled in as if knowing she'd done wrong. "She shows it straight and then with curls."

"Where'd you get that?" Joe came into the kitchen. He couldn't remember buying her a magazine or book in months.

"Dad." Sam slammed it shut and hid it behind her back. "This is girl business."

"Sam." The warning in his voice bounced off the bare walls.

Brittany touched his arm once before turning her attention to his daughter. "Sam has something to tell you about that book. And then if you say it's okay, I'm going to style her hair the way she wants it."

Sam froze.

"Tell the truth to your dad and if he says it's okay, I'll cut and curl your hair like in the picture." Brittany's smile was brittle. "Fair trade."

Sam frowned, except her frown looked like it could crumple at any time into tears.

"We don't barter," Joe reminded them. His Dad Radar was pinging all kinds of alarms.

"This is between Sam and me. And apologies will be involved." Brittany nodded. "Isn't that right, Sam?"

There were slow nods and there were slow nods, but Sam's nod was so slow it almost didn't qualify as an action. "I borrowed this book from Phil's."

Joe closed his eyes, counting to ten. "Borrowed implies permission. Did you ask Brittany?"

"No." Her voice was so soft, Joe almost wasn't sure she'd said anything.

But Sam didn't need to say anything. Guilt was written all over her face in cry-me-a-river pink.

"There will be no more girl time today," Joe

said evenly. "Messinas don't steal." Or lie. Or betray those they loved.

"I'm sorry. But, Dad…" Sam trailed off. She turned to Brittany. "We had a deal."

"Dads trump deals. I told you it was up to him."

"You tricked me." Sam smacked the book on the table and ran to her room, slamming the door behind her.

It was hard to believe that only a few weeks ago, a slammed Messina door was most likely caused by the wind.

Joe picked up the book. It was filled with different hairstyles for different lengths. He handed it to Brittany. "We'll make an appointment to have her hair cut." Joe managed to control the volume on that statement. "After she serves her sentence."

Brittany repacked the tools of her trade. "She didn't try to hide the truth once I confronted her."

He shook his head. "You dangled some bait."

"There were extenuating circumstances— her hormones, the move."

"She stole your book."

"And she came clean. I've had lots of clients steal hair books and never say a word." Brittany gathered her cases. "That says a lot about her character."

Joe was too angry to be proud.

THE DOOR BETWEEN the service bays and waiting room banged open Monday morning.

"Joe! You have a customer!" Irwin shouted the way guys did when their team won on the last play of the big game.

Brittany stood on the customer side of the service desk in blue coveralls, her orange-tipped hair captured in a ponytail threaded through a rhinestone-studded black ball cap. There was a tentative twinkle in her eye as she said, "I tried to tell him I have an appointment."

Joe almost smiled. It was the twinkle, more tempting than a Saturday night milk shake. After a weekend spent with a mulish daughter, he could use something as lighthearted as a twinkle.

Joe had been tweaking the timing on the party bus. He set his tools on the workbench, wiped his hands and turned off the engine.

"I can check her in." Irwin had his hands on the door frame and his butt on the door, as if it was a great effort to hold it open. "Just tell me what to do."

"Move out of the way." Joe waved him off.

"Donut, miss?" Rex held out his bakery bag.

"Cookie?" Brittany opened up her bakery box.

The two exchanged smiles.

Irwin scuttled back to his seat, staring at Brittany as if considering replacing Rose in his fantasy motorcycle ride.

The only way Joe was letting Brittany ride on the back of a motorcycle was if he was driving. The open road. Her arms around him. Sounded pretty darn good.

Except, she was looking everywhere but at him. That twinkle had been for Irwin's enthusiasm at a customer, not him.

Trying not to think about kisses or soft hair, Joe handed Brittany a clipboard with a work order. "Name, address and phone number. Year, make and model of the truck."

Brit filled out the paperwork, blocking Joe's view of Irwin. "How's Sam?" she said under her breath, making it hard not to remember their kiss.

"She wore a skirt to school and no zippered hoodie." Brad Hendricks wasn't going to be mistaking her for a boy today. "She also apologized again for taking the book."

"Nice." Brit put an appointment card on the counter as casually as if she was in Rex's gin game and couldn't make a play.

Joe read the card. "Tuesday at three thirty?"

Irwin gasped. "Oh, he's good. He's got a date already."

Joe leaned around Brittany and fixed Irwin with a hard stare. "I know her." *I've kissed her.* "I do not have superpowers with women."

Brittany mumbled something that sounded like *I'll be the judge of that.* And then she said in a normal volume, "It's an appointment for Sam in case she's no longer grounded. I was rearranging my schedule for this week and thought of her."

Softy. She'd probably thought two days at school with bad hair was punishment enough for taking something that didn't belong to her.

Joe was a softy, too. "We'll take this one, thanks. And pay for the service." He stuck the card on the bulletin board with a pushpin. Sam would be thrilled. "I can reach you at this number?" His mouth went dry thinking of all the reasons he could call—haircuts, dinner, helping scavenge the river bed for rocks.

"You don't need to call me. I'll be working along the river for about an hour." She smiled. "I'm still planning to take the grille, but I want to wait until I've got my workspace set up. Is Sunday okay?"

"Sure." In the whirlwind of bra shopping after their kiss, he'd forgotten he'd promised the BMW's grille to her. He felt uneasy. He didn't want her to take it until he knew he had the legal right to give it to her.

The sheriff was supposed to be free Tuesday afternoon. That left him plenty of time to back out if it wasn't Messina property.

Brittany headed toward the door, stopping to deposit the bakery box in front of the coffeepot. "Complimentary coffee? Is that new?"

"Yeah," Joe said. "Someone told me customers like free stuff."

"We do." Irwin nodded.

AFTER BRIT SETTLED up her bill with Joe, he followed her to her truck.

While he'd changed her oil, she'd collected rocks and crawled around the Volkswagen trying to figure out how to separate the body from the chassis. She was dirty and sweaty, while

Joe didn't have so much as a spot of grease on him.

"Something about you confounds me." He pitched his voice low as if he didn't want his office sidekicks to hear.

"Just one thing, Heroic Joe?"

He shot her a glance that let her know it was more than one thing. "You've been here awhile now and you haven't created anything. At least, nothing you've told me about."

She no longer worried about stained coveralls. She worried about her private insecurities, secrets only Reggie was aware of. "I've styled hair."

"Does that count?" The morning sun made his hair look like she'd put a blue streak in it.

Brit clutched her keys. "I can't exactly say I'm not in the mood to work on hair when a client comes in."

"So you haven't been in the mood." His gaze pierced hers, searching for the truth.

They'd reached her car. She didn't move to leave, to escape, to keep her secret.

"I was wondering if I could watch the next time you create a mermaid."

"Watch?" Her stomach fell. To her knees.

To her toes. Followed by her keys. "Me?" she squeaked.

The corner of his mouth quirked upward. He bent to pick up her key chain. "I'm curious about the cutting and shaping of metal. Welding it to a supporting frame. I bet Sam would be interested, too."

"I don't sell tickets." Immediately, Brit wanted to take the words back. She sounded cold, like Leona.

He stopped almost smiling.

She was going to have to tell him. She could feel the truth pressing against the back of her throat. "Because I...*I can't*." The words were bitter and loud. Oh, so loud. She wanted to cover her ears.

"Brittany?" Joe didn't hand over her keys.

"I can't do it. The mermaid sculptures. I made Keira for Dad, before he died." The words tumbled free, tangled with emotion. "He was on forced bed rest, but he'd sit up a few hours a day while I worked. And now he's gone and I can't... He brought out the best in me. Ever since, I've got nothing. I can do nothing but rocks and driveway gates. I'm not creative. I used to look at car parts and junk and see things. I used to hear a piece of metal sing what it wanted to be. And now…and now…I barely hear a whisper."

Those eyes. They sharpened like icicles hanging from delicate tree branches. "You. Not creative? That's a crock." He took Brittany's arm, towing her to a spot where she could see the BMW. "You wouldn't have fought me for the grille if you didn't hear it sing to you."

"It's just a driveway ornament. I'm not an artist." The words slashed their way out, branding her for the worst kind of liar.

"Is that your sister talking? Because that doesn't sound like you."

It was her. It was the deep, dark, doubting core of her.

"Aren't you the woman who defended the value of art and labeled herself an upcycle artist? Aren't you the woman who risked her life because she couldn't live without an old bicycle stuck in the river? Aren't you the woman who dyes her hair unusual colors?" Joe took hold of her chin, forcing her to look into his stormy eyes. "That doesn't sound like a woman doing arts and crafts in her spare time. That sounds like a devoted artist to me."

Brit heard his words, absorbed their meaning, tried to rally and believe, but she'd spent months doubting. "Do you think so?" she whispered.

"You're second-guessing yourself because your dad died." His touch turned gentle, a thumb stroke across her cheek. "It's easy to lose your way when things are hard. It's easy to doubt and belittle your talent. It takes courage to pack up and make a change, to leap out without a safety net." He pointed to the reddish-brown shell of a Volkswagen. "When you brought out your sketchbook there was passion in your eyes. It lit up your entire face. And I thought, wow, she's the real deal. Only an artist would get excited about building something with rocks." His hands settled on her shoulders at the base of her neck. Her keys hung from his ring finger, dangling within reach like his arguments.

And still she hesitated. "Stacking rocks doesn't take as much skill as working with metal."

"I'd argue that it takes the same amount of skill. There's geometry and load-bearing math in the rock Volkswagen. You're planning to stack stone in curves." His fingers worked the muscles in her neck and shoulders as if it was something he did for her every day. "Same amount of skill. Different skill set."

"Oh." She wasn't sure if it was his words or his touch that was swaying her.

"My uncle once told me that the great ones don't give up when the going gets tough. They don't crumple like a fiberglass fender at the lightest bump either. They hang tight and chip away at the task." He let his hands fall to his sides. "One sledgehammer strike at a time."

Her foundation shook without his touch. She struggled for balance. "Your uncle didn't say that last part."

"No, but he could have. He was the ultimate dream weaver." Joe's gaze drifted to the garage apartment. "He could tell me things… If anyone else had tried to tell me, I wouldn't have believed it. But from Uncle Turo…" He tsked, a sad sound. "The man had game."

A numb feeling of dread took hold of Brittany. Something bad had happened between Joe and his uncle. Perhaps not as awful as when Joe lost his wife, but something bad nonetheless. "Uncle Turo is the one in prison?" People were talking about it in the shop.

"Yeah. He loved fast, expensive cars." Joe turned his attention back to her. He slid her keys off his finger and pressed them into her hand, much as he had pressed his phone number into her hand days before. "He just didn't like to pay for them. The FBI says other chop shops would bring him parts and trade for goods. It didn't seem odd to me that we'd have go-karts and motorcycles, quads and Segways. They'd come and go in trade."

"In barter," Brit said, catching on.

Joe nodded. "Barter doesn't require a paper trail, which is an advantage when peddling stolen goods."

That's why he'd refused to barter the grille for a haircut. "I'm sorry."

"Don't be. He's in jail. We're here." He met her gaze. No smile on his lips, but warmth in his eyes. "And I met you."

They stared at each other. Not smiling. It felt more special without the smile.

Unsure of what to read into his look, she glanced away. Joe opened the truck door, an invitation for her to leave.

"You never said anything about the other day." Joe's gaze drifted to the river and then back to her, full of mischief. "About our own special way of sealing a deal."

Brit was *not* having a conversation about

his kiss. She could feel her cheeks heating and didn't want him to see that this ugly duckling longed for things she couldn't have. Like him. A man with too much on his plate. By the time his life was in order and the turmoil over his uncle's arrest was settled, he'd realize an ugly duckling wasn't the right choice for him. "Why do you think the Volkswagen got dropped here without an engine or dash or seats?"

"Someone stripped it." Joe let her change the subject, but didn't let go of her door.

"Maybe it was Mildred." Brit didn't believe it, but she tried to sound pert and chipper. It was how Reggie sounded when a good man was in her viewfinder.

"That's not even a good guess." Joe was looking far too serious and she had no idea why.

The mayor rounded the corner, whistling, wearing a purple-and-green tie-dyed shirt.

"We'll talk later." He closed her door and walked away.

AT PHIL'S HOUSE, Brit opened the garage door and stared at the empty spaces. Joe thought she could face down worry and uncertainty with hard work. She began setting up her workbench, attaching it to the studs on the far wall for stability. She unpacked equipment and taped her sketches for the BMW gate on the same wall. The grille wasn't fancy, but it'd be a statement. She also taped up her ideas for the river exhibit, the ones that included the mermaids she'd sketched last night, the ones she'd never thought would see the light of day until Joe gave her permission to hope again.

"This looks like Dad's garage." Reggie stood on the threshold of the driveway, elegant in black slacks and a long black tunic. "You took over there, too." There was hurt in Reggie's finely made-up eyes.

"He loved us both." Brit set her welding helmet on the workbench.

"I know he did." Reggie walked into the garage with fluid, graceful steps. "I misunderstood Dad." Reggie met Brit's gaze levelly. "I didn't mean to railroad you. And I'm ashamed that I lost my temper and hurt you. I was trying to live up to Dad's last wishes."

Brit knew she should wait for a better apology. She didn't. She rushed forward and hugged Reggie fiercely. "If Mom or Grandpa Phil or Leona ever say you need to watch out for me, talk to me first."

Reggie drew back, taking a lock of Brit's orange hair between her fingers. "I believe in your *art*. I really do. In my heart. What you create is unique and beautiful." She smoothed Brit's hair over her shoulders. "But when Dad said that to me, I fell into marching-order mode. I didn't think it through. I quit my job. I moved up here. I thought I could make you find a more traditional path." She blinked back tears. "I forgot that you're not just talented, but you're also no dummy. Being a beautician means you rent a station, manage a client list, balance your books. You're a businesswoman. If you don't make it in one world, you'll make it in another. But I really hope you make it as an artist."

"Thank you," Brit whispered, back to believing what her twin said was true. Her heart swelled with happiness. Everything was going to be all right. Brit had a growing support group, a solid foundation for creativity. She hugged Reggie again, smelling disinfectant, hair spray and home.

"I told Leona the deal was off." Reggie let Brit go. "I've wasted enough time here."

"You're leaving?" The peacefulness she'd felt a moment ago cracked.

"I want to be a CEO by the time I'm thirty-five. I can't make that happen in Harmony Valley." The old Reggie, the one with drive and hunger, was back. "And while I'm out conquering the world, you'll be here following your muse. You don't need anyone to do that. Not Dad and not me."

"I… How do you always know what I'm feeling?"

"Because I have the same fear about going it alone." Before she got uncharacteristically sentimental, Reggie's gaze caught on the river exhibit sketches. "So many mermaids. Aren't you afraid you'll be labeled as that woman who does mermaids?"

She wasn't. Mermaids weren't limiting. They were beloved. And she wasn't boxing herself in. The Volkswagen with rocks proved it. If anything, she was spreading her wings. But how could she make Reggie see it? A true artist could convince her. She eyed her sketches. "Do you remember me showing you a book on the works of Michelangelo last year?"

"Vaguely."

"The face he sculpted on *David*…" The certainty of mermaids and romance grew in Brit.

"It was a face he used on other sculptures. A face he loved."

"Michelangelo wasn't exactly a one-trick pony," Reggie allowed. "I may not know everything he did, but he was a master of many mediums."

Brit nodded, thinking of hair and metal and stones. "He was passionate about art, and curious beyond the limits of marble. He did everything from paintings and frescoes to the Sistine Chapel and the statue of *David*."

"But he didn't work full-time as a hair stylist," Reggie said, getting real.

"I'm caught in the rush, there not being a beautician in town for so long. Business at the shop will taper in a week or so." Brit didn't sound as confident as she'd like.

"Promise me that this—" Reggie pointed to her sketches "—this will be your priority. Not hair. Not Grandpa Phil. Not scruffy bad-boy mechanics. Make your dream your priority and you won't need anyone."

"I promise." Brit found Reggie's hand, sensing her twin needed some advice, as well. "But just because you don't need someone, doesn't mean you have to go it alone."

Reggie stared down at their hands. When

she raised her gaze, her eyes shone with unshed tears. "Thank you," she said softly. "I
know where to find you when I need a good
hug."

CHAPTER EIGHTEEN

"DON'T SCREW THIS UP," Joe muttered to himself as he drove the party bus through Harmony Valley Tuesday morning, palms sweating.

He'd dropped Sam off at school and then headed for his first pickup, not truly believing this endeavor could help his image around town, but unwilling to give up. "I need someone to give me a pep talk."

Like the one he'd given Brittany yesterday morning. Who'd have thought beneath all her bravado lay a debilitating fear. If you were a mechanic, you fixed engines. If you were an artist, you made art. End of story. But with Brittany, he hoped her story still had a plotline for him.

A figure in a jacket and knit cap waved at Joe. He came to a stop next to the man, wiped his palms on his jeans and opened the door. Only then did he recognize Will.

"Nice to see you, Joe." Will ascended the

steps like the royalty he'd become; only the uncertainty in his eyes seemed familiar. "Remember me? Will Jackson. We used to be buds."

"Congratulations. I hear you've become a millionaire." Joe shook Will's hand. "Me? I'm just a mechanic." And now a bus driver.

"It takes all kinds. My dad's a farmer," Will said graciously, taking a seat in the front row. "If you haven't guessed, I'm your concierge."

"So my passengers don't run from the sight of me?"

"Yep." Will grinned. "With that ugly mug of yours, you'll never need a mask at Halloween."

And just like that, they were thirteen again with the world at their bare feet at the edge of the river. "Still smooth with the words, I see."

"Still carrying that chip on your shoulder, I see." Will's grin faded. "The one that says you don't deserve any breaks you don't earn yourself."

"It's harder being a Messina than a Jackson." Joe faced Will. "And you didn't make it any easier last week when the mayor started talking about this job."

"I wasn't sure about you." At Joe's scowl, Will held up a hand. "Hear me out. I'm married now, got a kid on the way. All I knew was that your uncle had been arrested. I needed time to—"

"To check out my—"

"References," Will said firmly. "You said it was hard being a Messina, but there are still people in this town who're willing to give you a chance, the kid they knew as Joe before Turo showed up. They're willing so long as you're worth taking a chance on. Are you, Joe?"

It hurt that Will had to ask. It hurt that every time Joe talked to someone about Turo he felt he had to defend his own innocence. Every time except with Brittany. She'd taken him at his word. And Will should, too.

"I'm not going to answer that question." Joe put the bus into gear. "I've proven myself enough to you over the years."

"You mean like the time you decked the quarterback from Cloverdale because he called Jimmy the n-word."

"Tell me where we're going," Joe said through gritted teeth.

"Or when a couple of us were flinging matches in the gymnasium and it caught fire?"

"Destination, Mr. Moneybanks." Joe cruised

the back roads, past rows of neat vineyards, which Will probably owned.

"You know if you hadn't taken the blame, it would've blown my scholarship to Stanford."

Joe accelerated. "And yet you had to check my—"

"References. Yeah. I know a guy. I had him dig up your employment record. That's all. I swear." The gravity and urgency of Will's words got under Joe's defenses.

Besides, he had Sam to think of. He slowed down. "Where are we going?"

"Turn onto Madison. We're picking up Mrs. Stephens."

"The science teacher?" So much for hope. Joe had done okay in science. It was all memorization, although some of it was applicable to mechanics. And then they'd gotten to biology. You would have thought he'd be okay. He took engines apart all the time. But no. Dissecting live things turned his stomach. So he'd knocked his frog into Mrs. Stephen's lap and had been kicked out of class. He'd had to get creative to avoid the smell of formaldehyde and the spongy feel of preserved flesh. By his sophomore year, Mrs. Stephens had developed a no-tolerance policy where Joe was concerned.

"She's retired now. Spends her days baking and chairing the garden club."

The homes in this neighborhood could use some of the club's attention. "Everyone's gotta fill their time with something."

"Speaking of time." Will's tone turned serious. "Uncle Turo… That's gotta be tough on you. Sorry, man."

"It was. It is. I…uh." Joe sighed. Might as well come out and say it. "I had no idea."

"We like to think those close to us are above it all." Will gestured toward a green Craftsman home on the corner. "That's hers."

While Golden Boy went up to the door, Joe wrestled with feelings he didn't normally acknowledge, like gratitude and the bonds of friendship. How different would Joe's life have been if he'd followed Will by the river that day, if he'd left the Messinas behind? He might never have felt the depth of betrayal Uncle Turo's crimes caused. But he'd never have worked on a Maserati or met Athena or had Sam.

Sam made the bad parts of his life worth it.

"So this is how little Joey Messina turned

out? A bus driver?" His former science teacher used a five-foot wooden staff to help her walk down the driveway. Other than her gray hair, she'd stepped out of the past. That must have been the same ankle-length blue jean skirt, black peasant blouse and Birkenstock sandals that had made up her school uniform back in the day. Her hair was still long and thin, and swung to her waist.

"Good morning, Mrs. Stephens," Joe intoned like a good schoolboy.

Mrs. Stephens handed Will the staff and climbed the bus stairs using both railings. She sat heavily in the front row and arranged her skirt. "Leave the staff next to the mailbox, William, and get in. I don't want to be late for my appointment."

Will did as asked. He got in the bus, claimed the aisle seat in the row behind Mrs. Stephens and gave Joe directions to their next stop.

"You would've been a great scientist, Joey, if you hadn't had a queasy stomach when it came to dissection."

"You knew?" Joe reached a stop sign and glanced at his former teacher, ignoring Will chuckling behind her.

"You think you were the first student to act

out when we used the sharp tools in our lab kits?" She smiled like she was letting him in on a private joke. Which she was. "I was always grateful when my squeamish students didn't pass out. It was easier to send you to the office when you turned green at the gills."

Their next stop was so overrun with bushes that only the roofline was visible. Will disappeared into the shrubbery.

Mrs. Stephens shifted in her seat, groaning. "Darn hip. I'll be glad to get a new one tomorrow. Hopefully I'll be able to drive after this."

"Tomorrow?" Joe turned in his seat. "Should you be getting your hair done today?"

"It's not the Dark Ages, Joey. Besides, statistics show a significant chance that I could die during the procedure. I've always wanted colored highlights, and I hear Phil's granddaughter has some."

"She does." Strips of color as bright as neon and as soft as silk.

"I hear Rose Cascia wants to go red, but lavender is all the rage." Mrs. Stephens drew a long lock of gray hair over one shoulder. "I need to decide between tips, streaks and regular highlights. What do you think?"

"Tips have attitude. Streaks are surprising. And—"

"Tips it is." Her decisiveness was one of the reasons she'd been among his favorite teachers. "In honor of the town wild child coming home."

Joe was touched. "Did Will or the mayor pay you to say that?"

"Joey." She turned up her nose. "You know I can't be bought."

He knew, but he also knew she volunteered for any cause she felt was worthy of her time.

Their next rider wore a cannula beneath her nose and was tethered to an oxygen tank, which Will wheeled behind her. The woman's hair was white, short and slicked back over her head like Sam had worn hers last week. She shuffled toward the bus in red slippers and a long, shapeless, lime-green dress.

With Will steadying her and Joe reaching down from the second step, they got her inside.

"Mary Stephens, I haven't seen you since the cemetery run last fall." That gravelly voice. She had to have been a pack-a-day smoker. "When I heard there was an opening at Phil's, I snatched it up."

"Velma, isn't it nice to get out?" Mrs. Stephens glowed. "I might even have lunch at Giordano's. My neighbor told me the paninis are wonderful."

Joe put the bus in gear and drove as Will directed.

"I would've thought Becca would drive you to lunch now and then," Velma said in a raspy nasal tone.

"Becca has too many clients to make time for lunch," Mrs. Stephens replied wistfully. "Not that I'm complaining."

Velma hacked into a tissue, delaying conversation until she caught her breath. "Who's our chauffeur?"

"Why, that's little Joey Messina," Mrs. Stephens said in the deliberate way that teachers spoke when they caught a student doing something wrong.

Despite her denial of being paid by Will or the mayor, Mrs. Stephens had to be a plant. They'd made sure someone from his past who actually liked him was on the bus. Joe glanced at Mrs. Stephens in the mirror and gave her a small smile. Small smiles were about all he was good for lately.

Meanwhile, Velma was hacking again. Will rubbed her back and told her to relax.

"Messina?" Velma clutched her purse to her chest. "Is that why Will came along? As our bodyguard?"

Joe refrained from snorting, but he noticed Will didn't hold back a grin.

"Little Joey has grown up." Will handed Velma a tissue he produced from his pocket, because old habits died hard in nerds, even millionaire ones. "He's got a daughter and is running the car repair shop."

"I'm reformed." Joe played along. "And not too proud to ask for a second chance."

Velma clamped her lips together and white-knuckled her purse.

Their next pickup balked before she'd made it onto the bus. "Those Messina boys tried to kill my cat."

This…Joe did not remember.

"Dee Adams." Mrs. Stephens pulled herself to her feet and used her best teacher's voice. "If you make me miss my hair appointment, I will cross you off my Christmas card list and that includes the plate of Christmas fudge."

Mrs. Stephen's fudge must be something, because Dee climbed the stairs and sat in the rear of the bus. "Somebody call my son and let him know who I'm with in case I go missing."

"We Messina boys *were* a lot of things." Joe put the bus in gear, determined to get Mrs. Stephens to her appointment on time. Maybe then he'd get some Christmas fudge. "But we weren't murderers of people or pets."

"Really, Dee," Velma croaked, turning in her seat. "Everyone in town nearly ran over your cat. It was deaf and liked to sleep in the middle of Jefferson Street."

Now, that rang a bell in Joe's memory. Half the time, he'd thought the cat was already dead, and tried to speed by it without looking. And then it would leap up at the last minute and dart in front of his wheel, practically giving Joe a heart attack.

"I'm sorry if I scared you, Ms. Adams." Joe tried to look contrite as his gaze connected to hers in the mirror. "I was young. And, well, you know how my dad was." He had no qualms blaming his wild youth on his father if it helped him create a new life here for Sam. "For the record, is your cat still alive?"

Her thin lower lip trembled. "Harvey died of kidney failure at the ripe old age of twenty-two. It was the year I finally got him to nap on the driveway instead of the street." She sniffed.

"Twenty-two years?" Joe downshifted toward the center of town. "You must miss him."

"I do." She stared out the window. "I do."

"Well played, Joey," Mrs. Stephens murmured. "Well played."

WHEN THE MAYOR asked Brit to rearrange her schedule Tuesday to accommodate a new dial-a-ride bus service he was trying to launch, Brit hadn't expected Joe to be the driver. Or for Will to be his sidekick.

Joe and Will assisted her new clients into the salon, and then Will stepped out to make a phone call.

Joe leaned on the empty barber chair. "Where's Phil?"

"At the bakery in a snit." Brit tried to make light of the situation. "He says no one wants him here." It was the truth. Her clients couldn't care less if he was here or not. But the guilt was hard to shake.

"You okay?" Joe's gaze was warm, perhaps softened by the nice little old ladies he'd escorted inside. "You look rattled."

Francine glanced up from her gossip magazine. Her two-inch-long hair was spiked up with the ash-blond color Brit was applying.

Give her a nose ring and black eyeliner and she'd look like an aging punk rocker. She didn't care that Joe saw her in such a state.

"I'm off my game," Brit said. "My sister left town. My grandpa's deserted me." And Joe had kissed her. And given her a pep talk. And saved her life. Not in that order. "Maybe Felix is right. Maybe I do need a shop cat."

"Phfft," Francine said, returning her attention to her magazine. "You need a man."

"She's got me." Joe gave Brit that almost smile that made her heart want to faint. He offered his passengers coffee and cookies, serving them all.

"He's a keeper, that one," Francine said.

I wish, said the wallflower.

"Who is he?"

"That's Joe Messina. I tell all my customers about Heroic Joe." Brit finished applying color to Francine's hair, and began cleaning up. "Because of him, I'm alive, my truck runs great and now Joe's bringing me happy customers."

"Who'd have thought little Joey Messina would someday be good marriage material?" The woman wearing the long jean skirt raised her coffee cup in a toast.

She didn't seem to notice Joe had gone still. Or that his eyes had lost their warmth.

His reaction reinforced Brit's decision to keep her distance. She wanted to get married someday. He clearly did not.

"Oh, he's the one that people are talking about." Francine was eyeing the box of cookies. She'd been the first client of the day and Brit had hustled her directly into her chair without treats or caffeine. "Wouldn't a ready-made family be nice? Doesn't Joe have a boy and a girl?"

And.

Joe stood beneath Keira, a winter squall gathering in his eyes.

"He has a daughter," Brit said evenly. "She's coming for a haircut later."

The cookies were either very good today or her clients had sensed Joe's frosty air. Running a salon was like managing a three-ring circus. Brit shooed Francine to the coffeepot and asked for Mary next. The jean-skirted woman walked slowly toward her chair. Seeing her difficulty, Joe lent her his arm for support. The iceman had melted.

"How was Joe's driving?" Brit tried redirection when conversation still hadn't picked up again. "Did he break the speed limit?"

"He drove like an old lady." Mary chuckled. "Slow the entire way."

"That's what parenthood does to you," said the woman with the cannula and raspy voice. "Slows you down. It's only a matter of time till you're facing the grave."

The corner of Joe's lip inched upward. "I've never driven slow in my life. Just wait until I take you ladies home. You'll have to belt in."

That got them chuckling.

"Speaking of…" Brittany stroked Mary's long hair, learning its texture. "When are you returning for them?"

"One o'clock. They have time for lunch and shopping in town." He waved to his charges and left, driving away in a roar of pink.

"He's not the worst of the Messinas," wheezed the woman with the cannula.

"He's not bad at all," piped up the lady with the red slippers and lime-green dress.

"He's a diamond in the rough." Mary gave Brit a knowing smile in the mirror.

CHAPTER NINETEEN

"I'M HERE. I'M READY." Sam pushed into Phil's after school. She'd run over in her sundress and sandals.

Not wanting to miss the joy on his daughter's face, Joe had run after her.

Brittany was alone, sweeping white hair from beneath her chair. "Have a seat."

Sam climbed in, gripping the armrests as if expecting to blast into space. "Can you do curls, too? I want to sit under the dryer."

"Only if my four o'clock is late." Brittany put away her broom and dustpan.

Joe sat in the other chair. "Still no Phil?"

"Nope." There was something in Brittany's voice that made Joe peer closer. Her eyes had fine, tense lines around them as she swirled a tiger-striped drape over Sam. Was she tired from a full day of work and the demands of her elderly clients? Or was something else bothering her?

"Anything else I can do?"

She picked up a water bottle and began wetting down Sam's hair as if it was as thick as Joe's. "Grandpa Phil feels unwanted in his own shop. And I...I feel guilty that he feels like that."

Water dripped onto Sam's plastic-protected shoulders.

"He should retire," Joe soothed. "Phil's hands are a hazard with scissors."

"But he's my grandfather. And I'm the reason he decided to quit. He lives for this place." She combed Sam's ragged bangs and cut along a straight line. "I need to find a reason for him to come back."

"That's temporary. It doesn't heal the real problem." The old man couldn't do the job.

"When Uncle Turo gets out of jail, we're going to hire him." Sam's words were more wish than certainty. And there was an unspoken question at the end of her sentence: *Won't we?*

Brittany stopped snipping hair. Her gaze cut to Joe's.

"I don't know," Joe said carefully. "It's taken us a long time to get back on our feet after what Uncle Turo did in Beverly Hills. And he's part of the reason people here don't want to bring their cars to us."

Sam went silent, the gears in her head spinning at maximum speed. "What happens to people who get out of jail? How do they live?"

"They work in various places." Joe had no clear answer to the more difficult question. *What will Uncle Turo do when he gets out of jail?* Joe hadn't thought that far ahead.

"They ought to be able to come home." Sam crossed her arms beneath the drape.

Joe didn't know what to say. He wasn't sure Turo deserved a home with them.

Luckily, the sheriff opened the door and poked his head into the shop, saving Joe from answering. "I saw you come in. I'm ready to work on your list of cars."

Joe hesitated. He'd expected to have a good time with Sam and Brittany. He wanted to witness his little girl's hair transformation.

"She'll be fine," Brittany assured him. "I'll send her around to the station if we finish first."

Still, Joe hesitated.

"Go on," Brittany urged, pausing in her work to meet his gaze. "We're not going anywhere."

She was right. Something he hadn't known he'd been carrying lifted. They were staying in Harmony Valley. Not just Joe and Sam, but Brittany, as well.

Joe hurried after the sheriff, who'd been waiting on the sidewalk.

"Just so you know…" Nate's long legs kept Joe speed walking. "Agent Haas from the FBI called me today."

"I'm surprised—" Joe was suddenly as out of breath as Velma and in need of oxygen "—he waited so long."

"He didn't have a good opinion of you." Nate didn't acknowledge the sudden drag in Joe's step or that he'd fallen behind. "Actually, I got the feeling he didn't have a good opinion of most people. He wasn't happy when I said I thought you were a decent guy."

"I bet." Joe caught up to Nate at the corner. "I swear, I was strictly an employee. I didn't know what was going on. I have no idea where my uncle hid anything. I'd turn it over if I did. I'd never risk losing my daughter."

"I believe you." Nate unlocked the door to the station. "Car thieves don't come to Harmony Valley and certainly don't bust their butt to make a living." Nate sat behind a desk. "Pull up a chair and let's see that list."

The station was housed in a converted store behind the block that housed Phil's. Beyond the front counter was a desk and a jail cell. To one side was a door that looked like it might lead upstairs. A sign on it said Private.

Forty-five minutes later, they'd identified owners for all but two cars. Four cars were registered to Tony Messina. Sixteen cars were registered to Harmony Valley residents, living or dead. And the question marks? The Volkswagen Brittany had found in the bushes and the BMW.

Just Joe's luck.

"There are a couple more places I can check," Nate said as Sam ran in.

Her hair was cut neatly, short in the back and longer by her chin. Her bangs were fluffier than a poodle's fur, but Joe liked to imagine that Brittany had let his daughter play with the curlers she'd been obsessed with. In short, she looked like a girl.

She didn't act like a little lady. She ran in the open jail cell and put her face between two bars. "This is so cool." She spun around before Joe could argue that a jail cell wasn't cool.

"Wait. Is that the toilet?" She stared into the steel bowl. "Ew. Wait till I tell Brad about this."

"People who get locked in a jail cell don't have privileges like privacy," Nate said without looking up from the keyboard.

"Which is why Sam and I won't be breaking any laws." Joe refrained from knocking on the sheriff's wooden desk. "Did you pay Brittany?"

Sam put her face between the bars again. "She wouldn't accept my money. She said she owed us nachos and this way you wouldn't worm or squirm or something." She crossed her eyes and giggled, acting more like a carefree eleven-year-old than she had in weeks. "What does that mean?"

It meant Brittany was reneging on her dinner invitation.

And Joe was going to have to do something about it.

"You didn't come into the shop all week," Brit said to Grandpa Phil on Saturday night. She stood in the kitchen and tried not to think about how her feet and back ached. Foot and back aches tended to muddle the mind when it came to deciding what to make for dinner.

And when the mind was muddled, the hand reached for microwavable burritos.

"You had more customers in the past two weeks than I've had in three years combined," Phil lamented from his semipermanent position on the couch.

After a week of Phil avoiding her—leaving early for the bakery, pretending to be asleep on the couch when she came home—they were getting to the heart of the matter. "Is that when your hands started to shake? Three years ago?"

"Who can remember?" He stared at his trembling digits. "I saw Francine in the shop the other day. I used to color her roots and trim her bangs." He clenched his fists. "Do you know what it feels like to lose a skill? These hands…" His voice cracked. "They've betrayed me."

Someone knocked on the door. And then pounded with both hands.

It was Joe and Sam. They carried two boxes of pizza and a bottle of soda. Talk about bad timing.

"Delivery." Sam elbowed her way inside with the soda and shamelessly looked around. Her bangs floundered on her forehead, being too short to win the cowlick war over her right temple. "I hope you like pizza. I sure do."

"Me, too." Phil sat up, funk vanquished.

"This is because I wouldn't take Sam's haircut money, isn't it?" Brit scowled at Joe, blocking his entry with one hand on the door frame. "You can't just barge in here with dinner and expect me to roll out the welcome mat."

Unfazed, Joe lifted the top of the box. "Ham and pineapple." He angled the boxes to flash her a view of the lower pizza. "Pepperoni."

The smell of pizza filled the air. Hot and salty and more satisfying than a freezer-burned burrito.

Brit opened the door wider and stepped back. "Fine. You can come in, but don't make a habit of it."

"Never." He leaned over and kissed her forehead as he passed.

Brit froze. She was supposed to be wrong for him. They were supposed to be friendly, not friends. They'd had boundaries, of sorts, when he drove a second busload of women to the shop on Thursday. There was no kissing in Acquaintanceville.

Sam waved Joe toward the dining room. "I found plates and napkins."

"This is just what we needed to cheer us up." Grandpa Phil lumbered and swayed to the table. "Reggie moved to the city this week. We're feeling a bit sorry for ourselves."

Her grandfather didn't mention he'd been in the middle of a breakdown when they'd knocked.

Joe appeared at Brit's side, pizzaless, and closed the door. He directed her toward the dining room. "Sit down. Eat. You'll feel better." His fingers worked magic on her aching shoulders as he propelled her forward.

"Do you always pizza bomb people you barely know?" As Brit sat in the nearest oak captain's chair, she made a mental note to buy seat cushions.

"We know you." Sam grinned, wiping pizza sauce from her chin. "You're our neighbor. Our haircutter. And a mermaid lover."

Phil chuckled.

"I made that last one up." Sam was loving this.

It was hard not to smile.

Joe slid a plate in front of Brit with two slices, one from each pizza. He'd found the glasses. He poured everyone a soda. He was the perfect host. He wasn't glacial or frosty. In fact, both days he'd driven the bus this week, he hadn't scowled. Not once.

"There's green salad in the refrigerator." What was the use of buying vegetables if you didn't eat them?

"Don't even think about vegetables and sugar intake," Joe admonished. "It's Saturday night."

"We don't do vegetables on Saturday." Sam twirled a finger in her hair. "It's a rule. And before we go to bed, we have milk shakes."

Brit angled herself in the chair so she was facing Joe. "You didn't bring milk shakes?"

"It's a bedtime ritual. Not for the neighbors." There was a smile in his voice, plain as day. He just didn't let that smile out often enough. "We're here to celebrate the weekend and hear about what was accomplished in the art world."

Brit choked on her pizza.

Joe gave her a couple of sturdy backslaps. "I take it that means you were too busy to get creative."

"Shoot," Sam said. "I was hoping to peek at some mermaids."

Brit stared at her plate and wondered what Leona was serving for dinner.

"You know what this means?" Joe looked

at each of them in turn. "It means tomorrow we all encourage Brittany to take on an art challenge."

"We did papier-mâché collages in school on Friday," Sam said. "I have leftover paper squares if you want some."

"You've been complaining I don't have anything on my walls," Phil said when Brit looked his way.

She turned to Joe. "I suppose you're going to say I should get cracking on the BMW grille."

"I think…" For once, Joe looked almost wishy-washy. "I think you should do whatever makes you happy."

It was the river bike all over again. He was so sweet, Brit wanted to cry.

CHAPTER TWENTY

"I HAVE A lead on those last two cars." If the sheriff was excited enough to call at six in the morning on a Sunday, the least Joe could do was pick up the phone.

"Uh-huh." Joe yawned and rolled out of bed, padding to the living room.

They'd left Phil's house at nine last night. After putting Sam to bed, Joe had sat in the dark on his couch, wishing things were different and he could ask Brittany out on a real date. For now, family night would have to do.

"The BMW popped up first. It was stolen about seven years ago."

Joe stopped breathing at the word *stolen*.

"The Volkswagen fits the description of one taken about twelve years ago, but there's no clear match."

Joe drew a deep breath. "Taken from where?"

"That's the weird thing. Both cars are from

Southern California. I don't know why they'd have ended up here."

Joe thanked the sheriff and stared out the window at the barn in back. At the vines that didn't look healthy on one side. At the grass that didn't seem so thick on one side. At the isolation of the property. At the way Turo always insisted his nephews never sell this place.

Joe knew. He knew. Sadly and sickeningly, Joe was slow on the uptake where Turo was concerned, but now he knew.

The stolen cars were in the barn.

Jeans. Boots. Jacket. Joe raced downstairs to the supply closet and the chain saw. He only slowed down to fill the saw's tank with gas.

"Dad? What are you doing?" Standing in the doorway, Sam rubbed the sleep from her eyes.

"I promised you I'd check out the barn and make sure no cats or critters lived inside."

"Dad. It's like o-dark thirty." There was the preteen he knew and loved.

He was too upset to smile. "The sun's coming up. There's only a bit of leftover fog in the way." And they had no neighbors. They were bordered by a vineyard, the river and the highway. There was no one to hear and complain about a chain saw or a car engine at odd hours of the day or night. "Go back to bed."

He grabbed a pair of gloves and goggles, and hurried to the barn.

"Please be wrong." He knew he wasn't. Being right would explain the phone calls, which had stopped once Turo knew they were here. Once he'd said the words Harmony Valley and hadn't said anything about stolen cars.

The chain saw's engine startled a flock of red-winged blackbirds. Beyond that, nothing complained as he cut the vines at the base. The trunks were thin and seemed to have been bent before.

After cutting for a few minutes, Joe set the chain saw aside and began pulling the vines that clung to the wood wall. Some of them were stapled on. Thorns pierced his leather jacket and bit into his jeans. He ignored them and kept working, needing to see, needing to know.

Finally, he cleared the vines free of the door. It'd been made sometime after he'd moved away. It wasn't as much a door as a drawbridge. The hinges were on the bottom.

Made sense. Lowering it over the vines protected the tires.

It wasn't even locked. There were two latches—one on each side, each about six feet up.

He released the latches and let the drawbridge drop, dreading what he'd find inside.

Jaguars. Ferraris. Bentleys. A Tesla.

Eight cars in all. Each one worth several hundred thousand dollars and several more years to Turo's prison term.

Joe sank to his knees. He hadn't realized he'd still wanted to believe Turo was innocent. That this was all a huge mistake.

The truth gutted him.

He'd been played for a fool. Worse, he'd benefitted for his foolishness.

Family doesn't charge family rent, Turo had said.

I was buying a new TV and I thought, why not buy one for Joe, too?

Let the business buy you a truck, boy.

How close was Joe to losing Sam because he hadn't bothered to question why Turo was so generous?

And Brittany. She was coming this morning to take the BMW grille. The stolen grille. He couldn't let her.

The anger in his chest that he'd struggled to contain broke free.

Joe raced to the garage, hitting Redial on his phone. He darted in the open service bay and grabbed the extra length of chain he kept in the truck's toolbox. "My uncle's stolen cars are in my barn," he blurted at Nate when the sheriff picked up. He was almost too breathless to get the words out. *"In my barn!"*

Joe hung up and waded into the knee-high grass in the vehicle graveyard. He had to protect Sam. He had to protect Brittany.

"Dad? What's going on?"

"Go back inside." The sheriff would be here soon. And then the FBI.

There was no telling what else Turo might have done. No guarantee that he might not turn on Joe from prison, his lifetime mantra of family first forgotten, wiped out by Joe's betrayal. Joe wished he could send Sam away to Vince or Gabe, but they weren't in any position to take her in unless Joe was arrested.

And there was Brittany, with her penchant for trouble and fondness for stolen vehicles. She'd be a target if Turo turned vengeful and realized Joe cared for her. Brittany was stubborn enough that she wouldn't want to be protected. He had to make her stay away from him.

"Dad? What are you doing?" Sam followed him into the field. "Are we towing a car to the garage?"

Joe reached the BMW just as Brittany's truck made the turn onto his street. *Perfect timing.* "Stand back, Sam."

Joe swung the chain around and let it fly against the BMW grille.

"Dad, stop!" Sam screamed.

He didn't. The anger had broken free and he had a purpose. *Protect.* Joe kept beating the BMW's grille with the chain, filling the air with the sickening screech of metal on metal.

"Joe, stop. Please." Brittany's voice cut between the blows. "You're scaring Sam."

The chain slipped from his fingers. For the second time that day, Joe fell to his knees. His ears were ringing from anger, Sam's screams, the sheriff's siren.

A small body slammed into him. *Sam.*

Warm arms came around them both. *Brittany.*

"It's okay," Brittany kept repeating. "It's okay."

"TELL ME YOU didn't take anything from this field before I found you here that first day," Joe's voice was a breathless rumble.

Brit's arms fell away from him. "I didn't take anything." And now she never would. The grille was ruined. "Why, Joe?" What had made him so mad?

Instead of answering, he stood, lifting Sam into his arms. She looked small and helpless in her baggy football jersey and pink flannel pajama pants.

But Joe. Joe looked like he'd gone twelve rounds with the champ. And lost. "You have to leave, Brittany. Now."

What happened to her cheerleader? What happened to the man who'd told everyone she should be encouraged to create and to create whatever made her happy? Just last night, they'd sat around her grandfather's kitchen table like a family. And now he was asking her to go? Ordering her to leave?

Brit stumbled to her feet. Cold from the dew-moistened grass. Cold from the nip in the air. Cold from his words and his actions and the arctic look in his eyes. "Joe." His name was a strangled plea on her lips.

"You don't want to be around me." Joe gestured toward the garage. "You can't be around me. Stop procrastinating and create something as special as you are."

Sam watched Brit through dazed, tear-filled eyes. She lifted a hand, almost as if she was reaching for Brit.

"Turns out," Joe said woodenly, "the town was right. Messinas are bad news. Go away, Brittany. Now."

Sam's hand dropped to her father's strong shoulder. She buried her tearstained face in his neck.

The sheriff roared onto the street with squealing tires. He pulled around behind the garage.

"What's wrong? Joe?" Brit jogged after Joe. "Tell me what's wrong. Please." What had she done? What had happened?

He didn't answer and Brit stopped chasing him.

She turned, staring at the dented, ruined grille. It was as broken as her heart.

GRANDPA PHIL ENTERED the barbershop later that day. He sat in his chair and leaned on the armrest closest to where Brit worked at her station.

She was applying bleach to the tips of her

hair with a brush. She was on the fifth coat, stripping off the orange. Her hair lay across a formerly white towel draped around her neck. When the orange was gone, she planned to dye the tips black.

"Scuttlebutt says Joe's uncle hid stolen cars on their property."

Brit put the brush in the dye bowl.

"Everyone believes Joe's innocent, but they're searching the house and outbuildings for anything else that might incriminate the jerk. And they've requested a dive team to search the river tomorrow."

Brit felt a rise of curiosity that was immediately squelched by concern for Joe and Sam. "They aren't going to arrest him?"

"Don't believe so." Phil spun his chair to face hers and leaned forward. "You didn't take any car parts from that field you were picking, did you?"

"No!" She blotted the excess color from her tips. "Why would you ask that?"

"To protect you. Those FBI guys don't go after marshmallow criminals. If you have any stolen merchandise, the bad guys or the feds will come for you." There was real fear in his faded gray eyes.

It was reminiscent of the fear she'd seen in Joe's eyes.

Both men were trying to protect her. The morning's chill returned.

You can't be around me.

Joe's harsh words echoed in her head. He'd never gone on the attack. He'd never said she'd done anything wrong. It was just that she'd felt each strike of the chains on that grille on her very soul. She'd felt as if he was destroying the bridge they'd built between them.

And he had been. In the name of keeping her safe.

"Answer me, girlie." Phil's voice was unusually stern.

She cleared her throat, going for the joke. "Who's to say some of the junk your friends dropped off with me wasn't stolen?"

"Brittany."

She hung her head. "I don't have anything from that place." Not so much as a grille from a BMW. Or the love of a strong, hard man.

Phil nodded, studying her. "You missed a lock of hair." He stood and picked up the bleach brush, and slathered it on a tuft of orange hair. "I used to color your grandmother's hair."

"She doesn't color it anymore." It was odd to talk shop when her heart had been broken for all the wrong reasons.

He set the brush back in the bowl, wrapped the ends of her hair in aluminum foil and then put his palms on Brit's cheeks. "And why do you think your grandmother's gone gray? Pride. Don't you ever let pride get in the way of your happiness."

Pride. It was at the root of Brit's inability to create. Keira had been perfect. Brit had never created perfection before. Pride had kept her from trying again. She glanced at Keira. "You're right. I've been going about this all wrong." Pride kept her hiding from her passion in this shop. This busy, backbreaking shop. She should hire someone and free up her time to create.

"I could use a colorist." Brit fixed Phil with a steely stare that dared him to refuse her.

"Me? Be your assistant?" The sullenness traveled from his voice to the tight lines about his eyes.

"A colorist assists no one." Brit smiled, lips barely rising above the tightness in her throat. "A colorist is an artist. You have to cover every root without dying the skin around the face and neck. You have to let the color process without irritating the scalp. You have to turn clients with overprocessed hair away."

Phil preened, warming to the idea. "I am good at coloring."

"Is that a yes?"

Her answer was a big bear hug.

THE FBI WAS GONE, as were the expensive cars in the garage.

Joe sat on the apartment couch staring at the ceiling. Sam's head was on his shoulder. She'd fallen asleep after dinner, clinging to him as if she'd finally realized she couldn't have both her uncle and her father. One of them had to go to jail. She'd made her choice.

The pain and confusion in Brittany's gaze still haunted him. She'd wanted to stay. He hadn't wanted her to be involved in the FBI's investigation. It was bad enough they were skeptical of Sheriff Nate.

Next to him on the couch, his cell phone began to play "Jailhouse Rock."

Staring at the photo of Uncle Turo on the TV-less TV stand, Joe answered, vowing this would be the last time he did so.

Silence.

Joe sighed and lowered the phone, preparing to hang up. "It figures."

"I'm sorry."

Joe returned the phone to his ear. "What?"

Too loud. Sam stirred in his arms.

"I'm sorry." There was no mistaking the harsh rumble of Turo's voice. "I tried to protect you and Sam."

"You did a poor job of it."

"I'm sorry." Turo's breath rasped over the line. "I hope someday you'll forgive me."

The line went dead.

Turo hadn't been angry over Joe's turning state's evidence, over Joe alerting the feds to the hidden cars. Turo was sorry.

And asking for forgiveness.

Asking Joe to be the bigger person.

Joe felt smaller than Sam.

He'd destroyed one of Brittany's dreams when he trashed that grille. And then the FBI didn't even take the car.

"There's not enough there to say for certainty it's the stolen vehicle your sheriff thinks it is," Agent Haas had said. "And in the shape it's in, tracking down an owner is what my boss would call a waste of resources."

The federal agent had turned up his nose at the shell of a Volkswagen, too.

Joe had destroyed the grille for nothing.

He'd leaped ahead, and sent Brittany away, trying to shield her from what turned out to be nothing.

He doubted she'd ever forgive him.

The image of Keira floated back to him. Brittany had created a whimsical, joyous, beautiful creature. In his eyes, Keira wasn't as beautiful as Brittany. But that mermaid needed a firm foundation to float on. A sturdy Indian motorbike.

Brittany needed a firm foundation, too.

No one who came to Phil's shop in the weeks after the excitement on the Messina property had seen Joe, mostly because they didn't own or drive cars. With Grandpa Phil by her side, Brit reduced her workload. She spent her afternoons and evenings in the garage working on something that she knew wouldn't be as wonderful as Keira, but she hoped would elicit a deep emotional reaction.

Joe had shifted his dial-a-ride duties to Irwin and his sidekick, Rex. They came into the shop two days a week for free coffee and cookies. Irwin preened and blushed, complimented the women and asked about Rose, who hadn't found the time to go red. Rex just sat and enjoyed the caffeine.

Irwin reported that a regular stream of people were venturing to Joe's shop, mostly for oil changes, but beyond that there was little news of Joe. Rex was surprisingly mum.

And then one day Sam darted into the shop. "Can I put a flyer in your window?"

"Sure," Phil said, coloring a client's roots.

Sam hadn't looked at Brit. She'd taped the flyer to the window and ran off.

It was all Brit could do not to race to the glass and read the flyer.

A couple of the ladies waiting their turn stepped outside to see what the flyer was advertising.

"Well?" Phil asked.

"It's kid's stuff," Sandra said. "Makes no sense."

"What did it say, woman?" Phil roared, perhaps sensing that Brit was dying of curiosity.

"It said there's a future art exhibit opening at the bridge by the highway on Sunday. The real art exhibit won't be ready for another year."

Phil spoke to Brit in a hushed voice. "Isn't that where your exhibit is going?"

"I guess Mayor Larry gave it to someone else." Brit swallowed back regret. She'd dropped the ball with the mayor and Will, consumed by the act of creating. The opportunity had passed her by.

SUNDAY ARRIVED. BRIT GOT up before dawn, loaded up the truck and drove to the highway bridge. She didn't know what she'd find. For days she'd studied the flyer Sam had posted and been none the wiser. She could barely remember what the small meadow looked like.

All she could remember was Joe's face. His expressive eyes. His stern chin.

Stoic Joe. Shaggy Joe. Heroic Joe.

Protective Joe.

She parked and got out of the pickup. The sun hadn't yet risen above Parish Hill to the east. But she could see that everything had changed.

There was an old rusted swing set. A small rusted tractor. Four drag-racing tires stood in a flower pattern, like a merry-go-round.

And the Bug?

The body had been removed from the chassis and sat in the grass. But it was the frame that drew her farther into the field. Someone had laid a base bumper of concrete and re-created the curved body of the Volkswagen with river stone. There were no open windows. No windshield. But someone had painted blue headlights, blue windows, blue windshields. Someone who'd seen her sketches.

She touched a blue stone on the driver's window.

"We couldn't figure out how to leave the windows open without the entire thing coming down." Joe stood nearby, looking haggard and shaggy and oh, so kissable. "I figured you wouldn't be happy with a convertible. I hoped that you wouldn't be upset with us creating a platform for the real art. Your art. It was Sam's idea that the mermaids have a playground."

She was thrilled with what they'd done. All it needed was the magic of a few mermaids to make it come alive. "How did you collect enough rocks? I'd estimated it'd take me more than two months."

"Agnes organized the troops. We had twenty people collecting rocks every day, seven days straight. Will was my best worker. Turns out his nerdy mind comes in handy in the field."

"Why would they do that?"

"Well." Joe took a step closer. "The town council came the day after the FBI left. They offered their help. I don't think they expected I'd ask them to help you." There was a bit of wonder in his voice, as if he hadn't expected anyone in town to help him period. "I spent several sleepless nights after I sent you away. I didn't want to be the guy who stole your creativity."

He'd stolen something else altogether.

Joe took another step closer and laced his fingers with those of her right hand. "I lost it when I found the stolen cars because I knew everything came down to how my uncle reacted. Would he try to frame me? Would he send someone to take back the things he'd stolen? Nate and I suspect he stole that BMW and the Volkswagen. I couldn't let you take even one piece of it."

"I know," she whispered. "Turns out, I wasn't very passionate about that gate. I sent back my advance and recommended someone else."

He laced his fingers through those on her left. "I hurt you. And I had to do something to earn your forgiveness."

Brit didn't dare move. Not her fingers. Not her toes.

"I have no right to ask, but I hope you can forgive me." His words were deep and low and meant only for her. "I can't stand the idea of a life without you. Somehow, beneath all the anger and hurt when I first got here, my heart knew—" there was wonder in his gaze "—I fell in love with you."

Silence pressed her ears. Or maybe it was the weight of a wallflower flowing out into the universe, because Joe had fallen in love with the ugly duckling.

"Brit?"

It was the first time he'd called her by her nickname. Her chest was swelling with the fullness of her heart, and then she saw the rust and rock he'd brought to this strip of land, recognized the potential for more beauty still. Something flowing, something lovely, made of metal and worked with love. Mermaids. The mermaids Sam wanted. Her mermaids.

And then she was crying and his arms were around her and he was whispering the same thing over and over again.

"It's okay. It's okay."

When the burst of emotion had been released, Brit led him to the truck bed. "I have something to show you. I made this for you. I wanted you to know how special you are."

There was a merman in the truck, welded to the river bicycle. He had unruly black hair and icy blue eyes that somehow managed to be cold and hot at the same time. He was graceful and powerful, and though he was mesmerizing, he wasn't as magnetic to Brit as Joe.

EPILOGUE

THE MERMAIDS GARNERED most of the attention a year later when the Messina Family Art Exhibit officially opened.

But it wasn't the mermaids Brit treasured. It was the heart of Joe she saw in the foundation pieces of the display. The pieces he'd made and moved to win her back—a tractor, a set of tires, his childhood swing set. The love he put into every rock he'd arranged into the form of a Volkswagen.

They'd married in August in the field where they'd met. A field cleared of cars and mown to a short, tame green. Reggie had served as maid of honor. Sam and Tracy from the bakery were Brit's bridesmaids. Will stood up as Joe's best man, with Vince and Gabe as groomsmen. But the exhibit and the wedding weren't the only things keeping them busy. They were almost done remodeling the house Joe had grown up in. They'd knocked down walls and gutted the kitchen and bathrooms until nothing looked the same.

"I like the little mermaid on the tricycle best." Sam ran up to Brit, who'd officially become her mother last month. The breeze teased the hem of her blue flowered dress.

Sam's classmate and sometimes nemesis, Brad, accompanied her. He wore blue basketball shorts, a white T-shirt and a superior attitude. "If you have to choose the smallest one, I have to choose the biggest one. The merman on the tractor."

"I love them all, gorgeous." Joe draped his arm across Brit's shoulders. "The one on the swing set. The one swimming through the tires. But especially the one tugging the rear bumper of the rusty Volkswagen." He kissed Brit's temple. "She reminds me of you trying to tug that bicycle free."

They both looked back at the Messina Family Garage and the merman riding a river-salvaged bike that hung over the office door.

Joe's free hand slipped over Brit's swelling belly. "Are you happy, love?"

"Yes." Brit tugged him close for a kiss.

"Your parents are having a baby." Brad tossed the information like a taunt. "Your life is over, Sam. You'll be babysitting until you're thirty."

"I won't," Sam said stubbornly. "Mom promised. And my mom doesn't lie."

Brit grinned, breaking the kiss long enough to whisper, "Be prepared, Shaggy Joe, for the day they realize they like each other like we like each other."

Joe groaned, but he must not have been too depressed, because he kissed her again.

* * * * *

Don't miss the next
HARMONY VALLEY *romance,*
coming April 2017 from
USA TODAY *bestselling author*
Melinda Curtis!

LARGER-PRINT BOOKS!

GET 2 FREE LARGER-PRINT NOVELS PLUS 2 FREE MYSTERY GIFTS

Love Inspired® SUSPENSE

RIVETING INSPIRATIONAL ROMANCE

Larger-print novels are now available...

WESTERN WP PROMISES

YES! Please send me **The Western Promises Collection** in Larger Print. This collection begins with 3 FREE books and 2 FREE gifts (gifts valued at approx. $14.00 retail) in the first shipment, along with the other first 4 books from the collection! If I do not cancel, I will receive 8 monthly shipments until I have the entire 51-book Western Promises collection. I will receive 2 or 3 FREE books in each shipment and I will pay just $4.99 US/ $5.89 CDN for each of the other four books in each shipment, plus $2.99 for shipping and handling per shipment. *If I decide to keep the entire collection, I'll have paid for only 32 books, because 19 books are FREE! I understand that accepting the 3 free books and gifts places me under no obligation to buy anything. I can always return a shipment and cancel at any time. My free books and gifts are mine to keep no matter what I decide.

272 HCN 3070 472 HCN 3070

Name	(PLEASE PRINT)	
Address		Apt. #
City	State/Prov.	Zip/Postal Code

Signature (if under 18, a parent or guardian must sign)

Mail to the **Reader Service:**
IN U.S.A.: P.O. Box 1867, Buffalo, NY 14240-1867
IN CANADA: P.O. Box 609, Fort Erie, Ontario L2A 5X3

* Terms and prices subject to change without notice. Prices do not include applicable taxes. Sales tax applicable in N.Y. Canadian residents will be charged applicable taxes. This offer is limited to one order per household. All orders subject to approval. Credit or debit balances in a customer's account(s) may be offset by any other outstanding balance owed by or to the customer. Please allow 4 to 6 weeks for delivery. Offer available while quantities last. Offer not available to Quebec residents.

WPBPA16R

READERSERVICE.COM

Manage your account online!

- Review your order history
- Manage your payments
- Update your address

> **We've designed the
> Reader Service website
> just for you.**

Enjoy all the features!

- Discover new series available to you,
  and read excerpts from any series.
- Respond to mailings and special
  monthly offers.
- Connect with favorite authors at
  the blog.
- Browse the Bonus Bucks catalog
  and online-only exculsives.
- Share your feedback.

Visit us at:

ReaderService.com